Rescue from Innocence

Rescue from Innocence

JOSEPH FLINT

Cover Art provided by Kevin R. Karg
(kevinkargphotography@yahoo.com)

Library of Congress Control Number:		2013903271
ISBN:	Hardcover	978-1-4797-9906-0
	Softcover	978-1-4797-9905-3
	Ebook	978-1-4797-9907-7

This book was printed in the United States of America.

Rev. date: 02/20/2013

To order additional copies of this book, contact:
Xlibris Corporation
1-888-795-4274
www.Xlibris.com
Orders@Xlibris.com
130095

Preface

This novel was inspired by actual events; however, the characters herein are fictional and do not depict any persons who have lived. Any similarities to persons or entities are coincidental and the product of fiction.

The newspaper headline references were actual and set the timeline for the fictional plot and are intended to encourage the reader to research the true history of the participation of their governments and their fellow citizens in the events leading up to the 1990 Iraq War.

One

Bush Reluctantly Signs Bill on CIA Inspector*—New York Times, *Dec 1, 1989, p. D19, Nov. 30 (AP)

Walt Judge sat staring out into the cold night air from his window table at *Donut Express*, his hands wrapped around an ironstone mug of steaming coffee. Behind the counter, a teenager pushed a mop over the gritty tile, rap music beating incessantly in the background.

The café was deserted—not surprising for such an early hour. Sunrise was a long way off. Judge preferred the solace of very early morning—so quiet, save for the rap, and void of distractions. The perfect time as well for determining who was following him. He was being tailed, of that he was confident. Pauline's strange call had awakened his senses.

His survey of the area between the *Donut Express* and the Fort Worth Freeway yielded nothing. He kept his vigilance as his thoughts began to turn inward.

Closing his eyes, he dozed briefly as distant memories soothed his soul. He awoke immediately. That had not happened to him in a long time. He must not allow it again, he told himself.

Sighing, Judge noted it was well past midnight. Pauline was way overdue. Looking at his watch again, he wondered if perhaps her plane was held up. The weather was truly awful. He'd give it another hour.

Judge remembered meeting Pauline in England a few months earlier. Pauline Casey was a journalist working for *Aviation & Space* magazine, a weekly industry publication. He had been testing an Austrian military helicopter that had been modified by an engineering firm in Cambridge. The test had attracted the attention of the magazine, and Pauline Casey had been assigned to cover the story.

She and Judge had become acquainted; and it appeared, at least to Judge, that the gorgeous blonde reporter had been as interested in him as she had been in his test program. Despite his attraction to her, he had remained emotionally distant. Far from turning her off, however, his reticence had actually fueled her determination to seduce him.

She had followed him to Fort Worth "on a story," where, despite his best intentions, they had become better acquainted. It had been too much for Judge, however; and sensing it, Pauline had departed with the excuse of another lead.

To Pauline, Judge had been worth the risk of humiliation. He was the strong, silent type, with an obviously keen intellect. His mysterious background had intrigued her, and his stalwart moral character instilled in her an unwavering sense of trust.

She had gotten to know him well enough to realize that his intimidating presence was not of his control. It had come with the package and was for the casual observer to get over it or endure it.

Despite his disguised approachable nature, he seemed to have an arms-length force field surrounding his own feelings. He would suffer her obvious intentions with gentleness and a smile while at the same time making no advances of his own, as if he were not really there. He had a different agenda, it seemed to Pauline, and she was afraid enough of being outright rejected that she felt a period of distance might make him think more of her. At the very least it would give him time to get over whatever, or whoever, was occupying his most sensual thoughts.

If that did not work, she had enough experience with her fabulous looks and the effect that it had on men to know that another man like Judge, perhaps one not so aloof, would not be far off. Still, she longed for the comfort of him and left on the most pleasant of notes. There was just no disliking the guy, and one way or another, she would have to see him again.

Judge had not heard from her since. He had missed her company, but he knew he was not ready to respond to her sincerity. He could see through her obvious lust for him and realized she wanted him for the sex, that and much more.

The sex he could have dealt with readily, if not ravenously; but to him, it would have obligated him to more than his conscience could allow.

He let go of his coffee mug and gazed again into the darkness. Pauline had called him at the office the previous morning from London. All excited to hear his voice, she had asked, "But can we talk?"

"What do you mean?"

"You know, is the line secure?"

"All calls here come through a general switchboard, Pauline. What's wrong?"

"Nothing, sweetie, everything is good," she asserted blithely. "I need to talk with you." She sounded frustrated. "I can't talk to you on your company line."

"But you called me here," he pointed out. "Don't you still have my home number?"

"I tried, but you're never there, and I can't leave a message. I'd call you tonight, but I'm on my way to the airport. I leave London in an hour, so I have to hurry. You're not going to believe me, but I think you're about to have some serious trouble. You could even go to prison. I have some pictures to show you, Walt," she added. "I've stumbled across something really big."

"All right, let me pick you up at the airport," Judge offered. "When does your flight arrive?"

"I can't say! I don't even use my own name when I travel anymore. I have a meeting in Virginia in the mor—I mean this afternoon your time. Then I'm coming to Fort Worth. Can you meet me tonight at that café where we used to go last winter?"

"What time?"

"I should be there by ten," she calculated.

"Fine," he said. "Pauline, are you in trouble?"

"I could be. Ever since Baghdad, I've been a wreck. But I'm on a story that could be huge, Walt. This could be my big break. We'll just be in trouble together. I just need you to fill in some of the blanks."

Curious, Judge said, "I'll see you tonight. Have a safe trip." Hanging up the phone, he had shrugged. She had to be confused. He knew he had done nothing untoward, so there was no way he could be in trouble.

It was the last he had heard from her. More pointedly, it was the last he would ever hear from her.

Two

Walt stood in the strawberry field. Sweat glistened from his brow. He glanced over at Mrs. Gardner picking through the plants for the ripest fruit. The Gardners had moved not long ago from Georgia, and he felt strangely close with them. The Gardner family was warm and welcoming. He had a connection to them he couldn't explain. Here he was at peace. He loved Mrs. Gardner—maybe just a boyhood crush—and Dick was like a younger brother, and Mary was such a doll. Yes, this was refuge for him. Throughout his life, when he needed a safe place, if no more available than his nearest thought, this was the place he came home to.

Pinochet Era Ends as Chileans Vote*—New York Times, *Dec. 15, 1989, p. A1

Dr. Michelle Lofton slid behind the wheel of her Audi, set her valise on the passenger seat, and pulled the door closed. It was very late, probably past midnight again. She sighed heavily and leaned her forehead on the steering wheel.

"God, I am so exhausted," she whispered to herself. The strain of her double shift on the pediatric ward was taking its toll. The eternal sparkle in her bright blue eyes had faded, and her deep dimples had dissolved into what appeared to be simple age lines, belying her otherwise youthful appearance.

On nights like these, she wondered how she had ever considered taking on the double burden of motherhood and medicine. It seemed that the harder she tried, the more disappointed she became with herself. "You have a great aptitude for medicine," her father had always insisted. "It would be such a shame to waste it."

Michelle had specialized in childhood diseases, which had fascinated her when she attended Southern Methodist University. But later, when reality put little human faces before her, she found herself ill-prepared for the daily dose of sadness. Facing the innocent smiles of her often-ill tiny patients was often more than she could bear.

To compound her heartbreak, the more time she spent tending her patients, the less time she spent with her own child. Michelle's time with Heather, her six-year-old, had become nearly nonexistent.

Michelle leaned on the steering wheel and sighed again.

She knew she had to come to grips with a career that was crushing her soul. She had to come to terms with her own role as a single mother of a child whom few could understand and for whom she had less and less time.

Straightening up, she noticed the inside windshield fogging up. The chilly Texas winter air was heavy with late-winter moisture. Her warm breath was creating her own climate within the confines of the closed convertible.

She pulled the door shut again and started the motor, hesitating only long enough for the windscreen to clear. Quickly gaining the on-ramp to I-20, she no sooner hit the highway than the low fuel warning light flashed. She tried to calculate whether she could make her neighborhood near the Fort Worth Country Club, but at two in the morning, her brain had lost its edge.

The chill wind buffeted her small car as she made her way to the 820 turnoff. She noticed a few flakes of snow scurry past her windshield and then an occasional pellet of ice.

A flash from the sky momentarily lit up the dark highway, followed by another, and finally chased by the rumbling of thunder. *How unusual*, she thought, *for this time of year.*

Remembering that there was a station at the intersection of the 820 bypass and Highway 287, she turned up the heat, resigning herself to a quick fill-up there. Besides, a cup of hot chocolate would taste pretty good, she reasoned, recalling that there was an all-night coffeehouse adjacent to the gas station.

To her complete exasperation, the Audi gave no additional warning of impending failure. It merely sighed once and gave up, leaving Michelle a few hundred yards shy of her intended exit. "Damn!" she cursed.

The car ebbed to a stop on the shoulder of the highway, leaving Michelle shivering for her scarf. She trudged as quickly as she could into the chill wind towards the distant light of the station.

Only when she reached the edge of the station's parking lot did she look up into the biting sleet. Suddenly, she realized the light had come from the *Donut Express* and that the gas station was closed.

Swearing softly, she shoved at the glass doors of the little shop and felt a rush of welcome warmth.

No one, including the young doctor, could help but notice the man sitting quietly by the window. She hesitated when she saw him get out of his seat. He was looking directly at her.

The man acted as if he had recognized her, but then settled back in his seat just as quickly. He was no longer looking in her direction. A large but quiet man, trimmed and neat in appearance, he did not appear to Michelle to be a threat.

She proceeded straight to the counter. "May I use your telephone please?" Her soft voice quivered a little as she shivered, out of breath.

"Sorry, ma'am," said the teenager. "Phone's dead again tonight, but the pay phone at the station next door works. I used it earlier, so I know it's good."

She walked to the window and peered through the sleet, pondering the next move. Should she leave this cozy haven at so late an hour?

Michelle wanted to call her dad. As a surgeon, her father was used to calls at all hours. He would come and bring her a can of gas and get her car started.

She looked through the window and could barely make out the pay phone in the foreboding darkness. It was nearly out of view at the far side of the old gas station. Michelle shivered again.

The cashier handed her a cup of coffee. Sipping it, deep in thought, she tried to decide if she wanted to brave the cold again. She stood at the counter looking out into the darkness.

Pouring milk into her coffee, Michelle glanced at Judge, half expecting to meet his gaze. But he was staring out into the blackness. Even when he felt her eyes on him, he continued looking outdoors.

Michelle discreetly took him in. Although sitting down, he was very broad and easily six feet tall. His body was muscled, tight and toned, and his dark black eyes seemed to miss nothing. To describe him as handsome would be a bit of a stretch, she thought; but still, he was not bad looking.

Suddenly, a set of lights approached at high speed from the highway turnoff. She watched as the man by the window turned and glanced briefly at his watch.

Michelle realized he must be waiting for someone. Probably a woman, she guessed, maybe for an assignation. She began to fantasize; they would both be married to other people and met at this cozy way station at odd hours.

However, when the door opened, she could see that the new arrival was not a wanton woman, but instead a pair of unshaven men. Upon entering, they stopped in their tracks at the sight of her, a smile beginning to form on their ruddy complexions as if they were miners who had just uncovered a golden nugget. Slowly, they approached the cashier to make an order, all the while staring at Michelle.

With some apprehension, she looked worriedly at the pair, and then hesitantly at Judge, who had summed up the situation without taking his eyes from the window. Glancing over at her, he motioned for her to have a seat at his table.

Michelle was more than relieved—she was grateful. Clearly, sitting across from this man seemed smarter than standing in the otherwise deserted café alone. Without hesitation, she slid into the seat nearest to Judge.

The big man stared at the two ruffians at the counter. With a quick look at Judge's grim expression, out of respect, or fear, they turned their eyes from Michelle. Michelle's apprehension died as quickly as it had risen.

"Thank you," Michelle whispered under her breath, trying not to be overheard.

"Don't mention it," Judge said, again staring out into the darkness.

The two sat silently. Michelle watched the strangers' reflections in the window as they received their order. Meanwhile Judge was watching another vehicle, a dark sedan, slowly approaching in the distance, its lights off. The front of the café was all glass from floor to ceiling. Anyone observing from the outside could make out the entire interior clearly. Judge suddenly did not like being in such a vulnerable position.

"A bit of car trouble?" he asked Michelle, trying to sound sympathetic. He had turned his gaze on her for the moment, but his attention was still on the suspicious dark sedan in the distance. She had not sat next to him to make small talk he knew, but he didn't want her having any second thoughts about it. Somehow she had wound up in a vulnerable position herself, and he had offered her safe haven. Now he felt responsible.

Too embarrassed to admit that she had run out of gas, Michelle simply replied, "It just died." She took another sip from her cup as they momentarily explored each other's eyes.

To Michelle's relief, the scruffy-looking men gathered up their order and proceeded back to the Vega. After a few attempts at coaxing the starter, the engine came to life, and the pair roared off.

The Vega's headlights briefly caught the dark sedan. It was neatly hidden on the far side of the filling station. Only Judge had noticed it. The engine was off. Two figures could be seen for a split second through the windshield as the Chevy Vega passed.

"Well," Michelle said with a heavy sigh. "I guess I should venture out to that phone booth." She rose and moved towards the door.

Judge started from his seat momentarily with concern. He sensed the threat to the young woman had not entirely left with the two in the Vega. She had not seen the dark sedan. His sudden start, however, had given her cause to cast a worried look towards him. Dismayed, he realized that his reflex motion had in turn startled her. The comfort she had felt sitting next to him would not extend to being alone with him in the dark parking lot.

Not wishing to alarm her further, Judge stood at the door, watching her as she moved towards the phone booth in the distance. He knew if the men in the dark sedan had been the ones following him, any threat they posed should be directed at him and not the woman. He cursed himself for allowing his paranoia to give her cause to doubt his intentions.

As it turned out, he should have trusted his instincts.

Three

Occasionally dozing in the tall grass, Walt was slumped against the bank, perfect for fishing, or a nap in the sun. Mary sat nearby; a ball cap shielded her dove soft complexion.

She sat so close to him that her hair tickled his cheek, awakening him just enough to catch the pink and orange sunset, sneaking its way below the strawberry field. As if sedated by her presence, he drifted back again.

"Mom says you're going into the army," she said quietly, not looking at him, tossing a flower petal into the pond. "Dad says you might have to go to Vietnam. Mom's worried, why would you do that?"

"I don't have enough money to go to school," Walt replied, not opening his eyes. "You're twelve, what is going on in that little head of yours?"

"What if you don't come back?" She looked away.

"I'll probably be back before you get out of high school." He opened his eyes and looked over at her. But she was not looking at him. In the three years he had known the Gardners, they had become his second family; and Mary, well, he didn't know what to make of her. She climbed up the bank and ran back

to the house. His gaze followed her. She was very shy, rarely speaking to him.

Iraqi Army Is Accused of Attacking Civilians*—New York Times, *Jan. 31, 1990, p. A17

"I told you he'd lead us to her," the driver of the dark sedan said as he pointed to the *Donut Express* through the darkness.

"Too bad we didn't get here sooner. We could have nailed her before she got to him. Think she gave him anything yet?"

The driver lit a cigarette. "Don't think so. She just now sat down."

"You sure it's her?"

"How many gorgeous blondes you think are gonna meet a hulk like that out here in the middle of the night? 'Course it's her."

"How did she get here? The only cars here are his and the one those bums just got out of."

"Probably parked around back. The kid behind the counter probably parked back there too."

"I don't like it. Now we have to deal with Judge. Jesus, he's huge. I know you guys said he'd be a handful, but I thought you were exaggerating."

The driver took another drag on his cigarette. "Just relax. You're a shrimp. Everyone is huge to you," he sneered.

"We're not supposed to put Judge down. Just take care of the girl."

"We were supposed to get to her first so we wouldn't have to deal with him. If you had been at the airport with me, you could have helped me find her."

"You knew that was going to be impossible. All we were told was what time she'd get in and that she was going to meet with Judge later. There are four terminals at DFW, and we had no flight information. Besides I was supposed to keep track of Judge. Nabbing the girl was your assignment."

"OK, OK. So now we improvise."

They watched in silence from the darkness as two scruffy-looking men left the *Donut Express* and climbed into a Chevy Vega. It finally roared off into the night.

Moments later, the driver of the dark sedan tossed another half-finished cigarette out of the window and nudged his partner. The blonde was leaving the café. "Now's your chance. Keep out of sight and do it quietly." Silently, the man in the passenger seat opened his door and disappeared.

Judge had picked a tiny spot of light reflecting from one of the side corner reflectors of the black sedan. The car was almost invisible in the misty darkness. He knew that if the reflection moved in the slightest, it would be an indication that there was significant movement within the vehicle, like someone getting out. He was on his feet the instant he saw the reflection change.

He was so fast in fact that the two figures from the sedan had not noticed his lightning exit from the *Donut Express*. In an instant, Judge was invisible in the shadows.

To Judge's dismay, it was readily apparent that their target must have been the girl all along. One man remained behind the wheel while the other advanced on the girl, a white chord tightened between his fists.

Michelle was standing at the telephone, which was attached to an unlit light pole, shielded from the weather by the gas pump island's overhead canopy. Her back to the approaching man from the black sedan, she could not help but feel the ground shake as Judge pounded towards her out of the darkness. She caught sight of Judge through her peripheral vision an instant before the man behind her could get his cord around her neck.

Screaming, she ducked to the ground in a tight ball, inadvertently yanking the wires from the phone. Only then did she see the man behind her with a cord stretched between his fists. Judge sailed feet first overhead, delivering a striking crack to the would-be assailant. So unexpected was Judge's advance that the only sound the man could utter was the sudden rush of air that wheezed from his lungs.

Michelle was on her feet again as the engine in the sedan roared to life and the tires howled. The vehicle careened past Judge and swerved to run down the girl. It caught her with a glancing blow, spinning her backwards through the front glass window of the station.

The driver slammed on the brakes and threw the car in reverse before it had stopped its forward movement. The transmission complained with a deafening grind, and the vehicle clawed its way back in an attempt to recover its former occupant.

Judge sidestepped the snarling vehicle to the driver's side. For barely an instant, the driver, his neck craned around to his right, caught sight of his partner staggering to his feet. The big car screeched to a halt. He had lost sight of Judge, now only an arm's length from his door.

Suddenly, the driver's side window exploded by the driver's head, showering him with tiny shards of glass. Before he could move, a giant pair of hands nearly engulfed his head, and he was dragged through the opening. With his arms wedged at his sides, the doomed driver caught sight of the light from the *Donut Express* just before his head was snapped around, and what little light there was flashed out.

The other assailant, having managed to regain his balance, groped for his gun; but it had been knocked away by Judge's powerful kick. Realizing that any search for his weapon would have to wait, he quickly pulled a large blade from the sheath near his right calf.

The sound of his partner's neck snapping caused the knife-wielding attacker a split second's pause. Judge barely managed to deflect the blade wielder's thrust. The blade seared clear through to his clavicle, entering just below Judge's right collarbone.

Judge roared with pain and anger as he doubled over, dropping to one knee, spinning around with his back to his attacker. The knife remained lodged below his left shoulder.

Gritting his teeth, enraged, Judge leaned forward and put all his weight on his left foot, which was firmly planted on the ground. Touching his nose on his left knee, he snapped his right foot straight up in the air. His heel caught the little man squarely under the chin, cracking the man's jaw and lifting him off the ground.

Judge, still bent over with his head at his own knee, swung his right hand against the man's ankles, taking the man's feet out from under him.

The assailant crashed to the ground for the second time. His head struck a concrete parking curb and cracked like a fresh melon.

As he tried to stand upright, Judge nearly passed out from pain. His head swam as he swayed, struggling to remain conscious.

The girl's cries helped bring him back. He struggled with the delirium and began pushing the pain aside. Just like in Vietnam, he could separate the pain and isolate it from his consciousness, as he had been conditioned.

Michelle was struggling with pains of her own. Lying in a mass of shattered glass, she convulsed with agony whenever she moved her legs. Her head throbbed. She was not sure how long she had been out, but it couldn't have been very long.

The fender had caught her square in the butt. She knew something was broken. She curled up into a ball, shaking uncontrollably. Tears streamed from her contorted face. She was writhing with pain, shock, and anger. She clenched her eyes shut, trying not to move lest the pain worsen. Her head throbbed to the point where she feared she would vomit.

Michelle could hear a man panting heavily. Stealing a glance through tear-filled eyes, she could see him silhouetted through the shattered window. He was standing beside the dark sedan, his face invisible. He seemed to be reaching inside his jacket for something. Roaring, he pulled at a knife and wavered there, nearly faltering. He knelt again, leaning up against the car for what seemed a long time. Then he moved towards her.

Completely helpless, she pleaded, "Please . . . don't . . ."

"It's all right," Judge managed, dropping the knife. "They won't be bothering you now." He had found a light switch, but the station remained dark. Judge remembered it was common practice to shut down the main circuit breakers in service stations at night for fire prevention.

Michelle recognized the man's shadow as that of the man from the café. His voice was calm and reassuring, but she didn't trust anybody at this point. Still frightened and angry, she tried to push his huge hands away as he knelt beside her. He tried to place his palm under her head.

"How bad are you hurt? Can you tell?" he asked hoarsely. They could not see each other in the darkness. The only light coming in from the café fluorescence was reflecting off the sheets of icy rain.

"My tailbone . . . mostly," she replied, trying to get up. She was cut and bleeding; her clothes were nearly shredded. Standing, she stiffened and winced with pain; sucking in her breath, she faltered.

Before she could protest, Judge had lifted her, seemingly without effort. In an instant, he was carrying her through the sleet across the parking lot towards the café. She could see a man hanging lifeless from the driver's window of the black sedan. Another lay nearby like a soggy neglected sack of feed.

Holding Michelle cradled in one arm, Judge tried the door of the café. Finding it locked, he pounded on the door. The poor cashier must have seen the commotion and locked up. He was probably hiding in the back.

On another evening, the door would have proved no obstacle to Judge. He was weakening fast, and he knew there was no phone inside. They needed medical attention soon, or it would be too late.

Judge closed his eyes, wishing this night were over, then turned and carried his small bundle out beyond the café to the only other vehicle in the lot.

Still holding Michelle, he opened the passenger door of his Mercedes and gently placed her in the seat. Soaked and shivering, she suddenly realized he was driving off with her, uncertain as to where.

Judge, breathing hard, moved to the driver's side and sat on the far edge of the seat, one leg inside and one leg out, clutching his neck with his left hand. He was leaning against the seat with his head back. Without looking in her direction, he held out his woolen coat with his right hand, offering it to her.

He said softly, "Put this on before you freeze." His voice was calm, but raspy, as if he were about to cough.

Only slightly reassured, Michelle struggled to put the coat on, still shivering uncontrollably. The left sleeve was damp and sticky inside, but she welcomed its warmth.

He started the motor and pressed on the accelerator. "I'm going to get you out of here."

Michelle could see his shoulder was bleeding profusely. Slowly, with some hesitation, she instinctively reached up and applied pressure to the wound. "Don't worry," she said, "I'm a doctor. We need to stop this bleeding." There was no indication to Michelle that he had even felt her touch.

Judge pulled the big coupe out onto the service road and moved towards the highway with Michelle still reaching across his chest. He turned in the direction of Arlington, heading east. "Where are you taking me?" she asked, suddenly realizing that she had not given him directions to anywhere.

"Hospital," he said, so raspy she could barely hear him. "You're bleeding."

"Me? It's just a scratch." She exclaimed, "*You* need the hospital!" She lifted her head and looked at him and could see beads of sweat on his face in the light of the instrument panel.

He actually managed a thin smile. "It's just a scratch," he said. Secretly he hoped that he could make it that far. Judge knew that if he had to lift her again, despite her tiny frame, he would pass out.

Despite herself, Michelle had to fight back a smile. *Men*, she thought, *why couldn't they admit it when they're hurt? Wait until the pain sets in, then he'll start whining. Still, he had incredible self-control.*

Meanwhile, the ringing in Judge's ears was getting louder. He knew he could not hold the pain off much longer. The ringing always came on strong before he passed out. But now was not the time, he told himself, not just yet. He could beat this. He gritted his teeth, trying to focus on his goal.

Michelle leaned around in front of him, craning a bit to see his wound. Judge was still clutching it tightly with his left hand as he drove. Adjusting his hand to a better pressure point position, she noticed how soaking wet his chest was.

His car, ironically, was just like her father's, a big Mercedes coupe. She quickly found the correct switch and turned on the dome light from the overhead panel.

Fumbling with his shirt, she examined the wound just below his left collarbone, now bleeding profusely. "My god!" she said in alarm.

"Just a scratch," he lied again. But Judge was beginning to feel chilled. He shook his head to clear it and tried to focus against the pain. Bright pink foam was trickling from the corner of his mouth.

"It isn't either," she responded, horrified. "This is a serious wound." Michelle realized that he was going into shock.

Michelle tore at his T-shirt, managing to tear off a piece the size of a small handkerchief. She folded it quickly and forced it into his wound. To her amazement, he didn't flinch or even wince with pain.

She looked into his eyes with alarm. How could he still be conscious with pupils so huge? She could not see any iris, only pupil. "Pull over and let me drive!" she commanded. She turned to look down the highway. But to her surprise, Judge was in the middle of the lane, unwavering.

"No time," he whispered. "Almost there."

As she started to protest again, she saw the exit sign for Arlington Community Hospital. Watching him closely, she remained silent.

Judge could not remember much after that. He never recalled pulling into the emergency entrance or being carried from his car.

He had a vision of his tiny companion holding hands with a tall man with graying hair, standing in the emergency room. Suddenly, they were standing in the middle of the strawberry fields. It was becoming more familiar to him as the light began to fade. They were waving goodbye.

Four

"Rats!" Mary screamed, jumping out of the way. Walt and Dick jumped too to keep the scurrying rodents from running up their pant legs. They had been moving a pile of firewood, and the critters seemed to come out of nowhere. Major, their Dalmatian, was excited too and made quick work of them in rapid succession. Shocked at the dog's speed at dispatching them, they stood staring in amazement; it was over in seconds. They began laughing hysterically.

Walt looked at his friends and smiled. He loved it here. He wondered what must have possessed him to ever have left this place.

Dr. Richard Lofton stood next to his daughter's hospital bed, staring at her bruised, cut face. The morning sun was now streaming through the slits in the vertical blinds, giving the otherwise sterile room a hint of warmth.

Michelle was already sedated by the time he had arrived from Fort Worth. Suffering from a broken tailbone, concussion, and an inflamed lumbar disc, she was sleeping fitfully. The emergency room staff had applied a couple of sutures to her neck and forehead, followed by morphine to control her pain.

The police officer stationed in the emergency room had pieced together a report from some of Michelle's confusing and often contradictory statements. The receiving interns had provided little, if any, useful information.

Another officer had been called in and placed in the room of the man who had arrived with Michelle. That had probably been an overreaction on the part of the police, since the receiving intern had not expected the man, a Mr. Walter Judge, to survive the night. There was some discussion among the police as to who had done what to whom. They were keeping Judge under close scrutiny until they could sort out the facts.

Michelle's eyes flickered; and her father, having turned to leave, hesitated when she moaned. He picked up her hand and squeezed it gently. She opened her eyes.

"Hi, Daddy," she managed with a quivering smile. It was as if she were a small child again.

"Hello, Precious," he said softly.

"Daddy . . . I . . ." she began, trying to sit up.

Dr. Lofton gently placed his fingers to her lips and let her lay back against the pillow. "Shhhh . . . baby," he whispered, "I want you to lay still. We can talk later. I'm in surgery this afternoon in Fort Worth, and I'll come back after that. Your mother will be here shortly. It was her day with Heather, and she had to call Ms. Chi to change her plans and stay with the baby today . . ."

"How bad is . . . ?" Michelle tried to interrupt him and ask about the man that had brought her here.

"Oh, sorry, Honey," her father replied. Completely misunderstanding, he realized he had not given his daughter an inkling of the extent of her injuries. "You have a broken coccyx and possibly a herniated disc between L4 and L5. They've given you morphine for now. With any luck, it's just inflamed. You'll be working with an orthopedic specialist to get an MRI set up. Not much we can do for your tailbone though." He sighed. "It will be a bit painful for several days, but you should be up and walking around in a day or two if we get the inflammation in your back under control."

Michelle was not listening. "No," she protested. It was not her own condition that concerned her. "How is . . ." She searched her foggy mind and then realized that she had never gotten the stranger's name.

"You'll be fine in a few days, just plenty sore for a while." Her father continued. "We're going to keep you here for forty-eight hours. We don't want any pressure down there for a couple of days. I need to run." Kissing her on the forehead, he turned and hurried out.

Dr. Lofton nearly collided with his wife as he left Michelle's room. Embracing her, he assured her that Michelle would be just fine. Helen Lofton held back her tears. Her daughter, despite her privileged life, had had her share of personal tragedies.

As they were standing outside the closed door to Michelle's room, a man approached; a shoulder holster in sharp contrast against his white shirt. Dr. Lofton recognized him immediately.

"Hello, Tony," he said, still holding his wife. He reached out with the other hand and introduced Lt. Tony Gibbons of the FBI.

"Yes, I remember meeting you . . ." she began.

"Are you here to check on my daughter?" Dr. Lofton interrupted. Without waiting for the answer, he continued, "She's going to be fine. Had quite a bad time of it though."

"I'm glad she's going to be OK. It was a close call." The officer sighed, shaking his head. "May I speak with her?"

"I'd rather you didn't. She's still a bit groggy, and there's nothing you can do except upset her at this point by making her relive it. The Arlington policeman in the ER has the report. Can't that suffice for now?"

"I'm afraid it can't, Richard."

"Why not? What does this have to do with the FBI?" Dr. Lofton asked, becoming slightly agitated. "Look, I'm not going to let you upset her. Don't you have any sympathy for the victim? Do you realize how frightening and humiliating that was for her. Do you even know what they did to her?"

Lieutenant Gibbons held up his hand again; he had only just started. "Please, let me finish." He led the Loftons to the nearby elevator and pressed the button to the basement floor where the cafeteria was located. Getting the senior doctor away from Michelle for the moment would make him less confrontational.

"We found Michelle's convertible over on the 820 freeway," he continued. "A patrolman had ticketed it as an abandoned vehicle. Don't worry. I'll take care of that myself."

Helen Lofton spoke up. "Do you know anything about the men who attacked her?"

"We're not sure just yet," he replied as the elevator door opened, and they exited into the cafeteria. "Both victims had false IDs. We're running their prints to find out their identities." The trio walked to an empty table and sat down.

"Victims? You mean the man that brought her in? Michelle doesn't have a false ID." Mrs. Lofton was perplexed.

Gibbons held up his hand, trying to get a word in and explain. "The coffee shop cashier said that he had a late customer matching Mr. Judge's description, the man that brought her in. The cashier told us the man didn't talk much, but said he wasn't in any hurry and just wanted a hot cup of coffee."

"Well, a few minutes later, with Judge still there, a woman matching your daughter's description came in asking to use the phone. The phone was out, so she went next door to the filling station. It was closed, but it has an outdoor pay telephone."

"You think that's where she was attacked?" Mrs. Lofton asked.

"The front glass of the station is broken out, and it appears that Michelle was thrown through it," Tony said. "There was a lot, and I mean a lot, of blood, too much to be from only your daughter. Even with all the rain, it was a pretty gruesome scene. Most likely it was from Mr. Judge because neither of the deceased had any open wounds."

"Deceased?" the Loftons retorted in unison.

"We found a 30-caliber semiautomatic in the drive nearby, but we're not sure whose it was. It had not been fired recently. We also found a large dagger near one of the deceased. We're not sure whose that was, either. The ER staff said that Judge's wounds are consistent with a knife wound. The police are checking into everything, the blood, fingerprints, all of it."

"Do you think Judge had anything to do with it?" asked Dr. Lofton.

"It is definitely possible, but he might have gone to her aid," returned Gibbons. "The report from the officer in the emergency room says that Michelle brought him in, but we need to talk with her. The blood in his car is inconsistent with that report. It appears that Judge did the driving, despite his wounds."

"You said there were no open wounds on the deceased?" Dr. Lofton wasn't satisfied yet. "What caused their deaths?"

"One died of a crushed skull. The other one had a broken neck, nearly had his head torn off. The report I have is that one victim weighed over 250 lb. The guy with the fractured skull also had a broken jaw and several broken ribs. His jaw wasn't even attached at the joint."

"My god!" Mrs. Lofton exclaimed.

"Judge may have been waiting for the other two, and Michelle just walked into the middle of it. We have details from the scene, but not a clear picture yet from the only two who were actually involved who are still alive. I have to talk to them to get better details. You see where I'm coming from? It's going to be a while before we can talk to Judge, if ever, so Michelle is our only credible witness at this point."

"I'm sorry," Dr. Lofton apologized. "I know you're just doing your job. Tell me again why you're involved in this case?"

"The police suspect the two victims are from out of state. I can't tell you more than that right now."

Helen interrupted, "He must have been crazy to attack those two men completely unarmed. If the gun or knife were his, you would think the other two would have visible wounds."

"I'd have done it," her husband said grimly.

Helen looked knowingly at her husband. Of course he would have. Michelle was his daughter. But this man, Judge, was a perfect stranger; and in the middle of the night too. She shook her head in amazement.

They retraced their steps to the elevator in silence, each of them trying to imagine the scene. By the time they reached Michelle's room, Helen Lofton could no longer restrain herself. She was shaking, tears in her eyes, as she imagined what Michelle must have gone through.

But Michelle was not in her room.

"What the hell?" exclaimed her father. He stepped back into the hallway and moved quickly to the nurse's station, his wife and the lieutenant close at his heels.

Michelle had not been given a bed in the intensive care ward, as her injuries were not considered life-threatening, so the patients were not as closely monitored.

Reaching the nurses' station, Dr. Lofton loudly began demanding his daughter's whereabouts. She had apparently refused to stay put and had taken her IV and calmly left the floor. The drugs had apparently overcome not only her pain, but also her common sense.

"I know where she is," Helen suddenly announced, placing a hand on her husband's arm. Both men turned and looked at her. "She's gone to find Mr. Judge."

Five

Walt tossed the hay bale onto the wagon for Dick's dad to stack. Sweat was pouring from his forehead. Walt, Dick, and Mr. Gardner had nearly finished the field; and the wagon was piled so high Walt wondered if they could make it back to the strawberry farm without it tipping over.

Vietnam had been a horrible nightmare for him. Each night, no matter where he was, he retreated in his mind back to the strawberry farm.

Mary was decidedly absent, out somewhere with her boyfriend. Woody doesn't do hay baling, she had said to him.

> *"I think they're going to get married," Dick said matter-of-factly. Judge winced; she seemed way too young. He thought his heart might break. He knew the Gardners' were.*

February Pullout Set for Force in Panama; Troops to Leave Panama in February*—The New York Times, *Feb. 1, 1990, p. A1

Milton Fox shifted uneasily as he read the morning paper. Seated in his office at ARI, *Advanced Rotorcraft Inc.*, he had come across the article about Judge and the killing of the young doctor's attackers. It was not the facts in the article that bothered him.

No, the facts didn't even surprise him. He knew what kind of a man Walter Judge was. What made him uneasy was the byline "Associated Press." This meant that other newspapers across the country would have the AP article too. Soon one of his customers would learn that Judge was out of commission. They knew all too well, as he did, that ARI depended a lot on Mr. Judge's well-being. Judge had let Milt down once before, and Milt did not want his new customer to think it might happen again.

Milt had hired Judge as much for his background in the military's Special Operations Command as for his unique talents in developing aircraft for intelligence field work.

Milt's first "big" aircraft contract came from the Indonesians, arranged through the US State Department. The contract with the Indonesians had been secured, in part, because Indonesian president Suharto and his people had been alerted by Milt's "friend" in the CIA as to ARI's unique capabilities. Indonesia awarded the contract to Milt under the condition that ARI would train the Indonesian Special Forces Units and participate in its first "police actions" into East Timor.

But they had not counted on Judge's scruples. Judge had refused to be used as a mercenary. He wasn't in the military anymore and had insisted his civilian talents were strictly academic. When Milt had informed Judge that ARI was under contract and couldn't back down, Judge had packed his bags and returned to the US.

The Indonesian contract was never fulfilled, costing Milt all of his profit from that endeavor. Still, Judge was invaluable to ARI.

Milt turned back in his chair, looking out through his big picture window. Staring across the grounds, past his new flight ramp, to the new hangar with its big ARI logo, he sighed worriedly.

"I have Mr. Craig Wright on the line. He says it's urgent," the voice on Milton Fox's desk intercom said.

"It's OK. I got it," Milt replied. Picking up the receiver, he pushed the blinking button on the telephone.

"Well, hello, Mr. Assistant Ambassador Sir!" Milt feigned cheerfully, with an emphasis on "assistant."

"Oh, knock it off, Fox," Wright replied tersely. "What's this I hear about Judge being out of service?"

"It's just a temporary setback, I assure you."

"Is he going to make it?"

"You know how tough he is. He'll make it." Milt tried to sound more reassuring than he felt.

"You know, without him, the Chile deal is off."

"Don't say that. If he doesn't make it, we will have to find someone else."

"The director is not a stupid man, Milt. He knows that without Judge, you can't make it happen in time. You know the score. Too many people know about this program already."

"Have you told Carrillo anything about Judge?" Milt asked, referring to Hector Carrillo, his new Chilean customer.

"That reminds me," Wright said, ignoring Fox's question, "you better keep your staff away from any more reporters. Tell them it's classified, National Security. Read them the riot act. I'm not kidding, Fox. You keep Judge reigned in if he lives. He lets on about the weapons kits it'll be curtains for everyone. We had no idea he got all high and mighty about trivial shit like that."

"All right, all right, don't have a coronary! I got Judge back after the Indonesian program," Milt lied. "He doesn't know anything about Chilean deal, no one does. He thinks the kits are all for the Mexican Police. You just have to convince Carrillo that working the crop duster angle is the only way to go on his program, even if it costs a little more."

"Carrillo has already bought into that idea. In fact, he rather likes it, gives him another avenue for export sales."

"Good," Milt returned, "then Judge won't be a problem. Just leave him to me."

Milt finally relaxed, leaning back in his chair. Judge could be a hard case. Maybe this time he would be easy to deal with.

"Time is running short. Give me a call when he gets out of the hospital, if he gets out," said the voice on the phone.

"He'll get out . . ." reassured Fox, but the line had already gone dead.

Six

In his early twenties, he had already been through intensive military training and was reliving the worst of Vietnam almost every night. He was in the midst of attending one of the best engineering universities in the country, and he had never even been on a real date. Despite his aged and worldly continence, he was completely inept when it came to women. He still had the social skills of a teenager. In his mind, despite the years away, he had never really left the Gardners' farm. His teenage girlfriend Cheri and her wonderfully understanding parents recognized him for what he was and made him as much a part of their family as the Gardners had. They all knew each other, and it made his life complete.

"Dr. Lofton, please call IC extension six. Dr. Michelle Lofton, please call IC extension six." The hospital intercom repeated, in its usual unemotional monotone.

Michelle picked up the nearby paging phone and pressed the extension. "This is Dr. Lofton."

"Dr. Lofton, you asked to be paged if Mr. Judge's condition changed. He's fibrillating, ma'am. He was conscious for a moment, but they're working on him now."

"I'll be right there!" she said, hanging up and rushing towards the elevator.

It had been four days since that awful night. She was back doing her rounds, hampered occasionally by brief spells of back spasms. During that time, she had left the hospital only twice. Once was to spell Ms. Chi from Heather, and once was at the insistence of her parents. The Loftons nearly had to drag her from the hospital for a fresh set of clothing and a home-cooked meal.

Michelle had not admitted it to her father, although he suspected that she felt compelled to stay near the strange man lying in the ICU. His daughter had revealed that she was convinced a divine power had placed Judge in that café that night to watch over her. She believed it was her fault that he was sitting at that café table, waiting for fate to arrive.

Judge meanwhile was barely hanging on. His right lung had been punctured, but it wasn't inflating after surgery, as it should. If the knife had cut the aorta, it would have been all over for him. As it was, his blood pressure was not recovering as quickly as expected and remained rather unstable. His biggest problem seemed to be his slow recovery from such an enormous loss of blood. Many had died from less than half as much loss as he had suffered.

Judge's room was flooded with light when Michelle rushed through the door. The ICU staff was just removing the de-fib unit, and the heart monitor was blinking a steady sine wave. Except for a thin sheet across his hips, he lay naked on the bed with the gel from the paddles still glistening on his chest.

It was the first time Michelle had seen him in such bright lighting. Despite his gray complexion, his generously muscled shoulders, chest, and arms were still tightly flexed from the recent charge of voltage. Even his abdomen was tight and well defined. There was no hint of softness in his flesh, which could have been chiseled from stone for all anyone could tell without touching him.

There had been no record of Judge's medical history. Calls to other hospitals and clinics in the Fort Worth-Dallas Metroplex had yielded nothing about him. The hospital administration had allowed Michelle's father, a well-known local surgeon, to act as Judge's temporary primary physician.

"We may be using too much morphine," commented an intern. "Look at how his pupils are dilated." He lifted one of Judge's eyelids, and then squinted. "Oh." He added hesitating, "Never mind. He has black eyes. It was just hard to tell in dimmer light."

The patient winced at the onslaught of bright light. Michelle turned off the light and motioned the nurse to close the curtain. "He's not comatose right now, so let's keep the lights dim."

They all looked up to see Dr. Lofton Sr. standing in the doorway. "Just checking in on my favorite patient." He smiled.

Michelle said in a low voice, "He just had another close call." The rest of the ICU staff began filing out, leaving Michelle alone with Judge and her father.

Judge's right hand moved across his chest and gently grasped her right arm. Michelle caught her breath. His lips were moving slowly, his eyelids fluttered. She leaned slightly closer.

"Mistake . . ." he managed in a hoarse whisper. Judge swallowed, his parched lips almost smiled. Opening his eyes, he squinted, trying to focus.

Michelle placed the fingers of her left hand to his lips. He needn't try and talk right now. Looking up at her father, she gently tried to release herself from his grip.

Judge struggled to lift his head, looking directly at Michelle with unfocused eyes. He moved his right hand from her arm to her soft blonde hair, then to her forehead, then to her nose and lips. His touch was so light, like a blind person skimming braille.

Michelle finally managed, "I'm fine, and everything is OK now . . ." She spoke in her calm doctor-patient voice, but her heart was heavy, her throat dry.

Walter Judge settled back on the pillow, his glazed eyes still open, Michelle's hands still firmly held in one of his.

The senior Lofton was staring at the heart monitor, deep concern etched on his face. He began moving quickly towards the de-fib machine and slapped his hand on the call button on the wall. "Move over, Precious," he ordered his daughter.

Michelle seemed shaken as she suddenly realized what was happening. "No!" she whispered, but it was not directed at her father. "Oh no, no!" she cried softly to herself as she began helping her father with the de-fib paddles.

"Please, come back here," she begged Judge in silence.

The ICU interns reappeared in a rush, trying to untangle the de-fib electrodes that had become tangled in Judge's IV lines.

Michelle and her father worked feverishly on their failing patient. "Please don't trade your life for mine!" she almost cried aloud.

The strain and agony of the past days were catching up to her. She had faced down humiliation and death with the help of this quiet stranger. Helpless to help herself, she had found strength in being able to help him, maybe finally making the turn for the better in her personal strife for self-worth. She had shared the horror and pain of that lonely night with him. It was as if she was only enduring half of the nightmare every time she closed her eyes. She had found herself depending on his presence to ward off the terror of that experience.

For the first time in a long while, Michelle had briefly seen a glimpse of a different future. Fleeting as it was, it had given her hope and a purpose to help her change her life. As she and her father struggled with their still patient, Michelle felt the terror returning. Now it would be all hers to endure alone.

Seven

"I don't think I have ever seen anything like this," Walt commented.

"I think it's cool," Dick said, smiling. He stood back admiring his handiwork. He had just finished converting a Volkswagen Beetle into a pickup truck.

Walt wished he had more time to help him with Dick's project. His studies at the university were keeping him occupied, that and his girlfriend Cheri. Between the two, he was having difficulty getting out to the Gardners. Walt wondered what he thought he was doing with his life. He knew in his heart his young girlfriend would grow away from him as soon as he left the university, and then he would regret all the time he had spent away from the Gardners. But he found he couldn't help himself. She seemed to worship him, and that made her strangely irresistible to him.

Tony Gibbons sat reading the FBI data fax he had just received at his Burleson office.

"Good stuff?" asked Sergeant Jenkins, his partner.

"It seems that our Mr. Judge is really quite the Boy Scout," Tony began. "Decorated Vietnam veteran, top secret clearances, Army Ranger, pilot training, and not so much as a parking ticket in any police files." Gibbons finished scanning the fax. "Almost too good to be true," Gibbons said, mostly to himself.

"What?"

"Oh, nothing," Gibbons replied. Then, turning to Jenkins he asked, "What do we have on the other two?"

"They're Joe Cox and Dennis Atterbury. Their prints came up, but nothing else. And there's no info on the gun."

"Excuse me?" Tony asked.

"Computer won't let me in to their files. 'Access Denied' it keeps saying," Jenkins said, frustration in his voice.

"That's odd."

"Yeah," Jenkins remarked. "I would have thought those guys would have some sort of record. When the system blocked me out, I thought maybe they might be connected to the bureau, the CIA, or maybe the NSA. Usually, if they're CIA or NSA, we get a bureau or agency logo up here by the 'Access Denied' message," Jenkins explained, pointing to the screen. Gibbons moved around behind him to look.

"You're in the Bureau Intranet system." Gibbons suggested. "Get 'em on the phone. Ask them why those files are frozen."

"OK," agreed Jenkins, "I suppose it's a place to start. Why do you think they went after your doctor lady?"

"Before we get ahead of ourselves, we need to find out if there is a connection to these guys and Judge," Tony began. "They could be just some punks who've come across a doll like Michelle in the middle of the night."

"Really?" Jenkins was incredulous. "I think something else is going on here."

"I'm just saying," the lieutenant said, throwing up his hands. "We really need to talk to Judge." Walking out of the office towards the coffeepot down the hall, he called over his shoulder, "See if you can get an answer on those files."

Something just wasn't sitting right with Tony Gibbons either. Other than the obvious myriad of questions they had about this case, he felt an unsettling unease about it. He had long since learned not to ignore these feelings when they surfaced.

He thought about the file on Walter Judge. *Early forties, clean record, good job. He was too good to be true*, Gibbons thought. *If he looks too good to be true, he may be hiding something.*

"You know, it may be Judge who is connected to the agency?" Jenkins said to the lieutenant as Gibbons reentered the office.

"What? Who?"

"Judge."

"No. Where did you find that out?"

"His neighbors told us. They also said that he used to work for the government and then consulted for some helicopter outfit. So we called Bell, and I talked to their human resources department. They referred us to that other outfit up there, ARI, I think it's called. It's all there."

"Baloney! I've been through this file twice!"

"Uh, wait a minute." Jenkins shuffled through some papers on his desk. Finding a couple of pages stapled together, he added sheepishly, "Oops, sorry, I thought I had put this in there." He leaned forward, handing the sheets to the lieutenant.

Gibbons began reading. "Let's see. He tests experimental aircraft now. Did some operational testing with the military's Special Operations Command. Some of the aircraft are for the military. You know how the military likes to keep some of their projects under wraps."

"What do you suppose Judge was doing at that coffee shop so late?" Tony asked, changing the subject. "It's not exactly on his route between his house and the Bell Flight Test Center."

"Not sure. But he doesn't work at

Bell, like I said. However, he does interface with them all the time apparently. He works for that other helicopter outfit up in Hurst near Bell. ARI it's called."

Thumbing through the report again, then tossing it back to Jenkins in disgust, Gibbons spat, "Jesus, Jenkins, don't you ever write anything down?"

"Well, sorry, I didn't think it was important."

"Well, it might be, so put that in there and anything else they told you.

"You think there's more to this guy than just a Good Samaritan, eh?" Jenkins asked. "Are you sure you're being objective here, Tony?" he added rather hesitantly. He knew of Tony's prior relationship with the young woman doctor.

Jenkins was more astute than he appeared, and Gibbons knew it. Jenkins was often slow to catch wind of a real case. In fact, that seemed to be Tony's forte. But once he latched on, he never lost the scent and had an uncanny sense for who the guilty parties were. Together, they made a great team.

Eight

"Good morning, Joey. How's my favorite patient this morning?" Dr. Lofton smiled at the six-year-old, offering his palm for a good old-fashioned low-five.

The boy did not respond immediately. He was sitting on his bed with his legs crossed, looking into his lap. His head was down, and Dr. Lofton could not see the child's face because of the boy's baseball cap, which he wore to hide his bald pale head. "You say that to all the patients," he finally said, sulking, without looking up. He crossed his arms. "You're just looking for Dr. Michelle." Then he asked, "Is Dr. Michelle going to come see me today?" He looked up, his eyes mirroring this hope that Michelle would appear.

Dr. Lofton looked sadly into the little face. "Dr. Michelle is still not feeling well, Joey, but she told me to tell you she misses you." He rubbed the boy's ball cap with the palm of his hand.

His concern for his daughter had forced him to off-load his patients over in Fort Worth and move as much of his work to Arlington, a commute of only about twenty minutes.

Michelle believed that the pediatric ward was her sole responsibility. The senior Lofton thought he knew his daughter pretty well, however. He had concluded that Michelle was obsessed with guilt and was refusing to leave Judge behind.

Lofton finally gave in and adjusted his routine so that he could keep an eye on them both. Michelle's emotional state and compromised mental and physical condition did not make her a candidate for the best caregiver that either her young patients or Walter Judge needed right now.

Judge had barely survived his latest setback. His right brachial artery, just below his collarbone, closest to the rib cage, had been slightly pierced after all. It had been enough to lower his blood pressure.

The attending interns had not been successful at inflating his collapsed left lung. It had been Dr. Lofton who had deduced that blood was leaking into the chest cavity from the compromised artery, preventing the lung from inflating. An emergency surgery had corrected the problem, and now Judge was showing marked improvement. Dr. Lofton had kept him under a forced coma, much to the chagrin of the police. The drug would be wearing off soon, however, and the good doctor felt it was probably time.

Michelle, on the other hand, had been totally unnerved by the whole affair. Her sleep was fitful, haunted by visions of her attackers and the terror and helplessness she had felt.

She had always been highly independent and, save for her father, needed no one, especially other men, in her personal life.

Now, the boy was tugging at Dr. Lofton's white coat. "When will she be back?" he asked, pleading.

Suddenly, Dr. Lofton said, "What say we take a little walk and go find her?" Maybe this wide-eyed child would help cheer Michelle up.

The child reached up to take the doctor's hand, ready to go. Dr. Lofton smiled and knelt eye level to the boy. "Let's put on some slippers first. Shall we?" He found the child's hospital slippers, and together they slowly walked hand in hand towards the elevators.

It was no surprise to him when he found Michelle standing at the edge of Judge's hospital bed. The man had finally awakened. The head of the bed had been raised to put him in a half-upright position. Michelle stood with her stethoscope in her ears, listening to his chest. Judge was not her patient, but the senior Dr. Lofton and the staff had allowed her a lot of latitude given the circumstances.

Dr. Lofton and Joey stood quietly by the bed until Michelle noticed they were there. "Well, now," he finally said, "I see my favorite patient is finally awake."

Joey looked up at Dr. Lofton, frowning. "See, I told ya," he said, hitting the doctor on the arm with his tiny fist. "You say that to all your patients."

Michelle looked down at the little fellow, smiling. She looked fresh and pretty as she bent down to give the sick child a hug.

"You don't look sick," Joey declared, hugging her back.

"Neither do you," she lied, lifting the featherweight child in her arms. "There's someone I want you to meet," she added, turning the boy to face Walter Judge.

Judge managed a smile and held up a large hand for the boy to shake. The boy couldn't even make a fist around the big man's forefinger.

The child seemed mesmerized by Judge's dark eyes.

"Wow," was all he could say as he leaned over. He was not the least bit intimidated by the big man. He touched his nose to Judge's, trying to peer into his eyes as if trying to read something written inside the man's head.

Michelle looked oddly at Joey for showing no sign of shyness.

"What's wrong with you?" asked the boy, pointing to the man's bandages.

"Just a scratch," Judge replied with a weak smile. His voice was deep but hoarse.

"Joey," Dr. Lofton said, "why don't you take Dr. Michelle down to the cafeteria and get her and you some ice cream, my treat?"

"And some chocolate syrup?"

"Of course," he replied, reaching for his wallet.

As Michelle allowed the child to lead her from the room, the boy turned to Judge and asked, "Want us to bring you some?" He said it as if he had always known the man.

Judge turned his head slowly to see the boy. "You better," he said, trying to be gruff, barely loud enough for the boy to hear. The child seemed impervious to any false expression from Judge.

Out they went, with the boy talking to his long lost doctor friend and with her, looking at him curiously and then back at Judge.

The doctor shook Judge's hand. Dr. Lofton could barely span the man's palm. "Do you always have that effect on children?" he asked, smiling.

"It's a curse," Judge said, trying not to smile, but the doctor could tell that Judge had enjoyed the visit.

"Maybe you're a sheep in wolf's clothing," Dr. Lofton said, seeing right through Judge. Then he changed the subject. "I never thanked you for my daughter's life."

"I should have moved faster," Judge said hoarsely, a serious continence overcoming him. He felt mostly to blame.

"You did pretty well for yourself," the doctor said, sincerely. "What you did was pretty impressive."

"Not that impressive," Judge said, mostly to himself.

"Did you know the men who attacked my daughter?" the doctor suddenly asked.

Judge looked up at the man. The doctor's eyes weren't accusing, just curious. "No, they were waiting for Michelle."

Dr. Lofton's expression changed. "How could that be?" he asked suspiciously. "She ran out of gas. They could have had no idea that she was going to be there," he added, looking at Judge. When Judge did not respond, he asked, "You think she was being followed?"

"No," Judge responded quietly. "I was."

The doctor looked perplexed. "You said you didn't know each other," he said accusingly. He appeared completely confused.

"I was supposed to meet a friend, a lady that looked something like your daughter." Judge sighed heavily, a wet wheezing sigh. "They must have known about it. They must have been after Pauline, not your daughter."

Dr. Lofton looked grimly at Judge. "Does Michelle know?"

"She'll know soon enough. You might want to keep her away from me when she finds out."

"Michelle's not at all like that," the doctor responded. "You saved her life. That's all she cares about." Then he added, "You know, the police need to know you're awake. I'm sure they'll want to know all about it."

"I want to talk to them too. That officer outside the door has already called for the detectives," Judge said.

Dr. Lofton turned to leave the man in peace. He felt only somewhat relieved.

"Doc?"

Dr. Lofton stopped in the doorway and looked over his shoulder at the patient. "Yes?"

"Have the boy wake me when he brings the ice cream."

Nine

Suddenly it seemed, everything ended, and Walt was gone again. Graduation from college had come all too fast, and the job offers from across the country came flooding in. Dick too had graduated and moved to Chicago. Walt began work, testing aircraft in the Northwest, all the while longing to return to the Midwest. Cheri was only just beginning her university studies, and little Mary had gotten married and moved away from the strawberry farm.

East Timor Bishop Writes of Torture*—The New York Times, *Feb. 11, 1990, p. 23—LISBON, Feb. 10—

"I thought he was too good to be true," Gibbons said aloud, stepping into his office.

"Who?" asked Jenkins.

"Judge."

"I know what you mean."

"What?"

"You first."

"You know what he told me?" Gibbons asked with a curious look at Jenkins. He had just returned from an extensive but not very informative interview with Judge at the hospital.

"What?"

"He said that Cox and Atterbury had been following him."

"No fooling? So why did they go after the girl?"

Tony explained to Jenkins about Pauline Casey.

"What did they want her for?"

"Judge claims he doesn't know."

"Do you believe him?"

"No."

"No?"

"It doesn't explain what was so important that two people are dead over it. Could have just as easily been four. I put Pauline Casey's name on the wire. We'll see if anything comes back. I still think Judge knows more than he's telling."

Judge had a dark history, however honorable, with all the bad that had happened to him recently. No, that wasn't it, he said to himself; there was something else.

"What'd you find out about Cox and Atterbury?" Gibbons asked, changing the subject.

"A lot of confusing nonsense. 'Cept that they are, I mean were, connected. I mean, they used to be."

"To us? Or the Mob? Who'd they work for?"

"No, the CIA. Hold on," Jenkins said, raising a finger, shuffling the file that he was working on. "Cox and

Atterbury left the CIA nearly three years ago. Usually when a man leaves the service, the service portion of his file is kept classified. The rest is up for grabs."

"Yeah, so, what happened?"

"The Washington bureau is telling me that their files were deleted."

"Deleted? You know that's crap!"

"It's real curious," Jenkins continued. "I talked to an agent who put me in touch with the department that handles those guys' files. The clerk I talked to said he never remembers those two leaving. But he gave me a tip. The clerk said Cox's and Atterbury's names came up once a while back. They were arrested in New Orleans for a disturbance at a convention over a year ago. They were in some altercation with a big foreigner. The three of them apparently knew each other pretty well. The local cops tossed the three of them in the can to try and figure things out."

"Thought you said the files were deleted."

"That wasn't in the agency files. The clerk remembered he took the call from the police personally. He referred me to the New Orleans Police, as a gesture of professional courtesy, I suppose. The clerk said the local police might have kept something written down in their own local files, so I called New Orleans."

"Go on," Gibbons ordered.

"The local police had to let our two spooks go that same night. Someone from the Agency showed up and sprung 'em, but they kept the foreigner a while longer on a local warrant for beating up a prostitute. Got her name right here."

"Well, it turned out he had diplomatic immunity." Jenkins continued, "Some embassy staff member or something from South America. This diplomatic guy, Ponce Gutierrez, dragged this whore all the way from Dallas to New Orleans. He picked her up downtown Dallas after midnight and flew her to New Orleans on a private jet. After they did their thing, he attacked her, dumped her off, and went on to the convention. Very bizarre, beat her up pretty good. She called the cops in New Orleans for help, and the uniforms picked her up and put out a warrant for Gutierrez. Then the fight broke out at the convention later that night. They arrested him but had to let him go when it was confirmed he had immunity. According to the report, the girl said that when the guy had taken off his clothes aboard the plane, that's apparently where they had sex, he looked as if he had already been in a fight. He was all cut up and stuff. This was *before* his scuffle at the convention. She said she accused the guy of letting his wife get the best of him. He went crazy and started pounding on her."

"Picked her up here in Dallas, eh? Interesting."

"It gets better," Jenkins continued. "This Gutierrez is apparently a pretty big guy. So I looked into anything that might be on record around here that week. One thing popped up," he said, smiling.

"Well, what?" Tony asked, disdaining the suspense.

"A woman was found murdered in Arlington the night he left for New Orleans."

"Well, so what made you think she and this Gutierrez fellow were connected?"

"She was Korean and a licensed black belt karate instructor. She immigrated in '87 after meeting an American on assignment in Asia. Traveled back with him and set up a little karate school."

"Did she marry the guy she came back with? Was it Gutierrez?"

"No, not Gutierrez. She apparently lived with her boyfriend, the one that brought her to the States, and got her green card and then broke up with him a month or so before she was killed."

"I still don't get the connection with this case," Toni said. "So what if this Gutierrez guy killed her. Turn it over to the police. What's it got to do with our two dead perps, or anything for that matter?"

"The guy that brought her back from Korea, the guy she lived with for a while," Jenkins added, handing Gibbons a file, "was Walter Judge."

Ten

Alone and at loose ends, Walt learned that the Gardners had taken a sabbatical for six months to the Northwest, but on the eastern side of the mountains from where he was working. He took off across the Cascades in search of them and found the senior Gardners with their two youngest in Wenatchee trying to get moved into a new apartment. Even having them in the same state was comforting. Work kept them on opposite sides of the Cascades much of time, but they did get together for salmon fishing and exploring whenever they could.

The Windy Mideast—"It is becoming more fashionable to sound a bit moderate than to shout shrill defiance."*—New York Times, *Mar. 6, 1990, p. A23

Breathing hard, despite the cool air, Walter Judge walked slowly around the parking lot at Arlington Community Hospital looking in vain for his car. He leaned up against a parked vehicle and heaved a huge sigh, sweat dripping from his eyebrows. Dr. Lofton had suggested he could be released, provided he took it easy. She had not thought that Judge would walk out and drive himself home.

Just then, Michelle's Audi pulled alongside the vehicle he was leaning against. "Come on, get in," Michelle called to him. "What were you thinking?"

Judge pushed away from the parked car and opened her car door. "They told me I could be released today, so I checked out," he said, breathing heavily. He was soaked with sweat despite the cool weather. "Couldn't find my car. Must have left it somewhere else." He realized that he was panting.

"They were not supposed to release you without an escort," she declared. Then turning her eyes from the road, she looked suspiciously at him. "Did you intimidate them into releasing you?"

Judge shook his head. He looked as if his feelings were hurt. "I don't have an escort," he murmured.

Poor guy, Michelle thought. *He probably scared the registration nurse half to death and didn't even know it.* He was not particularly handsome when he was frowning. In fact, he looked somewhat fearsome.

"You should not be out walking like this," she said, changing the subject in her usual doctor-patient tone of voice. "Are you nuts? A cold is as bad for you as pneumonia right now." She sounded to Judge like a mother hen. Then, she added, "I'll drive you home." In an even softer tone she asked, "How are you feeling? You're really sweating."

Michelle turned slightly in her seat, enough to face him, and wiped his brow with a tissue.

Judge looked into her eyes. For a split second, he thought she reminded him of someone. He looked away embarrassed.

"I'm good," he replied. Something or someone from the past was pecking at his conscious thoughts.

They stared at each other for barely an instant, neither knowing quite what to say. Judge closed his eyes and leaned back in the seat. He forced his mind to stop its struggle. He had done it hundreds of times. Withdrawing, he said, "You shouldn't bother yourself about me," and then he was sorry he said it. Fact was he *did* want her to bother herself about him, but not as a doctor.

Michelle glanced at him, disarmed. What should she say to him? He should be just another patient, she tried to tell herself. But he wasn't, and she knew it, even if she wouldn't outwardly admit it.

She had not been looking for a man when Judge had shown up, and she didn't think she was looking for one now, especially this one. Still, he had been so powerful yet gentle with her during their ordeal.

"When they told me you had just up and walked out, I could not believe it. Why didn't you page me? I would have driven you home. You should not be exerting yourself yet."

Michelle stole another glance at him as she drove. He was too quiet. What was he thinking?

Judge stared out the window, then closed his eyes again. When he did so, he became aware of how good his chauffeur smelled. Her perfume was fresh and light, not at all like her reserved, almost sterile personality. She had seemed so attentive at times while he had been in the hospital, yet when he started showing marked improvement, she had begun to act more stern and professional.

Judge turned his head slightly to look at her, catching her gazing at him. She quickly turned her eyes back to the road. She was truly lovely, Judge realized. She seemed so different now than when she was in the hospital. There, she had been firmly professional. She now seemed unsure of herself.

"Of course," he suddenly realized. "She doesn't know were she's going. I never told her where I live," he told himself.

To his surprise, however, Michelle made the turn from the freeway onto Green Oaks Boulevard, and he realized she must know the way to his home. He sat up a little straighter in his seat. "Do you know where I live?" he asked her. "How did you find out?"

Michelle explained to him that a friend on the police force had driven his car home for him the day after he had been admitted. A car like that should not be sitting out in the hospital parking lot. This was supposed to satisfy his curiosity without letting him know that she had been in the car with the officer at the time.

Michelle did not tell Judge that her father had had Judge's leather seats and carpet redone. Judge would find that all out soon enough.

Now, she asked herself, why would she not want to tell him that? She wondered, *And what about Tony?* It was as if she didn't want Judge to know that she and Tony Gibbons had had a closer relationship. Michelle shook her head to try to clear the conflicting thoughts.

Tony Gibbons had let her into Judge's house so that she could gather some things for Judge in preparation for his being discharged, but she was not about to explain that part to Judge. That was too personal a thing that she had done for the man, totally out of character for her position as a doctor. After all, she was not his doctor, her father was.

She remembered being impressed with his home. The giant double front doors opened into an enormous marbled entryway. The front entrance outside and inside was guarded by two enormous marble pillars, easily two feet in diameter. The columns supporting the outside entryway were nearly twenty feet high, and the two inside the entryway were nearly as tall. She assumed he must be an ex-ball player, having done well with his brawn. She sighed. Men have it so easy.

The entryway, crowned with a magnificent glass chandelier, led through the marble columns into the living area, which in turn led through double-glass French doors to the backyard. The entire back wall of the living area was glass, providing a gorgeous view of his backyard from the front entrance.

The centerpiece of the backyard was an Olympic-sized pool. A beautiful fountain was situated between the pool and the French doors.

The house was beautifully decorated and to Michelle's thinking, a bit delicately. *Obviously, a woman had had a hand in the decorating*, she thought. Michelle remembered wondering if Judge was or had been married when she first entered his home. Not a soul had visited him in the hospital, so she had assumed he was a loner.

She had asked Tony if he thought Judge had a woman in his life, as he was poking around, taking advantage of the moment too. Tony remained tight-lipped about Judge. He had said he couldn't talk about the case, but knew inwardly he was uncomfortable talking about Judge in front of Michelle.

Gibbons had also stopped short of telling her anything else he had learned about Judge's life, past and present. He had not shared his interview with Judge with her either; particularly the big man's suspicion that he had been followed by the thugs who had attacked her. Gibbons noted that apparently Judge had not been forthcoming about his life to Michelle, either.

In the living area was an ebony black grand piano. Michelle wondered if Judge had once played. It occurred to her that a man with hands as large as Judge's would not have considered the piano an instrument that he could play.

It had taken less than ten minutes to cover the seven remaining miles to Judge's home, situated in the rolling hills south of I-20 in the posh Green Oaks area.

Pulling into his driveway, to his surprise, she produced his garage door opener and keys. "The policeman gave them to me to give to you," she said, dropping them into his hand. Obviously, the hospital's privacy policy did not preclude the police from taking whatever they felt inclined to.

"Delightful," Judge said solemnly. He frowned when the opener didn't work.

Michelle followed him to the front door and followed him into the house, carrying her medical bag. Looking at him standing in his own home, Michelle found him seeming older than when he had been in the hospital. Judge was still breathing laboriously and sweating.

"What's wrong?" she asked, suddenly concerned.

"The alarm," Judge replied. "It should be beeping until I type in the code to disable it."

Michelle had not heard any alarm when she and Tony were in the house earlier. Nor had she seen Tony do anything to one.

"Did you say Officer Gibbons brought my car home?"

"Yes, it's in the garage." Then she caught herself. "I mean, I think it is . . . I mean, yes, it is in the garage. He used the key on the keychain to let himself in. I do not remember an alarm being armed."

Judge looked at her suspiciously. "Something I should know?" he asked, raising an eyebrow.

"I . . . I saw him put it in there," she confessed. "I was with him when he came here. The power was out, so he opened the garage from the inside. Your key was in your belongings. I'm sorry. I just thought I would gather some of your things for you so you had something to wear when you were released from the hospital."

"But you didn't bring me . . ."

"No, I chickened out," she replied. "Dad, I mean, my father picked out new clothes. He also had your car cleaned. Really, don't be angry, it was the least we could do."

"I'm not," Judge replied, looking down into her eyes. Again, a familiar face looked back at him, but not Michelle's. He turned to break his gaze, disturbed. "But," he continued, "I am concerned about the electricity and why my alarm is not working. Let's take a look around."

Forcing his mind back to the present, he retraced his steps to the entryway and leaned against a large planter near the front door. The clear imprint of a key was visible in the dirt under the pot, but no key.

"If you have an alarm, why put a key in such an obvious place?"

"It keeps the doors and windows from getting smashed. The alarm would still scare them off if they didn't have the code. If the alarm isn't enough to scare 'em off, windows and doors wouldn't slow a professional for very long."

A search of the house revealed that the power to the house had been cut, as well as the telephone line. There was no power to the alarm and no phone line to call the alarm monitoring company.

Chagrined, Judge and Michelle walked into the backyard. The power to the house came from an underground cable leading from the light pole at the rear corner of the lot. It led under the foundation to the circuit breaker panel inside the garage. The conduit stemming from the bottom of the pole had been neatly cut.

The phone line too was underground; however, it led only to a plastic box on the outside of the house. Although it had been padlocked, it had not taken much force to break it open and cut the wire.

"The house seems so undisturbed," Michelle finally said.

Judge stood silently for a moment, rubbing his neck. "There must be a reason for this," he said.

It did not take them long to find it. Judge led Michelle to the kitchen, where he positioned himself in front of the refrigerator. Placing a big hand on each side of it, he gently slid it forward. It moved easily as it was on well-oiled rollers. To Michelle's amazement, a combination safe was beneath the refrigerator, mounted flush into the concrete floor. He turned the flush-mounted handle and pulled open the door.

"It's not locked!" Michelle exclaimed.

"No," Judge said. "I keep it unlocked. I figured it would keep any thieves from pulling it out of the floor and having it opened somewhere else."

"What difference would that make?" she asked puzzled, "If you leave it unlocked anyway?"

Together they peered into the empty safe.

"Was there anything in it?"

"Yes. They must think they got what they came for because they didn't trash the house."

"What do you mean, *think*?" she asked. "It is empty," repeating herself a little louder.

Judge reached into the safe with both hands and, pulling upward on the lips of the inside of the safe, lifted it out of the foundation.

"Stop it . . . stop that right now," Michelle cried in alarm. "That's too heavy."

Judge set the safe down beside its hole. "It's OK," he insisted, but he sat down heavily on a nearby chair.

Michelle looked at Judge, frowning; then she peered back into the hole. Reaching down, she removed a small metal box.

"That's very clever," she said, looking at Judge, impressed. "The good stuff was *under* the safe!" she exclaimed.

"There was another one in the safe just like that one. It was my decoy. It had useless drawings, gibberish notes, a few bucks, and meaningless codes on disks." He tried to explain briefly. He held up his disc that contained his cipher for the encrypted data system that he used to digitize the technical data that his instrumentation system recorded when he was testing a prototype. It also contained his encrypted solutions to the problems that he had uncovered as well as codes for bank accounts, blueprints and diagrams, and his software code for a helicopter missile tracking system. All of which were modified to be useless on the decoy.

"You are so ingenious!" she exclaimed, "but won't they be back when they discover that you fooled them?"

Judge didn't reply.

Michelle was watching him with concern as he sat down. He was still mumbling something about the contents in his hands. His shirt was moist from sweat, and he looked exceedingly tired. Not to mention his recent exertion in pulling out that heavy safe. She pulled him from his seat and led him out of the kitchen. He resisted halfheartedly, looking over his shoulder at the safe and the refrigerator, still out of place.

"Never mind that," she insisted. "You can deal with that on another day. The power is off, and I must fix that now," she said. "I'll call it in to the power company as soon as I get back to the hospital. I'll drop by on my way home tonight and make sure they came over. C'mon, let's get you cooled off," she said, unbuttoning his shirt.

"Really?" he protested, but didn't stop her. Judge looked down at her as she removed his shirt; she wasn't being shy at all. He closed his eyes. *This couldn't be*, he thought to himself. "You're not who my mind wants you to be," he said in silence.

"You have to stop," he finally said.

"Oh be quiet," she said. "You shouldn't be embarrassed. I've had a nurse giving you sponge baths for nearly three weeks now."

She half led him to the master bedroom and into the huge master bath. She seemed to know her way around. Michelle turned on the bath water and made Judge sit on the edge of the tub while she attended to his bandages in preparation for sponging his upper body. He sat, silently watching her, as she worked on him.

With only cold water running and him sitting on the edge of the tub, she sponged his neck and shoulders around his wound until he visibly stopped sweating. The water was cold, and it didn't take too long.

When she was finished, Michelle tried to coax him to lie down, but he wouldn't hear of it. He found himself trembling, and he needed her to leave. He would see her to the door.

After she was gone, he returned to the bedroom. Removing his slacks, he slipped into his own bed for the first time in several weeks. Judge sighed sadly with his eyes closed, trying to pretend that his caregiver had not been here out of a feeling of obligation. He forced himself once again to put her out of his mind, and with her, the young phantom as well.

He wondered who had broken into his home. Maybe the two that had attacked them had been to his house before they had showed up at the filling station. They might have wanted to make sure he couldn't pass anything on to Pauline in case they could not get to her. If that were the case, it would also mean that the thieves were somehow connected to his work and that he ultimately must know who the master criminal was.

Judge realized that the two men were most likely only after Pauline for something else she was working on, but what she had said to him on the phone haunted him. He could go to prison, she had said. He was getting into something pretty deep. He realized that, at some point, he had stopped worrying about Pauline Casey. She had not called and had never showed up. After all this time, after everything that had happened, he feared the worst had come upon her.

Eleven

Walt was not looking forward to his first Thanksgiving alone since Vietnam. His nightmares had been subsiding, but with their diminishment came an increasing withdrawal of his personality. He was keeping to himself more and more. He found himself missing the Gardners and Cheri's family and kept away from other people to keep from feeling he was betraying them. As if to sense his falling into oblivion, Cheri's mom called him to ask if he would like company for the holiday. They had decided it would be fun to meet him and the Gardners in Seattle for Thanksgiving.

As soon as Judge was well enough to return to ARI, Milton Fox arranged for Hector Carrillo to fly up to Fort Worth.

Although reportedly Latin, Carrillo looked more like an American businessman than did Milt. Educated in the US, he spoke excellent English. Few would guess him to be a foreigner.

Milt talked with him as if they were old friends, the usual stiff cordiality absent. These two had to have known each other for some time, Judge mused as they were introduced.

Hector was quick to get down to business. He produced a set of 8 by 10 photographs. The pictures were of different views of a single-engine helicopter. It appeared obvious that some serious modifications had been made to one of Bell's designs.

"Where was this built?" Judge asked, although he suspected he knew the answer.

"They are being built in my country near Santiago, Chile," Hector replied, the pride in his voice showing through his otherwise businesslike demeanor.

"What is it that you would like for us to do for you?" Judge asked, glancing at Milt. Milt knew Judge had recognized the aircraft as a gunship and could sense Judge's apprehension.

"We need ARI to certify it with the FAA," Carrillo replied.

"You've got to be kidding," Judge replied. He disliked being mistaken for a gullible rube.

"Look, Walt," Milt stepped in, "this isn't what you think. We are going to present the project to the Southwest Region as a crop duster," he continued, referring to the lead FAA Helicopter Certification Branch located near Meacham Airport in Fort Worth. "It should be a simple matter of a few handling qualities flights," he finished, reflecting his usual lack of understanding of the real requirements.

Standing before these two men, Judge could not help but look around for the hidden camera that surely must be there to record this ridiculous conversation. He turned to David Barkley, ARI's chief engineer, always the quiet, sane one.

"I have already talked to the region," David said, referring to the FAA. "They think the project has merit. In fact, they have been hoping for a project like this for some time."

"What do you mean?" Judge was having trouble believing any of this.

"The FAA Southwest Region is excited about the program. The FAA is going to assign Designated Airworthiness Representatives to the project to oversee quality control in Chile." Milt was grinning.

"Have they seen these pictures?" Judge wanted to know. He appeared now unsure of himself. Maybe this would make a good crop duster. What sort of market for it was there? He began to wonder.

"They have seen them," Milt said quietly.

Judge turned to Carrillo, who had been sitting silently the whole time, grinning. Carrillo had known the outcome of this meeting before it had started. Milt had assured Carrillo of success, and the Latino's admiration for Milt was obvious.

"Are you planning to sell these aircraft in the US?" Judge queried. He was not finished protesting yet.

Carrillo looked at Milt, then back to Judge. "No," he replied, hesitating. "I have no plans at present."

"Then why bother with the FAA? Why bother with such a huge expense?" Although the services of the FAA are free to industry, ARI's were most certainly not. The flight test portion of the project alone could cost a million dollars. "Let's be on the level for a minute. This is a gunship, OK?"

Milt and Carrillo exchanged knowing glances. "It could have some military applications, like any aircraft," Carrillo offered cautiously, still refusing to commit a full admission to Judge. "It really does not matter," he continued. "Few countries will buy an aircraft from Chile unless it is either FAA certified or has been qualified for airworthiness by the armed services of the US, Great Britain, France, Germany, or Italy."

"Third World flight standards departments are not as prehistoric as you might think," Carrillo continued. "Most have laws and regulations setup to control, restrict, or prohibit the flight of experimental and noncertified equipment. Up until now, Chile has had no aircraft manufacturing capability. The Europeans won't even talk to us," he said.

Judge knew there was more to this than he was being told. He returned to his office and slumped into his chair, looking out of the huge windows, past the parking lot to the empty flight ramp and beyond to the distant stand of oaks. He wondered if this program might somehow be connected with his previous projects at ARI. The Indonesian fiasco and the turreted gunship conversion he had completed in England at the behest of the US State Department. Maybe this was what Pauline had alluded to. If so, he would find himself dealing with whoever had interfaced with the other programs. He wanted more answers to old questions. As the day wore on, he brooded over his growing feeling of unease. He was getting into another hornet's nest.

The sky had darkened considerably as he wrestled with the remainder of the day. The wind was beginning to kick and thrash the trees in protest to the premature end of what had begun as a beautiful morning. It was decaying into a miserable, cold, windy, late-spring storm.

Twelve

The holidays had risen quickly and with it Walt's spirits. Everyone arrived in Seattle, but Cheri. She had remained behind at the university. She would join them for Christmas and have a great break from school and him from work. His continence fell as fast as it had lifted. By New Year, it was all too evident to Walt that Cheri had moved on with her life as he knew in his heart she had to. Her parents and the Gardners returned home and receded with Cheri as the seventies' recession waned. It was the last he ever saw of them. By the beginning of the new decade, no one could reach the man they once new as Walter Judge.

Dr. Lofton Sr. had asked Judge to join him and his wife for dinner at their home in the Fort Worth Country Club Estates. It occurred to Judge that the tone in the senior doctor's voice had been very businesslike. The dinner was a final thank-you and farewell for his helping Michelle, in Judge's view.

He at first had tried to decline, but his refusal had been weak, and when he learned that Michelle was to be there too, he accepted. There was something about her, pulling feelings he had long since decided could never again be. Feelings that came only once in a lifetime, and he had had his chance at it, and it had died a long time ago. But somehow he had to face the fact that he wanted to see the young doctor again. He could not help but feel an attraction to her. She was young, beautiful, well bred, and educated. Her attitude towards him on occasion confused him, and he did not like guessing whether she might be interested in him or not.

Helen Lofton greeted Judge at the door. It was her first time meeting him when he was standing, and she was obviously taken aback by his bulk.

Tonight he was wearing a gray wool tweed sport coat, which blended well with his graying temples. He presented not a particularly handsome picture, but not altogether bad looking either.

She tried to shake his hand, which went a bit awkwardly, since she could barely get her dainty hand around two of the big man's fingers. Judge, however, was accustomed to greetings like that and barely noticed.

It was easy for Judge to see where Michelle's pretty face and eyes had come from. He struggled with déjà vu as distant memories began flooding back to him.

He guessed Michelle's mom to be no more than ten or twelve years older than himself, unlike her husband, whom he judged to be about sixty.

Helen Lofton led him to the den, where her husband was kneeling by an open fireplace, a drink in one hand, a poker in the other.

Upon seeing Judge, Dr. Lofton stood smiling and raised his glass in greeting. Unless Judge had missed his guess, he could hear the music of Strauss coming from the stereo. He listened as Michelle's voice, from somewhere, called in the tone of voice that she used with her young patients.

A little girl with long curly blonde hair and dancing blue eyes skipped into the room wearing a red plaid jumper and white blouse. She wore a pair of white silk stockings, but one of her little black patent leather shoes was missing. Judge guessed her to be about six.

She was rocking her head from left to right, touching each ear to her shoulders in turn. Her fingers were busy drumming the air as if she were playing an imaginary musical instrument. She stopped dead in her tracks when she saw Judge standing in the room, her happy smile replaced by a look of sheer surprise.

Michelle entered the den from the opposite side of the room holding the child's other shoe. "There you are, Muffin, come here." Then, seeing Judge, she straightened, surprised. "Well, hello! Sorry, I didn't hear the bell," she said. "How are you?"

Heather had stepped in front of him and was staring up at the big man's face. Judge knelt in front of her, but even while kneeling with one knee on the floor, his head was well above hers.

"Ohhhhh," the child said with wonder as she stared up into Judge's eyes. She approached slowly, until her eyes were too close to his for him to focus. She peered up into his eyes as if she were looking for something.

The senior Lofton gazed at them with amusement.

Heather backed up a step, clasped her hands together, and said, "Hello. Nín jiào shén me míng zi?" she said, asking his name.

Surprised, Judge's jaw dropped slightly. Recovering, he replied in Mandarin, "Wō jiào Walter Judge."

"Hĕn gāo xìng rèn shí nín," the child said, telling Judge that she was glad to meet him.

"Hĕn gāo xìng rèn shí nín," Judge replied.

Mrs. Lofton burst out in surprise, "You can understand her!"

"She speaks Mandarin Chinese," Judge said, himself amazed.

"Yes, we know, but we don't speak it, at least not well enough to understand her most of the time," Helen admitted.

Michelle raised her eyebrows. A second language, who would have thought, she said to herself. She had felt embarrassed at first, for her curt greeting.

Judge still looked miffed. *Who taught the child to speak Chinese?* he wondered. The Loftons were wondering who taught him.

Although Michelle had rehearsed in her mind a greeting at the door that would have been warmer and more familiar, she had not heard the doorbell and had been caught off guard.

"Heather, this is Mister Judge," Michelle's father introduced them, as the two women looked on. The child was suddenly stricken with shyness and scurried over to her mother.

"Mr. Judge, when is your birthday?" Helen Lofton asked. The look on her face told Judge that she already suspected the answer and was anticipating Judge to simply verify it.

"April 5th. And please, it's Walt."

"An Arios!" she exclaimed. "Of course. No wonder! Heather is a Taurus."

"Oh, Mother, really!" Michelle exclaimed, rolling her eyes. "I'm sure that astrology has nothing to do with Mr. Judge's manner around children. It's weird I know, but it's nothing to do with astrology!"

"Says you. I think it has something to do with Heather's attraction to him," her mother countered, dismissing Michelle's disbelief.

Helen Lofton had barely met Walter Judge, but she had heard about him from her husband. Still, the man remained somewhat of a mystery. Her concern for her daughter made her cautious about any man in whom Michelle seemed interested. However, as Michelle was now in her thirties, Helen's apprehension to new men in Michelle's life had been more open-minded. It had indeed occurred to her over the course of the past few weeks that Michelle spent a fair amount of time thinking about him. She sensed that there was something to be said for Walter Judge if he had earned her daughter's admiration.

Helen Lofton knew it had taken more than the usual bystander's courage to intercede, on Michelle's behalf. She, for one, was grateful, and she wanted to believe there was even more that was good about him. His apparent natural rapport with her granddaughter was a welcome hint of more good to come.

In fact, it seemed that he was more comfortable with the child than with the rest of her family. Helen was a true believer in astrology, and the Arios's natural parenting and protective nature seemed so obviously exhibited by Judge as to not be second-guessed.

The senior doctor, however, had remained more clinical in his opinion of Judge, at least for the time being. Despite Judge's involvement in Michelle's recent experience, the doctor still considered him more a patient than anything else.

Most any man, in Dr. Lofton's viewpoint, would have risked his life to help Michelle; and this did not particularly elevate Judge above any other in the doctor's opinion. He knew from talking to Tony Gibbons that Judge had a dark and mysterious past and should be approached with some caution until more was known about him.

Judge did, however, have a unique magnetism with Heather, and now, it seemed he spoke a foreign tongue. Intellect and wisdom commanded more respect from the doctor, who rarely gave his respect easily. Mr. Judge, here, was becoming a rather interesting fellow.

Judge was asking the doctor, "Who taught Heather to speak Chinese?"

"Her daycare nurse is a lovely little Chinese woman. She doesn't speak much English, and Heather is picking up quite a bit of Chinese. It seems to have slowed her grasp of English a bit, but she'll get it figured out in time. Michelle thinks a second language, especially Chinese, will be invaluable to Heather."

"Nín rèn shì wō de péng yōu Ms. Chi ma?" Heather asked Judge if he had met her Ms. Chi.

"Bù, hái méi ji huì," Judge replied, telling her that he had not had the pleasure.

Heather mixed in some English words, but Judge could understand her perfectly. Her hands began drumming the air again.

"Is Ms. Chi your nanny?" Judge asked, curious as to how much English the child could understand. He was watching her hands intently. There was something about the way her fingers danced that seemed familiar to him.

"How precious," Mrs. Lofton said softly, "how they understand each other." Then she whispered to Michelle, "Look how she gravitates towards him. I've never seen her do that with anyone before."

"She's never had anyone, except for Lin Chi, who could communicate with her," Michelle replied clinically. "Besides, Mr. Judge has a strange effect on children. I've seen him a few times visiting the children's ward at the hospital."

The Loftons stood watching in amazement. A big smile suddenly warmed Walter Judge's face. "Little One, what music is it that you are playing with your fingers?" he asked. The little girl seemed to ignore his English question and turned, dancing out of the room.

Judge did not say anything. He stood quietly looking after the girl. He was sure she had understood every word.

Dr. Lofton was looking straight at Judge watching him intently.

"She understood you," Michelle said. "She understands more than you might think even though she speaks a lot in Chinese. She does it more for attention than of habit."

Mrs. Lofton said, "You're right, look at this." She nodded towards Heather, who had just reentered the room from the doorway behind Michelle. The child approached Judge, holding up a sheet of piano music. Handing it to him, she made a little curtsy and danced back out of the room.

"Ragtime," Judge said, looking at the sheet of music.

Michelle and her parents stood watching Judge's reaction. Judge had a smile on his face, one he rarely displayed. He was a good bit better looking when he smiled, she admitted to herself.

"Your daughter plays ragtime?" Judge asked, but it was more of an impressed statement than a question.

"She's really quite a savant," Mrs. Lofton said in an admirable tone.

"Which one of you is the teacher?" the big man asked.

"Actually, Ms. Chi teaches her. She plays much more than just ragtime, of course, but that is her favorite," Michelle continued.

"You should hear her play, Mr. Jud—excuse me, *Walter*. Too bad we don't have a piano. I swear, sometimes when I pick Heather up from Ms. Chi's I think I'm entering an old saloon."

Dinner was finally served after a translation session between Heather, her family, and Walter Judge. Judge did much of the translation for Heather, when he realized that the child indeed understood most of the English that was spoken. It also became apparent that she could speak a lot more English than she was letting on to Judge, preferring to concentrate more on the Chinese language, for which she received lots of attention.

Heather ate at the table in her booster chair with the rest of them. She insisted on sitting next to Judge. Sometimes she spoke mostly English sentences with only a couple of Chinese words until she felt she was being left out of the conversation. Then it was the other way around.

"So, Walter," Dr. Lofton finally turned the conversation towards Judge, "Tony Gibbons tells me you were a Green Beret?"

Michelle looked up in surprise. Tony had not shared any of that with her.

"Army Ranger," Judge corrected. "That was a long time ago."

"We thought you must have been a football player," the doctor's wife quipped. "Did you ever play sports?"

Judge shook his head. "Only as a little kid. I was too small in school. Pretty much of a bookworm, I guess."

"Too little?" Mrs. Lofton said in surprise. "You've got to be kidding."

"I was pretty average until my teens," Judge continued.

"A late bloomer," Michelle said matter-of-factly, looking at her father, who nodded in agreement. "Special Forces?" she said to herself. She now realized where the man had learned his self-control when under excruciating pain.

"Tony says you're a pilot?" the elder Lofton asked, trying to keep the conversation going. Michelle looked at her food and shook her head. Seems like Tony had had quite a conversation with her father, she thought to herself.

"Well, yes and no. I became a Ranger pilot with the Office of Special Operations after Vietnam," Judge continued. "When I finally left the service, they kept me on as a civilian contract pilot, basically doing the same thing. I left the Special Ops in '84. I went to ARI after that. We did a lot of experimental work with the military. I've been consulting in the flight test business for the past several years."

Michelle was silent as she listened, as if watching Judge from a distance. There really was more to him than met the eye. This man's air of confidence had come from having nothing left to prove to himself. She should have realized it from the way he had rescued her.

The man had no ego, it seemed to her. There had been no witnesses that awful day, except for her. He could have walked away had it not been for his conscience. He had never brought it up to anyone, never bragged. When asked what had happened to him, he merely brushed it off as having had an accident.

It then occurred to her that Judge never acted like anything more than her patient. She had always known that he was not her patient, but that might not have been clear to him. Her treatment of him, checking up on him during his hospital stay and cleaning his dressings, was something she had been doing because she wanted to. Judge might have thought she was doing it because it was her obligation as a physician.

It had sometimes bothered her, perhaps even irritated her that he had responded to her attention as if he had expected it, like a patient would. He had never called for her even while bedridden at the hospital. He simply endured whatever discomfort befell him and accepted her attention as he would have from any doctor.

During the remainder of the evening, she listened and watched intently as Judge comfortably interacted with her parents and her daughter. She remained quiet and distant. She watched as her daughter chatted with this solemn stranger in her own private language and hung on his every word.

He spoke quietly without elaboration. There was no hint of braggadocio. He offered nothing beyond the answers to her parents' continued questioning. But her mother's curiosity and fascination with the man finally reached the point of embarrassment for Michelle.

When Mrs. Lofton asked Judge if he had ever been married, Michelle interrupted.

"Mother, really! I'm sure Walter has had enough of twenty questions."

Mrs. Lofton laughed and apologized for being so inquisitive. Even so, there was a pregnant pause as the Loftons all waited for Judge to answer the question. Judge smiled but offered nothing further.

Heather was growing fidgety, and the attention turned back to her. She had not eaten much of her dinner, and Michelle asked her what was wrong.

"Wō bù xi huān zhè gè," Heather said, making a face.

"She doesn't like her food," Michelle said before Judge could translate. Then looking at Judge, who had almost uttered the same words, she said defensively, "It's OK, you needn't translate for her all the time. I understand some of what she says."

"Michelle, when shall we go piano shopping?" the senior doctor interrupted the exchange.

"We don't really know for sure that she wants to," Michelle replied.

"I'd lay odds," Judge added. Then he continued, "I know, because she says she does."

Dr. and Mrs. Lofton burst out laughing. Even Michelle was amused.

"Well, Walter has a piano. A great big beautiful one," Michelle said with a twinkle in her eye. She was beginning to feel more comfortable.

"Whenever were you at Walter's home?" her mother asked, surprised.

"I saw it when I was giving him a . . ." She stopped in midsentence as she took in the looks from her parents, suddenly realizing what she had been about to say. She turned red, stammering for the words to make time go backwards.

"Giving him a what?" her mother asked, her mouth still open.

Judge sat quietly, a look of amusement on his face. Michelle looked at him and was clearly irritated with his expression.

"A lift home from the hospital," Walter said easily. Words flowed better when one's mind wasn't confused with the truth. It had really been nothing, but then, her parents had not been there; and he was sure Michelle did not want them imagining for themselves.

"Oh, well, for a minute there . . ." Dr. Lofton said, mocking his daughter. It was too late. The good doctor already suspected that his daughter had provided Judge with special attention, and at this point, it seemed little more than good humor to him.

Michelle's jaw jutted ever so slightly as she glared at her father. "So," she began slowly, changing the subject while turning her gaze back on Judge, "when shall the recital be?"

"Whenever you wish," Judge replied quietly, "but you all must stay for dinner afterwards."

"And he cooks too!" Mrs. Lofton said loudly, looking directly at Michelle, who just rolled her eyes at her mother and shook her head.

Then, turning to Heather, Michelle asked, "Heather, would you like to play Mr. Judge's piano?"

Heather sucked in her breath in exaggerated surprise as she caught her mother's words. She looked at Judge with an expression of delight. Everyone laughed.

The man was clearly taken with the little girl, and she with him. She refused to leave his side even when prodded by her mother that it was time to leave. Judge spoke to her in Chinese, and she agreed to have him walk her out to Michelle's car. Her mother followed at a distance.

When he had buckled the child into her car seat, he gently ruffled the child's hair and said goodbye to her in Chinese. Heather squealed in delight and waved as Judge closed her car door.

Michelle was standing beside the Audi. "Walter," she began hesitantly, "I was serious when I suggested a recital for Heather."

"Honestly?" he asked.

"Of course," she said, "Heather would be really disappointed if we didn't. She won't forget."

"I just didn't think you were too serious about it."

"What makes you say that?" Michelle asked.

"I just thought you were uncomfortable," was all Judge would say. He shrugged.

Michelle put her fingers on his lips. "Please," she said softly, "the only thing that makes me uncomfortable is you calling me 'Dr. Lofton.' After all we've been through together, can you call me Michelle?"

She stood silently, gazing at Judge standing before her in the moonlight. How he could have such an opinion of her feelings, she wondered.

"Listen," Judge continued, "I'm leaving for South America in a couple days. I'll be gone a week or so. You know where the key is, and I'll call you in the morning and leave you the alarm code. Bring Heather and your folks over and make yourself at home. She'll love playing that old piano."

"I wouldn't think of doing that," Michelle said softly, a look of hurt on her pretty face. "It would break Heather's heart if you weren't there. Don't you pay any attention to my moods? I'm a case."

To his surprise, she reached up and gently pulled his head down. She kissed him gently on the lips, barely touching him. It was so sudden that he hadn't a chance to respond.

As she turned to open the driver's door, she said, "Oh, Dad asked me to tell you to drop by his office so he can have those staples in your chest removed. They need to come out. We'll get together with Heather as soon as you get back in town." Sliding behind the wheel, she gaily waved at him and was gone before he could say anything. Michelle's mother and father stood in the drive and waved as she drove off.

Dr. Lofton looked at Judge standing with a perplexed look. "You look like you could use a drink." He laughed.

Judge smiled. "I accept," he said, following the Loftons into the house for a nightcap. They talked about their respective livelihoods with the senior Lofton being particularly fascinated by Judge's occupation and exploits. Dr. Lofton too was a Vietnam veteran, and both talked for nearly an hour as if they had known each other for years.

Their conversation eventually came back around to Michelle and Heather. "I think my daughter might be taken with you, Walter," Dr. Lofton said.

Judge shook his head in disbelief. He smiled. Perhaps, he thought, but he wasn't sure that it mattered to him. OK, well that's not true, he told himself. It did matter to him. He was just having a hard time believing that it was happening.

"By the way, Walter, stop by my Fort Worth office in the morning, and I'll get someone to remove those staples. It's high time they were removed. We'll run a blood series and put this thing behind us."

Wondering if he had enough time before his flight, Judge said, "If you say so." Then he dismissed himself, finally bidding the Loftons a good night.

Thirteen

The Burleson field office of the FBI was nearly deserted. Jenkins sat reading a fax he had just received. "Got something interesting for you," Jenkins said, addressing Lieutenant Gibbons.

"What's that?" Gibbons said, looking up from behind his desk.

"Judge is flying to South America tomorrow."

"How'd you find that out?"

"I went over to DFW and had each of the airlines put a flag on his name in their reservation computers to fax me if he made any reservations, period."

Gibbons had to hand it to Jenkins; the guy was thorough, never wrote anything down, but was a great sleuth.

"Where to, exactly?" Gibbons asked, reaching for Judge's file.

"Now get this, Santiago, Chile. Ring a bell?" Jenkins asked suggestively.

"Sure does," Gibbons replied, suddenly very interested. He set Judge's file down and reached for a different one.

"What did you say the name of that huge foreigner was, the one they released because of diplomatic immunity?" Gibbons was frantically shuffling files, looking for the right one.

"Ponce Gutierrez," Jenkins replied.

"Ah yes, here it is," the lieutenant said, smiling. "That guy once lived in Illinois on a work visa. Came up on an FBI search of Visas. Says here that he worked for some security agency. In parenthesis it has "bodyguard." Strange, it doesn't list who he was guarding. Look at this picture they sent us. Gutierrez is the big guy standing in the back to the left of the podium." Gibbons handed Jenkins a photo that had arrived from the Illinois State Police.

"Jesus!" exclaimed Jenkins. "What a gorilla! Who's that at the podium?"

"No idea. Get with the Illinois State Police and see if they can come up with the names of everyone else in the picture."

"Says here that Gutierrez got himself reassigned to the Colombian Embassy," Gibbons continued.

"Sounds odd," Jenkins mused.

"According to the file, there were accusations of 'roughness' between Gutierrez and a couple of the women in the Agency. The charges were dropped when Gutierrez left the Illinois job to join the embassy staff." Looking up from the file, he asked, "So he's working in Colombia?"

"No, we assumed he had moved from Colombia because the embassy told us he was 'in Chile' on assignment."

"Fascinating," Gibbons said, almost to himself, deep in thought. Then, looking again at Jenkins, he ordered, "See if you can find out what Judge is working on."

"I checked with ARI," Jenkins replied. "They're being pretty tight-lipped about Judge. He's due back the end of the week. I'll get with our friends over at the Dallas Bureau and see if they can find out anything," he said. "Something else that's really curious too," he added, handing Gibbons an additional file. "Headquarters sent this over. You were right about your suspicions of Pauline Casey. She turned up dead in a Virginia hotel the night the Lofton girl was attacked here. The locals called it a 'suspicious' suicide. They're looking into it at our request."

"Hey, Lieutenant," a uniform called from the office doorway. "That chick you wanted picked up for questioning is here. They just brought her in downstairs."

"Thanks, I'm on my way," Gibbons replied. He stood and motioned for Jenkins to follow him.

Descending the stairs to the holding area, he explained that he had been looking for the prostitute Gutierrez had beaten up on the way to New Orleans the year before. On a hunch, he figured she had probably returned to the Dallas-Fort Worth area.

Now, here she was, sitting beside a clerk's desk, in a short black leather skirt, tight halter top, and high boots.

Noisily chewing a wad of gum, it seemed obvious to Gibbons that she had not changed her profession.

She fixed Gibbons with an aggrieved look. "So, Mr. Man, what's this all about? I wasn't doing nothin'. I got my rights, ya know."

Gibbons and Jenkins each took an arm and coaxed her to her feet. Neither was smiling. "Let's have a little talk," suggested Jenkins. "I know the perfect place." They motioned her towards an adjoining interrogation room and urged her to sit down when they were inside.

Gibbons had dealt with suspects before who had a chip on their shoulder. He knew he could get the most information from her by letting her know that he was not fooling around. Absolutely nothing would happen to her if she cooperated.

"We just have a few questions for you. Afterwards, Sgt. Jenkins will take you anywhere in the city you want to go," Gibbons said, his voice amiable, but his eyes hard.

Lighting a cigarette, the girl, a seasoned veteran of police stations, asked, "What's in it for me?"

"A free lunch and a lift," he replied, snatching her cigarette and stuffing it under his foot. "Otherwise we'll hold you for 24 hours on suspicion of pandering."

She frowned. "You got nothing on me."

"Take it or leave it."

The girl thought about it for a moment, then said, "Dinner at the Old San Francisco Steak House."

"Lunch," Gibbons replied sternly.

"OK, whatever." She shrugged, resigning. "What d'ya wanna know?"

Gibbons questioned her for over an hour. She didn't hesitate to share her entire ordeal of the year before. Ponce Gutierrez, whom she identified for Gibbons from the photo that he had shown Jenkins earlier, had picked her up in Dallas around midnight. He had driven her to the Addison Airport, where they boarded a private jet, which, according to "Mr. Ponce," belonged to a friend of his boss. He was flying to the Big Easy to collect pay for a job he had just completed in Arlington.

"You're sure he said 'Arlington'?" Tony interrupted.

"Arl-ling-ton," she said, exaggerating the pronunciation. Gibbons glared at her.

"We had sex on the plane on the way, really rough sex," she said continuing, like it had been no big deal. "The guy was a brute, if you know what I mean," she added. "When we got to New Orleans, a big limo met us at the airport and drove us to the convention downtown. Big political fund-raiser or something, lots of bigwigs, congressmen and all."

"Why did he rough you up?" asked Jenkins.

"Rough me up? The bastard tried to kill me. He met with some guy at the convention center, who I never saw. Apparently, the big ape didn't get his money 'cause he was madder than hell when they threw him out."

"What do you mean he didn't get his money?" Tony interrupted.

"For the job he done in Arlington. I dunno, he just kept saying that it was the last time he does somebody without getting paid in advance. I overheard him hollerin' at the two guys they arrested with him."

"Did you tell that to the police?"

"They never asked. Look, there must've been a hundred girls picked up downtown that night, what with the convention and all. All the cops did was charge us for trick'n and took a statement if we was beat up. I just told them he wouldn't pay and then he beat me up. I got rent to pay, ya know."

"Why did he beat up on you?" Jenkins asked again.

"I started askin' him for my money." She tried lighting another cigarette, but hesitated after detecting a glare from Gibbons.

"He was all scratched and cut up, you know, from fightin' with someone before he picked me up. Whoever he 'done' in Arlington must have put up some fight."

"Before he picked you up from Dallas? It was in your statement to the police." Gibbons wanted it clarified.

"Well yeah, 'cause after they arrested him he tried to say he was just defending himself from me. What a crock. I never put a mark on him, not like what he had. Some of his cuts couldn't have been made with just fingernails," she defended. "He'd been fightin' with somebody before we ever left. Probably that job he said he did in Arl-ling-ton," she added, glaring back at the lieutenant. "The one he didn't get paid for."

"Go on," Tony urged, ignoring her expression.

"Well, when he wouldn't pay me, I told him I'd have him worked over worse than that last person he'd fought with. I was only bluffin' 'cause I don't know anyone who could kick that monster's ass."

"Then what happened?"

"He grabbed me 'round my throat and said, 'Yeah? Well, maybe I'll do to you what I did to her,' and then he started whuppin' on me 'til I almost blacked out."

"You said 'her.' He'd been in a fight with a *woman*? You're sure? In Arlington?"

"*ARL-Ling-Ton*," she hollered at Gibbons, clearly irritated with the lieutenant. "Sure I'm sure. I'll never forget them words."

"Where did this happen?" Gibbons tried to keep his cool. He felt like slapping the bitch.

"Right there in the limo. He'd of killed me if the driver hadn't started hollerin' at him. He threw me out and stomped back into the convention center. He was all fired up about getting his money. He got arrested for trying to fight his way back in. I got away from there figuring he was going to kill me when he came back empty-handed. I didn't have no money and was hurt. Some cops picked me up and took me downtown. I saw them bring him into the station later on with them other two," she said disgustedly. "Had to find my own way back to Dallas too."

Gibbons stood and pulled Jenkins aside. "Go ahead and take her to lunch. After you drop her off, find out where Judge is and call me on the radio. I need to talk to him before he goes on his trip."

Fourteen

Jenkins found Judge at his home. When he knocked on the door, he could see through the window, a small duffel bag lying on the floor. Judge greeted him stiffly when Jenkins introduced himself.

Rather than having to entertain Jenkins while they waited for Lieutenant Gibbons to arrive, Judge agreed to accompany Jenkins to the field office in Burleson. They drove in silence. He was irritated at this last-minute inconvenience on the eve of his trip.

"I have some questions I want to ask you," Tony said with no introductions when Judge entered Gibbons's office with Jenkins trailing behind.

Jenkins led Judge to the same interrogation room where the two police officers had been earlier in the day with the little hooker.

The room had a large mirror on one end, which Judge stared at momentarily. *Just like on TV*, he thought. "Delightful," he muttered under his breath.

Jenkins held up a file, which Judge's dark eyes quickly caught the title of from nearly six feet away. "Judge," it read.

"You have a file on me?" Judge asked.

"We'll get to that," Gibbons said.

Judge glared at him.

"We just have a few questions for you about Ms. Lofton and your deceased girlfriend," Gibbons said.

"They're not related . . ." Judge began but cut himself short. *Now would be the time to listen*, he thought. He had heard about Connie Lin's death. He had been overseas at the time of her murder. But it had nothing to do with him, and they had not exactly parted on the best of terms. He had not thought much about it since.

"I think they are," Gibbons continued, handing Judge the photo of Ponce Gutierrez that the Illinois State Police had sent.

Judge's veins on his neck stood out. "What are you saying to me?" he asked slowly, turning his gaze onto the picture.

Judge looked at the picture; the two policemen looked at Judge. They could see no expression on his face.

"What is your relationship with this man?" Gibbons asked.

"There is no relationship," Judge said.

"Did you know he was in town the night your girlfriend was killed?"

"Who was?" Judge asked. "What would anyone want with Connie?"

"Him, that guy, the one that looks like King Kong!" Tony said, pointing to the biggest man in the picture, somewhat exasperated.

"Never met him," Judge said flatly. He knew the FBI wanted to get information, not give it. He, on the other hand, wanted to know what the FBI knew.

Tony threw up his hands in frustration.

Jenkins, in an unusual display of leadership, stood up and pulled his lieutenant aside. "Tony," he hissed, "get a grip. I think we're on to something, and Judge just might not be the bad guy here. Try to be objective for a moment and snuff out that torch you've been carrying for that Lofton broad."

Tony looked at Jenkins. The man he saw was not the absent-minded sergeant that Jenkins usually portrayed. The sergeant, older than Tony by some years, father of three, solver of more crimes than Tony had years on the force, was gazing back at Tony like his dad used to when helping him with his homework. Tony felt suddenly ashamed.

Jenkins turned to Judge with his hand on Tony's shoulder. "Mr. Judge, have you ever met anyone in this picture?"

Judge, welcoming the calming influence of Jenkins, looked again at the photograph. He shook his head.

Looking first at his lieutenant and then back to Judge, Jenkins asked, "Do you have any idea why any of these men would have been in Arlington the night your girlfriend was killed?"

Judge squinted at Jenkins, as if trying to see into Jenkins's mind. It had suddenly occurred to him that these two knew something that he wanted to know, and he wanted to know it as much as he had wanted anything in his life.

Jenkins looked at Judge, and he suddenly knew that the big man standing before him could tell they were holding something back. He was ready to share information with Judge. If Judge was involved in any untoward way with either crime, Jenkins felt confident that he could tell. Suspects always slipped up eventually, and he for one, did not suspect Judge of a crime. At any rate, they could learn more than they knew now.

Jenkins also knew that his lieutenant was being influenced by his past relationship with Michelle. He was being highly unprofessional in his dealings with Judge. Jenkins had therefore decided to take the initiative. He hated to go to their captain about Tony's lack of professionalism, but he would if it came to that.

After taking a big sigh, Tony said, "We have a witness that says that big guy there was in a fight with a woman in Arlington, by his own admission, the night your ex-girlfriend was killed, and hurt her pretty bad."

Judge stood up, towering over the two officers. "Excuse me?"

"It would appear," Jenkins said in a calm voice, "that Gutierrez may have suffered a significant beating at the hands of the woman he fought with."

"You forgot one other thing our witness said," Tony added, looking at Jenkins. "The girl said that Gutierrez flew to New Orleans to get paid for the job." Tony had said more than he had intended to placate the towering man before him.

"So why have you not arrested him?" Judge asked angrily.

"Calm down, Mr. Judge," Jenkins ordered. "Gutierrez is not in Texas and as near as we can tell, not in the country. We only have a weak theory and a very unreliable witness at best. Even if we could haul him in for questioning at this point, he'd be out again in 60 seconds."

"Even if we find him," Gibbons cautioned. "Our evidence is pretty thin. We still don't have a motive and so far, we can't connect enough of the events to hold him on anything. If we catch him in Texas, you can bet we'll only get one crack at him."

Judge was nonplused. "I don't get it." He smiled inwardly. His act of emotion was working.

"You don't get it?" Tony asked angrily. "If Gutierrez really attacked your girlfriend, it appears he got paid to do it. His buddies then try to knock off your reporter friend, who they think is Michelle, and here you are right in the middle of it." Tony was becoming emotional again and, despite Sam Jenkins's repeated gestures for Gibbons to cool it, persisted in completing his statement. "How is it that someone with your background can be in the middle of all this and act so completely innocent?" he cried.

Well, finally! So that was it! Judge had his connection. Jenkins winced at Tony's revelation to Judge.

"Mr. Judge, can you explain your business in South America for us?" Jenkins asked calmly, giving Gibbons a warning look to remain silent for the moment. "We know you ran a shady program in Indonesia. You can help allay the lieutenant's suspicions if you can tell us as much as you know. Your folks at ARI have not been very forthcoming."

Judge wanted information in return. He described his role in conducting a test. "I don't set programs up," Judge said. "I get presented a contract, and if it is something I'm interested in, and legal, and the price is right, I accept it," he added.

Judge kept his cool. "Lieutenant, I very well could be 'right in the middle of it' as you suggest. I would just like to know what it is that I'm in the middle of." Judge spoke as politely as he could manage to the lieutenant.

"Tell us about your trip tomorrow," Jenkins interrupted, changing the subject. "We know you're headed for South America."

"The program I'm working on is with a company from Santiago, Chile. Carrillo Industries, S.A. I believe.

We're working with the FAA on an aircraft that Carrillo is building, for agricultural purposes." Judge said it as if he believed it.

"We haven't definitely made a connection between those three men." Tony wasn't even listening to what Judge was saying. "It's loosely circumstantial at this point," Tony admitted.

"Is it possible that ARI is using you to conduct illegal foreign activity?" Jenkins asked.

Judge shrugged; they weren't saying anything that hadn't already been through his mind hundred times. "All of the programs have always been set up through a State Department Liaison. We have to deal with the Commerce Department for Export licenses, US Customs for visas and equipment shipping and inspections, and contacts with foreign dignitaries, like Habibie in Indonesia. All of that requires someone versed in foreign business law and practices. ARI doesn't have anyone like that. We always worked through contracts that were received through some liaison with the State Department."

"Who was your liaison?" Gibbons asked.

"I don't know. I've seen US government official vehicles parked at the front offices on several occasions, but I've never been introduced."

"So, Mr. Judge, in your opinion, this project you have going in Chile is with the US government's approval?"

"Well, the FAA is involved. The FAA even has designated representatives ready to go to Chile once I'm further along with the development."

Jenkins had withdrawn his attention. Deep in thought, he began to realize that this case was getting beyond the capabilities of the local FBI field office. He looked at his partner, and then to Judge. Jenkins suddenly had the feeling that Pauline Casey would not be the last corpse to turn up in this case.

Fifteen

Baghdad Rages On—"PARIS. The conventional Washington argument on Iraq is that President Saddam Hussein is totally impervious to official complaint, but may mellow when handled with velvet."

—New York Times, ***Apr. 28, 1990, p. 25***

Flying south beyond the equator, the pilot had difficulty with the cabin temperature control or had not bothered with the numerous complaints from the freezing passengers. By the time Judge disembarked, his apprehension of his arrival had changed to anxious anticipation of climbing out into the warm sunshine, only to be disappointed by the briskness of the air when the moment finally came. He had forgotten about the reversed seasons when flying south of the equator, which he had left behind some hours before.

Judge remained patient as he suffered the Chilean customs inspectors and then, after being nearly strip searched by the entry police under a sign that simply read "CNI," he made for the main terminal. He quickly exited the large station and, having learned years before to travel as lightly as possible, tossed his only carry-on bag to the first taxi waiting in line.

"Carrera Hotel," Judge said to the driver.

"Ah, Si senor." The driver smiled happily and darted into the traffic.

The city of Santiago seemed alive with the excitement of their recent election. Chile, a totalitarian government since before the Allende fiasco of the mid-1960s, was in the midst of a change in power.

The driver, who nodded his head at Judge's every question, obviously was not fluent in English. Would they make it to the hotel or end up outside the city zoo? Judge wondered.

To his great relief, the driver swung into the narrow courtyard just outside the lobby of the Carrera Hotel. Having at least recognized Judge's pronunciation of the name of the hotel, he most certainly deserved a decent tip. He stuffed a few thousand pesos in the cabby's shirt pocket as he lifted his bag from the trunk.

The little man's face lit up; and then, just as suddenly, it disappeared. "No, no, senor. Too much . . . too much." He handed the bills back to Judge.

Their route to the hotel had been direct. The cab, Judge noted, was quite old but had been meticulously cared for. He looked at the driver's clothes, threadbare, but neatly pressed and clean. The man's belt was drawn to its first hole, adding to its owner's gaunt appearance.

Judge smiled and handed the bills back to the cabby. "Not too much for me," he said.

The driver remained by Judge's side as he checked in. He insisted on taking Judge's bag all the way to his room, to the consternation of the hotel bellhop.

It was getting dark as Judge stepped down to the hotel lounge. He looked over a sandwich menu as he motioned for a waiter. None came, so he moved to the bar.

He ordered a cup of coffee at the bar and chose a low-slung table in front of the only window facing the street, which ran in front of the hotel. The street was fairly quiet now, lit only by the fading blue sky. The sun had slipped below the horizon, leaving a dull pink trail behind it.

The bar was fairly dark and empty, save for one fellow in the corner talking on the only telephone in sight. He kept looking over his shoulder at Judge, cupping the mouthpiece to prevent his conversation from being overheard.

The man referred occasionally to a small notepad that he kept pulling from his shirt pocket. He was speaking English and appeared quite Anglo. Judge could not discern specific words that he spoke, but he thought that he might be British.

Judge had seen that look before. He had been located. Perhaps not followed, but the man had been looking for him, and Judge knew when the man hung up the phone that he would either follow Judge or approach him.

The man did the latter.

When he had hung up the phone, he stood, somewhat hesitantly, and moved towards Judge, stopping only when Judge stood to meet him, towering over him, ready for anything.

"You're Walter Judge," the man said in an obvious British accent. "I'm William Duffy. Pauline told me to look you up here in Santiago if something should happen to her."

Stunned, Judge stood motionless but for a moment. Pauline could not have known weeks ago that he would be in Santiago. He hadn't known it himself. He motioned the man to a booth.

"I'm working on a story for a little aviation publication, *Global Helicopter* magazine," Duffy began. "I'm here covering the FIDAE Air Show." He seemed to have a bit of a swollen lip, occasionally touching it with his fingertips and then looking at his fingers, as if to be checking for blood. "I'm sure you've never heard of it . . ." he continued.

Judge raised an eyebrow. "On the contrary," he said, "I'm in the business myself."

Duffy stopped. "Yes, I know. Pauline spoke very highly of you. Told me I could trust you. Said you were real big in the industry. She was right about that," he muttered under his breath.

For the first time, Judge noticed what appeared to be a bruise on the side of the man's temple. The man looked to have been in some fight, Judge thought.

Duffy leaned forward and almost whispered, "You're working on the Carrillo thing." He whipped out his little notepad again.

"Pauline!" Judge interrupted. His usual patient manner was absent for the moment. "What about Pauline?"

Duffy looked at his watch. "I say, can you talk about it? You know, the Carrillo thing! I mean, without getting upset? I've had enough of that for one day." Duffy was almost talking to himself.

"I'm not upset. Had enough of what? Tell me about Pauline. How do you know her? Where is she?" Judge demanded.

"Well, she and I covered some of the same stories together. Met mostly at the world aviation exhibitions, you know, Paris, Farnborough, Singapore, like FIDAE, the one being held here."

"Have you heard from her?" Judge asked.

"Well," Duffy began again, ignoring Judge's last question for the moment. "She first mentioned your name when we were in Baghdad last April. She seemed excited. As soon as she found out that you were working with the Iraqis, she wanted to talk to you right away. She was afraid you wouldn't talk to her."

"What? The Iraqis, I'm doing no such thing," Judge insisted.

"That's what she was afraid you'd say. She said she overheard your name being mentioned as doing the work . . ."

"Last April? That couldn't be . . ." Judge interrupted again.

"No, I mean, well yes. You see, she said you did the work on that Indonesian thing. Got the system all developed and then the turret and sighting system in England. She said it was all part of the plan."

"What plan?"

"The Carrillo thing. You did it all in preparation for the Carrillo aircraft."

"Nonsense!" Judge insisted. "That aircraft doesn't have any weapons on it. It doesn't even fly yet." Judge began to feel like the gullible rube again, this time for real.

"All I know is Pauline said she was sitting at a table at the Baghdad Exhibition at a luncheon and overheard a conversation at a nearby table. They were talking about 'the final product,' like it had been planned all along. She smelled a story when they mentioned your name because she knew some of the stuff you had been working on."

"She told me on the phone that I wouldn't believe it," Judge said slowly, thinking back to his conversation with Pauline. "I've suspected that weapons could go on this aircraft, but I knew I wasn't going to have anything to do with it. Pauline told me that she had proof of something, but she never showed up."

"They killed her before she had a chance," came Duffy's grim reply.

Judge was suddenly deflated. "Goddamn it," he said grimly. It was as if he half expected it. He had feared the worst ever since that night when she had not appeared. Hearing it for certain hit him hard just the same.

"You're sure it was murder?"

"Well, the police first said it was suicide, but later I read that they had discounted it," confirmed Duffy. "They must have gotten her pictures too."

"Pictures of what?"

"Last month, in Singapore, she told me she found that same group of men together in the Chilean Chalet at the Singapore Air Show. She took a picture, you know, trying to act like a tourist. They chased her and took her camera, but not before she had switched films. Clever girl she was."

"She had the roll developed and showed me," Duffy said. "She was very excited. Said it was her big scoop."

"Who was in the photo?"

"Pauline knew most of them, but the only men I recognized were Carrillo and a Palestinian. I can't remember his name."

"Palestinian?" Judge asked.

"Some wheeler-dealer, sort of a go-between for Carrillo. He introduces Carrillo to dignitaries interested in arms."

"Why would Carrillo care about that?"

"Why would . . . ?" he mocked Judge, sounding incredulous. "Don't you realize Carrillo is the largest arms manufacturer in South America, not to mention one of the richest men in Chile? Next to the United States, nobody in this hemisphere exports as many arms!"

It was Judge's turn to be surprised. He had never heard the name Carrillo associated with arms sales. He had been fooled after all.

"You said Pauline recognized the others that were in her photograph?" Judge asked. "Besides the three you mentioned."

"I swear, old boy, I didn't write it down, and she was just sharing her excitement."

"Can't you remember their names?" Judge said anxiously.

"Well, I remember she said one of them was the head of ARI, your firm . . ."

"Fox?"

"Yeah, that's right, but the ones that had her so excited were an Iraqi general and a member of your government."

"My government, you mean like someone from the FAA? Are you sure? Who?"

"Sorry, ole boy, I just can't remember the name. Pauline seemed to think he was a lot more important than a guy from the FAA. A politician I think."

Then Duffy added, "I think I can find out. It's risky, mind you. Seems like every time I ask questions about the Carrillo project, or the Iraqis, I get my chops cracked."

"How can you find out their names?"

"They're here," Duffy whispered.

"What?"

"They're here, for FIDAE! You know how these exhibitions work. Lots of deals go down at these things. Strangest thing you've ever seen, been that way for years. The guys selling just love us journalists, but the guys buying hate us. They'd kill us soon as gander at us. 'Cept on the Carrillo project, that is. Pauline warned me that both sides hate us. Won't even talk to us. She said even the Americans got upset when they found out who she worked for."

"You can find out the name of the American in Pauline's picture?"

"I'm sure I saw him. Just can't think of his name. I'll find out for you."

"Pauline shared her scoop with you?"

"I've known Pauline for years. She knew I'd never steal a big story from her. We helped each other out from time to time. I was going to follow up on her story after she died you know, get the goods and make a big headline sort of thing. But every time I'd get close to a good source, I'd get my head kicked in. You were going to be Pauline's inside source, the one to tie it all up for her. Can't go to press without solid evidence, you know. She said if anything ever happened to her that I would find you in Santiago working on Carrillo's project. She said you'd show up sooner or later. I decided I'd follow up when I came to cover FIDAE. But hell, you know less than I do."

"What's the big deal? That the Chileans are selling arms to Iraq? Where's the story in that?"

"No, Mr. Judge, that's only on the surface. It's you Americans that are behind it. Chile is just the middleman. And the topper is, as Pauline would have quipped, that she could prove that the US government is paying for the development!"

Sixteen

The next morning, Judge left the hotel to catch a cab to Carrillo's facility, in the foothills south of the city. He was still deep in thought about his meeting with Duffy the night before and more than a little depressed at the reality of Pauline's death.

It had not been difficult for Duffy to find him, knowing that Milt had always used the Carrera Hotel on his trips to Santiago. It was also one of the most popular establishments for government and industry specialists attending the FIDAE Air Show.

Carrillo's directions had been very good, but Judge wondered why Carrillo had not sent a car for him instead. Perhaps he had wanted to distance himself from any public association with Judge and ARI. Reporters and secret agents were always looking out for private associations between arms dealers and private industry representatives, and Judge was recognizable, to say the least.

Associating with ARI at FIDAE presented a different perspective to any suspicious observer. The aviation and arms exhibitions were like a shopping mall of technology where dignitaries and generals cruised and asked questions.

Private liaisons were viewed differently however and, if discovered, created a high degree of speculation in foreign intelligence circles. "Back room" deals among dignitaries and merchants were always being sought by the journalists and spies.

The road leading to the airfield was gated. An armed guard motioned for Judge to get out of the cab. After checking his passport for identification, the sentry checked Judge's name against a list he held on his clipboard, then sent the cab on its way. A second sentry motioned Judge to a jeep. They climbed in and proceeded onward.

The sentry had taken Judge directly to Carrillo's office. Judge was ushered in immediately by a rather attractive girl, presumably his secretary, or one of his secretaries.

Carrillo, dressed in a white shirt and dark slacks, looked as if he had just stepped from his favorite haberdashery. Not a wrinkle was in sight. His expensive Italian shoes matched his belt, completing his "casual" business attire.

He said a few words to the girl in Spanish and closed the door behind her as she scurried off. Carrillo welcomed Judge cordially and motioned him to a seat. "I trust your flight to our great city was comfortable, yes?" he asked. Before Judge could answer, he continued, "You look tired. I must apologize. The Carrera is fine for most men, but a man of your, eh . . . stature, well . . . I will see what I can do."

"Everything was fine," Judge replied. "I am just anxious to get to work." However, he nodded when Carrillo motioned to a cup of coffee and pressed a button on his telephone to speak with his secretary in Spanish.

Carrillo folded his hands together and quietly began to speak more seriously. "So you will give me an evaluation of my design. Yes? How much time do you think you will need?"

"A day or two at the most, maybe less," Judge replied. "If I see problems, however, it will take some time to get any required changes designed and the parts made."

"The first prototype must be shipped to Dallas as soon as possible, to be used for development flight tests. It is of utmost importance that the project be kept on schedule."

"What's the rush?" Judge asked.

"Time is money," Carrillo replied quickly. "I want to see you again Friday morning, before your flight back to Texas." He then called for his chief engineer, who was to give Judge a brief tour and get him settled in.

"It will take a week to ship the prototype north," he said to Judge while they waited for the engineer to arrive. "A precious week that ARI can use, for designing remedies for any problems that you discover now."

The cute secretary opened the door. She held the door with one foot while passing two cups of coffee to Carrillo. A young man of about thirty stood quietly behind her. When she was balanced again on both feet, she motioned him to step in. He nodded to Carrillo and introduced himself to Judge as L'eon De Padilla, chief engineer.

L'eon led Judge out to the big manufacturing facility. Judge's brief tour consisted only of a walk through that particular building, which was one big hangar with numerous shop workstations stretched along its length. Unmodified LongRangers were being brought in through the hangar door on one end, where they were systematically dismantled and rebuilt as they moved along the line.

Judge counted a dozen fuselages in various states of assembly, with two more LongRangers sitting on the flight ramp outside, awaiting their transformation. By the end of the week, there would be more.

The prototype aircraft, intended for shipment to Texas, was located just off to the side of the line, near the exit hangar door.

The flight controls workstation was the area of Judge's greatest concern. It was there that he concentrated his first efforts. By the end of the day, he had identified a serious control system design error that would prevent the aircraft from being flown.

He pointed this problem out to De Padilla, who had been curiously watching with several other assembly workers and engineers.

"Watch the flight controls at the swash plate as I move the cyclic forward and aft," he commanded L'eon. The group of engineers and technicians watched the swash plate. It tilted right and left in response to Judge's fore and aft inputs. There were several groans from the group as they began to understand their error in properly phasing the rotor controls.

A buzzer sounded as the afternoon wore on. "It is time for the second shift," announced L'eon. "We will talk to the engineers and give your changes immediate attention. They must continue the necessary changes to the blueprints."

It was evident the project received around-the-clock attention. A new group of assembly workers and supervisors had arrived, and De Padilla quickly explained to his supervisors what he expected of them during their shifts.

L'eon escorted Judge to his jeep as the tired first shift began filing out, some running for bicycles, in an attempt to get to the gate ahead of the crowd.

They drove through the gate and immediately turned away from the road leading to town and headed towards the hills east of the airfield.

"I'm sorry, but I forgot to mention that Mr. Carrillo wants me to take you to a different hotel for the remainder of your stay. I have already sent a man for your bag. Of course, Mr. Carrillo will take care of your bill."

Judge's earlier suspicions seemed to be confirmed, and he wondered how many more times he'd be moved before the week was out. He also wondered how he might contact Duffy, who was to get him the name of the American official at FIDAE whom Pauline had photographed.

Judge had surmised that there was a serious effort afoot to keep news of Carrillo's real intentions for the aircraft away from him. To that end, he knew his presence at FIDAE could create a confrontation that he wished to avoid for the time being. As long as Fox and Carrillo thought he was still in the dark, he could move about more freely.

"I decided that instead of a hotel," De Padilla continued, "that if it is OK with you, you would stay at my home. It will be easier to get to work in the morning, and it is very quiet where I live."

"Wouldn't a hotel be less trouble for you?" Judge protested. Being in town would make it easier for him to get in touch with Duffy.

"I have not asked permission from Senor Carrillo. Perhaps, you might not mention it."

"No problem." It was not as though he had much choice. Judge was not sure what the big deal was, until he learned later that they were to leave for work at five in the morning. No wonder L'eon wanted to avoid an extra long drive to and from work. The only other hotels in the area were on the opposite end of town from Carrillo's factory. The airfield seemed to be halfway between the hotels and De Padilla's villa. De Padilla would have had three times the drive to pick him up from a hotel and then drive them to work.

L'eon must have thought he might get in trouble with Carrillo for being lazy and taking Judge home with him instead of to a hotel, just to save him some commute time twice a day. Judge also wondered if in fact that was the case. Perhaps he wanted to keep a better eye on him and limit the number of contacts he had outside of the airfield.

They drove east and slightly south until the road began to wind through the foothills, leading to some very rugged terrain. Dusk was turning to nightfall, and as they rose in elevation, the lights of the city behind them added sprinkles of starlight to the base of the fading sunset.

L'eon had remained silent ever since leaving the Carrillo airfield. He did not appear nervous, but seemed content to drive and look about. "How long have you worked for Carrillo?" Judge finally asked.

"I have worked for Senor Carrillo all my life. He has been very good to me, senor," L'eon offered. Judge was glad he had asked. L'eon's loyalty to Carrillo would affect how the man could be questioned.

"Senor Carrillo paid for me to go to the university. Now he gives me the highest priority programs," L'eon continued.

"This crop duster that we are working on must be pretty important then?" Judge asked.

"Crop duster, senor?"

"The helicopter."

"Oh, I do not believe . . ." L'eon suddenly became silent, wondering how to continue.

"It's OK, L'eon." Judge laughed. "We know we should not say too much about it." His laughter was for L'eon's benefit.

The road soon switched back to the west and turned to gravel. Within a quarter mile, a small bungalow appeared on the right. The surrounding hills were covered with tall grass and shrubbery. Another road from the south intersected the road that they were on barely an eighth of a mile from the bungalow.

"When we have the control system design finished, the aircraft will be ready to prep for flight. Will you be coming to Texas to help me test it?" Judge asked as he reached behind the seat for his bag.

"Oh no, senor," L'eon replied, "I must go to Europe to help Senor Carrillo on another project," L'eon said as he parked the jeep.

Judge had been studying as much of the local geography along the route, noting everything while he conversed with L'eon. The terrain sloped steeply downward behind the villa, providing a wonderful view of the distant city lights.

L'eon showed him in. The cottage was quite cozy, consisting of a small kitchenette, a den, and two tiny bedrooms.

Apart from a single radio, the bungalow had no appliances, save for a telephone, an oil furnace, a small stove in the kitchen, and a little furniture. A bookcase stretched along the wall opposite the fireplace in the den. There were shelves from floor to ceiling, stuffed with books. In fact, there were so many books that some were laid sideways on top of other books. It was evident that he lived a simple life. He seemed very content.

Their brief supper of stew and bread was interrupted by a knock at the door. A man had arrived with Judge's belongings from the hotel. Judge recognized him as one of the workers at the airfield. L'eon introduced him as Roberto. After a short conversation in Spanish, which Judge was too slow to follow, Roberto said goodbye and departed.

L'eon was not much of a conversationalist; however, Judge continued to try and get more information. "Roberto looks a lot like you," Judge lied. Roberto was better looking than L'eon, but Judge needed a segue.

"We are not related," L'eon responded.

"Do you have family around here?"

"Si, I have a sister. She is married. We see each other often now."

"Now?" Judge prodded.

"Si. She and her husband were away for many years. Now they are back in Santiago."

Judge tried to continue to ask questions about his employer, but felt uncomfortable with L'eon's short answers, so he gave up lest L'eon became suspicious. He decided to retire for the evening.

The bedroom was chilly. There was an old steam radiator standing against the wall not far from the window, and it too was cold. Turning the knob at its base produced a flow of hot steam within the radiator, and it was soon warming to the touch, creaking and groaning, protesting like a submarine that had descended too deep.

Judge sat on the edge of an old feather mattress. Depressed at what he had learned. The intent of the Carrillo project, if true, would mean the end of his involvement at ARI. He had already been deceived once, which he had shrugged off as a misunderstanding. Now he felt that he was becoming part of another deception.

Judge rested his chin on his palms with his elbows on his knees as he glumly sat staring out at the faraway city lights.

He had been tempted to postpone his trip, but Gibbons had urged him not to raise suspicion by doing so, but to see what he could find out in Chile. Now he was glad that he had.

It had been one thing to think that someone had orchestrated the death of his friend Pauline. It was quite another to think that he was on the edge of a giant conspiracy that stretched to the corners of the Middle-East and South America. Utmost on his mind, however, was the suspicion that Connie Lin's death might somehow be tied in to this mess.

Seventeen

Judge had to admit it—he was having difficulty concentrating on his work at the aircraft factory. He had an overwhelming desire to get home to Texas.

But for the time being, he forced himself to work at the plant, trying to rush his evaluation along and assemble his report.

As he looked around the factory for L'eon, two men he had not previously seen appeared. Both had very black hair and appeared to be Middle Eastern. He noticed them watching him closely from the production line. From the corner of his eye, he watched them disappear into Carrillo's office.

When they reappeared, they were talking with Carrillo and began inspecting work being done on the production line. They were too far from Judge for him to hear them. Carrillo looked in his direction and obviously answered their questions. Satisfied for the moment, they continued in the opposite direction.

When they were out of sight, Judge called, "Roberto, who are those two foreigners hanging around Carrillo?"

"I do not know, but I can tell you they cause much trouble for us. I believe L'eon knows who they are."

Frowning, Judge asked, "What sort of trouble?"

"They watch us a lot, and then they go in Senor Carrillo's office. When Senor Carrillo comes out of his office, he comes to me and tells me we do not work fast enough. Sometimes he tells us not to stop for siesta," he said, shaking his head. He led Judge to the aircraft workstation.

"Do they live here?" Judge asked, referring to Chile, not the airfield.

"Oh no, senor," he said, shaking his head, "they always stay at the Carrera Hotel. They have been here since just before your trip."

As the first shift was winding up work for the day, Judge caught a glimpse of the two men moving towards the guard gate. L'eon was parked off to the side, waiting for him. Judge followed the men at a distance and climbed into the seat next to L'eon. Judge asked him to wait a minute while he purposely fumbled with his lap belt until he had seen the two drive away.

The week was nearly up, and Judge realized he was running out of time. His anxiety over not meeting up with Duffy finally forced him into action. He turned to L'eon, suddenly thinking of a plan.

"L'eon," Judge said, "could you drive me to the Carrera Hotel? I forgot a pair of slacks in the laundry." The lie seemed to work. Without speaking, L'eon sighed and turned in the direction of the Carrera Hotel.

The sedan that the men were driving was already parked when L'eon and Judge drove up to the front of the hotel.

Judge quickly ran in, trying to remain inconspicuous. Fortunately, the men were just entering the elevator as he passed the lobby desk.

Judge stepped in front of the elevator as the doors swished closed and watched the numbers moving above the elevator entrance door. The elevator stopped on the third floor.

Judge raced for the stairwell, bounding up the steps three at a time. Luck was with him as he peered through the glass of the door leading onto the third floor. Both men were just entering a room down the hall.

Rushing over to the elevator, he got in and rose to the fourteenth floor, where Duffy was staying. Tapping gently on his door, he was not surprised that there was no response. He scribbled a note explaining his sudden checkout of the hotel. "Enjoyed our chat of last," he wrote, not signing the note in case it was intercepted. He added that he would try to catch him later in the evening.

A cantina of sorts was just up the street, and Judge had no trouble talking L'eon into a free meal at the Café de Brasil.

The cantina was alive with young people. Laughter, music, and the tinkling of glasses filled the air as they entered. L'eon's usual expressionless attitude changed as the scantily clad waitresses began hovering about, taking their orders and bringing their drinks. Judge, observing with satisfaction the usually quiet L'eon enjoying his Pisco Sour, made sure the young man's glass was never empty.

Judge waited until L'eon had drunk a couple of glasses before bringing up the subject of Carrillo. To his surprise, it was L'eon who spoke first. "Senor Walt," he began. "Do you know that Senor Carrillo happens to be one of Patricio Aylwin's best friends? Do you know who he is?"

"No," Judge lied, wanting L'eon to do most of the talking. It was evident that the drink was affecting the otherwise discreet L'eon.

"He is the Presidente," L'eon boasted drunkenly. Judge had learned that Pinochet had been defeated in a plebiscite in late 1988, and there had been a yearlong campaign, leading up to the recent election. Pinochet's government was in a shambles, and he had agreed to step down if the people voted against him. Changes of power in Chile had rarely occurred peacefully, and Judge figured Pinochet had thought of a way to ensure his longevity without getting killed.

So, Judge thought to himself, *Carrillo must be supporting Aylwin, or the other way around.*

"So Aylwin and Carrillo are very close, are they?" Judge asked, wanting to keep L'eon talking.

L'eon looked over his shoulder and then whispered loudly to Judge, "Senor Carrillo married Aylwin's sister!" Then he laughed aloud. "I should be so lucky!"

Judge decided that L'eon was sufficiently drunk to press him a little harder.

"L'eon, who are those two foreigners in the aircraft plant? They seem to cause your workers a lot of worry."

"Shhhh!" L'eon motioned with his finger over his lips, looking over his shoulder again. "They are Mukhabarat!" he whispered loudly. "Iraqi secret police. Very bad men! You must not talk about them," he added, scowling.

Judge was not surprised at L'eon's statement. He sipped his drink while L'eon downed his and then waved his arm drunkenly for the waitress to bring him another.

L'eon tried to put his arm around the bare waist of the girl while she poured him another Pisco Sour. Smiling, she deftly slid out of L'eon's reach and moved to another table.

"Do you know a man named Ponce?" Judge asked.

"Who?" L'eon was drunkenly staring after the waitress.

Judge's heart sank. If Ponce worked for Carrillo, L'eon would know about it.

Suddenly L'eon burst into laughter. "You English." He laughed aloud. "It is pronounced Ponth, not Ponce," he added, chuckling. "Sure I know of him. That man is even bigger than you, senor." Then, L'eon's face clouded, and he looked over his shoulder again. "Ponce is always chasing the women and being rough with them. He is a bully. I do not know why Senor Carrillo likes him."

"Where can I find him?" Judge asked. There were few things that Judge feared, and none of them were men. Gibbons and Jenkins had given him reason to think Ponce had something to do with Connie Lin's murder. Judge knew if he could get his hands on him that he would get some answers.

"You do not want to find him, senor. Oh no, not him. Besides, he does not live in Santiago, I think. I have not seen him in many days. But someday he will show up again."

"Why do you say that?"

"He comes to visit. Usually I see him with senor Carrillo and a man from the US. I do not know his name."

Discouraged, Judge realized Ponce would probably not show up before he returned to Texas. He wondered if L'eon was drunk enough that he wouldn't remember telling him about the Iraqis. The Mukhabarat were Hussein's elite secret police. Pauline had been right. As L'eon staggered to his feet and made an unsteady search for the restroom, Judge decided that the young man wouldn't remember much of anything of the evening.

When L'eon's inhibitions were sufficiently absent that he began fondling a buxom waitress, much to her displeasure,

Judge decided it was time to go. He gently lifted his inebriated companion to his feet and moved him towards the door. By the time Judge had driven to the Carrera Hotel, L'eon was snoring soundly, slumped over in his seat.

Passing through the lobby, he glanced towards the lounge. Finding it deserted, he stepped to the elevator and up to the fourteenth floor. Again, there was no answer to his knock at Duffy's door.

According to his watch, it was nearly ten o'clock. Duffy could still be out. On a whim, he turned the knob. Maybe he had just dozed off. He peeked inside the room. The light was off, and he was about to close the door when he noticed an overturned lamp lying on the floor, the shade broken.

Judge entered quietly, closing the door silently behind him. He called Duffy's name, but there was no response.

The room was a shambles. A suitcase had been emptied, its contents strewn about. There had been a clock radio beside the bed, but it too was on the floor. The sheets and mattress were hanging off the bed, as if somebody had been looking under them for something.

The room had no closet. Like Judge's, it contained a large wardrobe. One of its doors stood slightly ajar. He slowly approached and opened both doors.

William Duffy stared at him from the wardrobe. He was bent in an awkward position within its confines, his hands bound behind him. His lifeless eyes pierced through the cellophane that had been wrapped around his face. His mouth was open, teeth bared, expressing his last agonizing attempt to gain a breath that would never come.

Eighteen

Saturday—Judge arrived back at DFW. He did not remember much about the flight and even less about his drive home. Duffy's murder was proving to be particularly troubling. Closing his eyes, he suddenly opened them as the vision of Duffy's agonizing stare appeared again.

He felt especially guilty for asking Duffy to get him some additional information under such dangerous circumstances. He brooded throughout the flight over what he was getting himself into.

As Judge had thought, Ponce had not surfaced before he had to catch his flight to Texas. He sorely wanted answers to Connie Lin's death, and he struggled to piece together a connection between her murder and the situation he now found himself in.

The message machine was blinking when he dumped his bag beside his bed and briefly tried to remember if the front door had been locked. Shrugging it off, he tumbled into bed. His curiosity was stronger than his fatigue, however, so he extended an arm and laid a thick heavy finger on the playback button.

A tiny voice said, "Hello?" And then, a long pause. Judge sat up on the bed and listened intently. He could hear a voice whispering to the caller from the background, but he couldn't make out the words. Then the little voice continued, "I come to your house to play piano." It is followed by another long pause and a giggle. The sentence was a mixture of Chinese and English, but Judge could make it out perfectly.

He lay back on the bed and sighed, a smile on his lips. Heather had been about the cutest child he had ever seen. He was smiling too, because he knew her mother had coached her.

Sitting up again, he picked up the receiver and called Michelle. After a few rings, it was answered by a machine, which had a recording of her voice. He hesitated after the beep and finally hung up, unsure of what to say.

Sitting on the edge of the bed for a moment, he picked up the receiver again and redialed. This time when he heard the beep he began to speak, only to have his message immediately interrupted by Michelle.

"Hello, Walter," she answered. "Welcome back."

"Thank you, it's good to be back," he replied in a quiet tone. "I was returning Heather's call." Judge found himself smiling again.

"She's taking a nap," Michelle replied. "May I take a message for her?" If one could hear a smile, Judge felt certain that Michelle was wearing one also.

"Could you ask her if she might be available for a dinner recital tonight or tomorrow evening?"

"I know she has a pretty busy schedule," Michelle said, coyly. "I believe her grandparents could accompany her if it were tonight. I know they were coming here, so we'll just meet at your place."

"Would six o'clock be acceptable to them?"

"Well, I'll call them and ask."

"Six it is then, unless I hear from you."

"Really, Walter, you don't have to do this." Michelle suddenly sounded very formal.

"Ever notice how bright the sun shines when that child walks into a room?" Judge asked.

"I've certainly noticed how she looks at you," Michelle replied. "Can we bring anything?"

"Just your appetite."

"Then we'll see you at six."

After hanging up, he moved to his desk and rummaged around in his box of business cards. Finding one for a Van Warren, attorney-at-law, he put it in his wallet and walked back into the den.

Sinking into confines of the big Italian sofa, he went over the events of his trip, the project that he was about to undertake, and the strange night that he had met Michelle Lofton. His mind was swimming as he tried to make sense of it all. Finally, he drifted off to sleep.

He awakened with a start to the sound of the doorbell. Groggily, he stood and stepped to the door, realizing he had overnapped.

Opening the door, he found the Loftons standing at the entry. Heather stood with her hands cupped over her mouth as if she were surprised to see Judge. He knelt, trying to hide his embarrassment at not being ready for them, but he was unable to hide his look of just having been awakened.

"You've been napping," Helen Lofton said. "We thought that we would come a few minutes early to help you prepare dinner."

Michelle bit her upper lip. Shaking her head slowly, she said, "You must have been exhausted. I am so sorry."

Reaching out for Heather, who allowed him to grab her, he picked her up in his arms in a big bear hug. She squealed in delight.

"Please come in," he said. Holding Heather in one arm, he reached out to shake the senior doctor's hand.

Immediately, Helen remarked, "My, what a beautiful home you have."

Judge looked at Michelle and said, "I'll just run down to the store and pick up a few things. You know your way around. Give your folks the nickel tour and make yourselves at home. We'll cook up a storm when I return."

"Mind if I go along?" Richard Lofton asked.

While the women explored Judge's small mansion, the two men headed down Green Oaks Boulevard to the supermarket.

"My daughter thinks you try to avoid her," Dr. Lofton said, eyeing Judge. He still had not made up his mind about the big man.

Surprised, Judge remained silent for a moment. Then, he replied, "Actually, I thought she preferred it that way."

"What gave you that idea? I thought she gave you quite a bit of attention in the hospital."

"Sure," Judge replied, "I was a patient."

"You weren't her patient," Dr. Lofton countered. "You were mine! Michelle is a pediatrician."

Judge gave a start. It had never occurred to him. He thought about it for a while as they drove. His opinion of Michelle's motivation to be around him was suddenly changed. Dr. Lofton thought he detected a smile on Judge's lips.

"Have you been able to prove that Michelle's attackers were really after someone else?" Dr. Lofton asked, suddenly changing the subject. He had been wanting to ask Judge without the women present and realized he might not get the chance if he didn't hurry up.

Judge nodded his head as he stepped out of the car, and the two men walked into the market. "There's no question anymore," Judge replied solemnly. I'd prefer it if you gave me time to tell her myself."

"I can appreciate that. What could your friend possibly have done worth killing her over?"

"She apparently took some incriminating pictures. Of whom and why they were so incriminating, I may never know."

Deep in thought, the two quickly selected a few choice fillets and couple of pounds of steamers, along with some condiments Dr. Lofton guessed the women would like.

Arriving back at Judge's house, they could hear piano music coming from within.

They opened the front door to find Heather playing ragtime music on his grand piano, rocking her head from side to side, and grinning happily. Helen and Michelle were sitting nearby.

To the ladies' immense surprise, Judge handed the groceries to the senior Lofton, slid onto the bench next to Heather, and picked up the accompaniment without missing a beat. Heather looked up at him with surprised laughter and stayed right in step. Judge joined in, and they played as if they had played together before.

Her tiny fingers missed an occasional stretch for a big chord, and his huge fingers randomly nailed two keys instead of one. Their mistakes made her giggle, but she kept right on playing. Her mother and grandmother vacillated between laughter and tears as they watched and tapped their feet to the lively tunes.

When their playing was finally over, Heather jumped up and ran into Michelle's lap. Then she was up again, babbling in Chinese and English and running through the open French doors into the backyard. Michelle chased after her fearing that she might fall into the pool. Heather had her heart set on explaining all the colors of Mr. Judge's new spring annuals, in Chinese of course.

"Isn't that child just amazing?" Helen asked. "I'll be glad when she can better distinguish between the two languages."

"Heather spends a lot of time at Ms. Chi's, doesn't she?" Judge asked, anticipating the obvious answer.

"You have to understand Michelle's schedule. Some weeks she would only see Heather when the child was asleep. We feel so ashamed that we only spent time with her on Sundays, mostly," Helen concluded.

As Judge watched Heather and Michelle through the huge picture windows, Helen looked over her shoulder to see if they were out of earshot. Then, turning, she placed her hand on Judge's knee.

"Walter, that girl is taken with you. We have never seen her so happy. I don't suppose you've noticed?" There was laughter in her eyes.

"Which one?" Judge asked, thinking she was referring to Heather, but hoping that she meant Michelle. It was obvious to him that the child adored him.

Mrs. Lofton laughed again. "Both of them, silly!"

Heather, who was still chatting away, was leading Michelle from the yard.

Richard Lofton, who had found his way to the kitchen, had taken it upon himself to begin the meal preparation.

"Are you guys hungry?" he called, making himself quite at home.

Everyone, save for Heather, moved to the kitchen to help with the dinner. Heather remained behind to retake her position on the ivories. Her playing could be heard throughout the house.

"So how was your trip?" Michelle began.

Instantly Judge's expression clouded. *Something had happened*, she thought, *something terrible*. She could see the deep worry in those coal black eyes and the furrow on his forehead. Michelle watched him intently.

"It was OK," he said, slicing an onion and avoiding her eyes.

"Yes, Walt," Helen prodded, "tell us about your trip."

The Loftons listened, fascinated, as Judge explained the changing political climate in Chile. He told them very little about the technical aspects of Carrillo's project but spoke briefly of L'eon and his cozy bungalow.

They gathered up Heather and brought her to the table. She began tugging on the big man's wrist. Judge looked down to see the little one pointing to the white untanned area where a watch had been.

"Yeah, little one, I left my watch in Chile. I forgot to put it on this morning. I remember taking it off at night and tucking it away. With it out of sight, I must have forgotten it. I'll have to get L'eon to send it to me."

Michelle responded, "That's too bad. It was a beautiful Breitling. I remember it from the hospital."

"Walt, you said you were mostly a bookworm as a child," Helen said, changing the subject, "and you didn't get your size until after you were in the military."

Judge nodded.

"The military does not strike me as a pursuit that a bookworm would undertake. Were you drafted?"

"No," Judge replied. "I didn't have the money to go to college, couldn't save enough earning minimum wage at the local gas station. The GI bill was my only option. When I realized that I could be sent overseas, I figured that Special Forces training would give me my best chances of survival."

"But it also would put you in more dangerous situations, wouldn't it?"

"That was twenty years ago. My definitions of danger and excitement are a lot different now than they were then."

"So how would you classify the situation you have before you now?" Michelle asked.

"Politically explosive, maybe," Judge replied thoughtfully.

His comment led the conversation back into politics.

"I read that the President and Secretary of State are stopping in Chile on their South American tour," Dr. Lofton said.

"Do you think the program you are working on has anything to do with that?" Helen asked.

"I doubt it," Judge lied. "I suspect that money is at the root of the whole affair." He was muttering mostly to himself.

Judge stood, insisting everyone stay seated as he began cleaning up the dinner table. His guests would have none of that, however, and within seconds had cleared the table. When they completed cleaning up the kitchen and loading the dishwasher, they gathered up little Heather and settled into the living room for a final piano recital.

When Heather had completed her third tune, Dr. Lofton and his wife stood and thanked Judge for the evening.

Judge escorted them to their car and stood with Michelle as they chatted briefly. A breeze was rising, and they began to feel a sprinkle of an approaching rain.

He was holding Heather in his arms, and the child soon fell asleep on his shoulder as he quietly chatted with Michelle. Then they waved to Michelle's parents as Dr. Lofton and his wife drove away.

They stood watching the car's lights disappear around the bend. Judge was silent, wishing Michelle and Heather did not have to leave.

As if to prod him along, Heather shivered in his arms. Noticing, Michelle suggested softly, "We should take her inside so she doesn't chill."

Judge smiled and led the way back into the house. He lit a fire in the master bedroom fireplace and gently placed the child on his bed. He covered her with a fresh blanket and led Michelle to the den, where he lit another one.

"I've never thanked you for saving my life," Michelle said, as Judge brought her a glass of wine. She pressed her fingers softly to his lips so that he could not protest. She set their glasses on the mantel and reached up, placing her hands behind his head. She pulled him to her and gently touched his lips with hers.

He drowned himself in her arms, lifting her gently as she wrapped a long beautiful leg around one of his. The raindrops in his hair sprinkled on her rosy cheeks.

They settled onto the pillows of the sofa. Michelle lay with her head on his chest, locked in his embrace. Turning her head, placing her chin on his heart, she looked into his face. "I was afraid you might not want us to stay."

He lifted his head with a look of surprise. "Why would you think that?"

"Because of how I've thrown myself at you, because . . ."

He stopped her by placing his fingers gently on her lips, but she protested.

"You've never asked me about Heather's father. It was nothing, really . . ."

Again, he placed his fingers on her lips.

"It does not matter. We are both different people than we were years ago, even months ago. I can't judge you. If you judged me on my past, you'd leave in an instant."

"So where do we go from here?" she asked softly.

"I don't know," he whispered. "All I know is that I like being with you."

Kissing him softly, she said, "I don't wish to just be a visitor."

"I don't want either of you to just be visitors," he replied. This was more than true, but her unexpected burst of emotion had overwhelmed him just the same.

She stared into the deep blackness of his eyes. She could see pain in the depths of that darkness, the same look he had earlier in the kitchen. Something was still troubling him.

"Something's wrong," she said, a statement rather than a question. "Why can't you tell me?"

He wanted to protect her from the nightmare that seemed to have erupted around him. How could he explain it? The realities of the world were beginning to shatter his naïve attitudes about the country that he had worked for all his life.

"I have a problem at ARI to work out," he said. "It has nothing to do with us."

"You promise?" She just knew there had to be more.

"On my life," he whispered.

The deep red embers glowed under the dying coals. Michelle pulled his chin back to her face. "Are you ignoring me, Mr. Judge?" she asked softly. "Something else is wrong."

"I'm not sure how to continue with this project," he started. "I guess I just have a really bad feeling about it." It was not the truth he knew, but he was not going to bring up Connie Lin's death.

They rested quietly on the sofa for a while. Soon, she had become quite still, having drifted off, free from reality for a few hours.

Judge gently rose and carried her off to his bed. He laid her gently beside Heather, covering them with the down quilt as she softly clung to him. She kissed him softly in her sleep, as if to assure him that he would not be alone while she was away in her dreams.

As the ebbing rain gradually gave up tapping on the window, he pried her arms from his neck and, closing the door behind him, softly made his way back to the den.

Nineteen

Parking his car by the side entrance leading to ARI's office complex, Judge ascended the steps and headed along the corridor towards his office and the nearby coffee machine.

He was feeling particularly upbeat this morning. On a whim, Judge had called Michelle the day after Heather's "recital" and invited them to spend a weekend on his boat, berthed at Eagle Mountain Lake Marina. Michelle had agreed.

As people filed by the coffee machine for the first shot of the day, they appeared to be unusually jovial. It had been some time since the laughter and jokes flowed quite so freely.

Noticing Judge's expression, a young secretary asked quizzically, "Haven't you heard?"

"Heard what? What's going on?"

"We've been saved!" she replied excitedly. "An investment firm just bought fifty percent of our outstanding private stock. We're out of debt!"

"Well, that *is* good news," Judge agreed. Several times there had not been enough money to cover the payroll.

Judge had even refused a paycheck on occasion, insisting that others be paid first.

"So who saved us?" he asked.

"Some European firm, SwissInc, I think.

He wondered what new contract was coming in from Europe, assuming for the moment that SwissInc was a Swiss firm.

Turning and pointing towards the conference room, he said, "Let's gather the first team together, and I'll tell everyone about the trip after you bring me up to date."

Judge related the control system problem to them and presented Carrillo's blueprints of the faulty design. He had redlined over the drawings to show the changes that he wanted to make and instructed the CAD guys to get started so they could get some parts built. The fit checks of the yet-to-be-made parts had to be conducted as soon as the prototype arrived.

ARI's instrumentation engineer was given the necessary drawings to get him started on the instrumentation that would be required to conduct the flight testing. The man was so resourceful; he would be finished and waiting for the aircraft to arrive.

The remainder of the day was devoted to roughing out the test plans for the girls to work into the word processor. They would be instrumental in the data reduction and assembly of the final report.

At noon, Judge called Van Warren. The attorney's secretary set Judge up for a 4:00 PM appointment.

"Hey, Walt, did you hear about Milt's son, Chad?" It was another staffer, whispering to him over the partition as he hung up the telephone.

"I didn't even know he had a son," Judge replied. In fact, there was a lot he did not know about Milt.

"He's a helicopter crew chief," she went on. "Chad had been stationed in Panama since the Noriega thing. He's coming home on leave before reporting to a new station and bringing his Panamanian girlfriend with him."

"So?" Judge was not really interested anymore.

"She can't speak a word of English, and he can't speak Panamanian. He's going to announce their engagement. Milt doesn't have a clue yet," she added excitedly.

"I believe they speak Spanish in Panama," he added dryly. "And how is it you are privy to this tidbit of information?" he asked, not really wanting to continue this line of gossip.

"I was answering the phone for Milt's secretary," she whispered, "when Chad called in to tell his dad he was being transferred to the Persian Gulf. Milt was not in, and he was so excited, he told me the whole story."

Judge shook his head, smiling. Relationships were difficult enough when you could communicate. Those two were in for it.

On the way out the door, he ran into Milt. Judge scanned Milt's eyes quickly, seeking a clue that Milt knew about his adventure in Chile. He sensed nothing. Was it possible Milt was not aware of what had transpired?

Milt suddenly stopped Judge as they passed each other in the lobby by the front office. "I'm throwing a party at my place next Sunday night," he said excitedly. "It's for my son," he added. "You know Chad? I'm inviting everyone from the office."

"I've never met him," Judge replied. "But I understand he's on his way to a new duty assignment."

"Why, yes," he admitted, impressed that Judge had shown interest in his family. "Can you make it?"

"I'm going to join some folks at the boat Friday after work," Judge began. He was stopped by the disappointment in Milt's eyes. "But it's not that far to your place. I'll try to drop by."

"Thanks, Walt." Milt grinned. "See you there."

Judge swung out of the parking lot and proceeded to the 820 freeway, trying to catch state road 287 into Fort Worth. He might be a bit early for his appointment with his attorney, but with afternoon traffic, you could never be sure.

Van Warren was a short heavy man in his late fifties. Balding and a heavy smoker, he was the sharpest attorney Judge had ever met. Few attorneys ever return a call when they say they will. Even fewer send out a document or court report as promised. Van was punctual to a fault and exceedingly accurate in his legal analysis.

Van greeted Judge at his office door, pushing his cigar to the side of his cheek in order to speak. Not being much for small talk, Judge related the project that ARI was involved in, producing a copy of ARI's contract with Carrillo.

Van interrupted only once to pull a fat legal book from the perfectly arranged bookcase on the wall facing his desk. He held up his hand briefly to read a short passage to himself and then tossed it on his desk.

After reading the documents that Judge had given him, he turned and looked out the wide office window, looking down on the traffic below.

"Have you heard of the Anti-Terrorism and Arms Export Amendments Act of 1989, or maybe the Arms Export Control Act, or perhaps the Kennedy Amendment of 1976?" he asked, still looking out the window.

"No," Judge replied. "Enlighten me."

"Basically, it forbids any American from consulting or providing information or advice, either directly or indirectly, to the government of a terrorist country. That includes Chile, in the case of the Kennedy Amendment."

He turned pointing to ARI's contract with Carrillo. "That contract alludes to the potential military end use of the helicopter. Chile is not on the list of terrorist countries, but Chile is specified in the Kennedy Legislation—no military end-use hardware or help. Who are they selling the aircraft to?"

"It could be Iraq," Judge replied, "but Fox is buying the certified material to complete the modification from ARI. We may not be selling him the actual aircraft, but we are assisting him in turning the aircraft into a potential gunship, in my view. At the very least, we're making it possible for him to sell them to another country."

"Are you selling the weapons kits to him?"

"Not that I know of. I think we know better than that." Judge hesitated, realizing he wasn't one hundred percent sure. His expression clouded as he remembered that ARI did build weapons systems and that kits were being shipped, although not to Chile, that he knew of.

"And you have no proof that Fox's intentions are anything but honorable?"

Judge was pretty sure on that point but couldn't prove it.

Van turned again to look out the window, his cigar smoke taking a stranglehold on Judge's throat. "It means," he began slowly, "that if Carrillo does sell these aircraft as gunships to a terrorist country, such as Libya, or Iraq, it would violate a clause of the Kennedy Amendment. If it could be proven that you knew of their intended end use"—he hesitated, glancing over his shoulder at Judge and taking a breath—"then you could go to prison for years."

He turned and stared directly at Judge. "Now you listen to me, Walter," he began, pointing his finger. "I know you. You and I go back a long way. You're not working for the government anymore. You're on the other side. If you fight against something like this, as I know you're capable of, the wrong side would be against you this time. If the government is involved in this affair, illegitimately involved, and you end up interfering with a clandestine national security operation, regardless of how wrong you think it is, you'll be charged with treason as their fall guy—and the penalty for treason is death!"

Twenty

When Judge returned to his office, he tried to concentrate on his test plans. Van's words kept echoing in his mind, and he found himself pacing. Finally he left his cubicle, deciding instead to work on something less mind-intensive. The engineering room seemed deserted. "Where the hell is everyone?" he asked.

"They're all upstairs packing up a shipment of those Mexican Police Kits," came the reply.

The Mexican Police had been the first ARI customers to order the weapons kits after Judge had returned from Indonesia. Sales of this nature had to be approved through the US State Department, however. For sales to Mexico, approval had been easy enough to get.

Judge ran up to shipping and receiving. There was not enough time in the Chilean schedule to have all the engineers stuffing boxes. He felt guilty as it was that he had taken time off to talk to Van Warren.

Reaching the top of the stairs, he was amazed to see virtually every employee except Milt, putting parts in boxes, taping, and labeling.

"What's all this?" Judge asked.

"We got an order for these 'Tube in Tub kits' for the Mexican Police," a secretary said, wiping her brow with her sleeve. "Milt said to get everyone together and get it out right away."

The kit was nicknamed the "Tube in Tub Weapons System" because of its unique shape and how it fit the fuselage "tub" of the light helicopters. It could be fitted with special racks for holding rocket pods, guns, and TOW missiles.

"But we filled that order weeks ago," Judge protested.

"I guess they wanted spares," was her dubious response.

"That order was for six sets. There must be a dozen kits here."

"Two dozen," someone corrected.

"Two dozen?" Judge stammered. "The entire Mexican Police Force only has a dozen helicopters. Did this order come through the State Department like the others?" he asked, suddenly wary.

"As far as I know," came the reply.

"The purchase orders are right over there," an engineer said, pointing to a stack of documents on a nearby desk. Judge picked them up and started thumbing through them. He immediately recognized the official logo of the US State Department. The order was from the government, as all foreign military type sales had to be. He shrugged and set them down slowly. He didn't like this latest development at all.

"Fax coming in for you, Walt," a girl called from the foot of the stairs. He descended the stairs to the fax machine and glanced at the cover sheet coming through.

It read:

Cambridge, UK, from Mr. Blake Johnson. One sheet to follow—attention Mr. Walter Judge.

Walt,

I caught this article in the Times this morning. Friends of mine are keenly interested. Knowing you are from Texas and in the rotorcraft business, I thought perhaps you might check your sources and see what's up. The lads at the Times have hit a dead end. Give me a bell if you come up with anything.

Regards Blake

What could Blake Johnson be up to? Judge thought to himself. Blake had been his M.O.D. witness during the gun turret program that they had conducted in England for the Austrian Government and Luke Aerospace.

Blake and Judge had become fast friends during the course of the testing and had kept in touch after the project through letters and faxes.

The next page began scrolling up. It was a photocopy of a newspaper article, which had been cut from an issue of a London newspaper. The article was written by Times's writer Casey Richards. To Judge's dismay, it read:

Chilean Magistrates Suspect Cover-up in Death of British Reporter.

Santiago, Chile, by Casey Richards.

Chilean magistrates in Santiago today have ruled the recent death of William Duffy, investigative reporter for Global Helicopter Magazine, to be a case of homicide, not suicide as the local police had reported. They cited evidence in the case such as the victim's hands being bound behind him and his head being wrapped in plastic in such a fashion as to cause suffocation. The Magistrates ordered the police to reopen the case.

According to Cambridge businessman and financier, Edward Duffy, father of the victim, William Duffy had telephoned his father shortly before his death. The son had been in Chile investigating a lead he had received from an undisclosed source. He reported that arms manufacturer and exporter Carrillo Industries

of Santiago was building a new type of helicopter gunship. The younger Duffy had received several recent threats while investigating the story including a brief bout with one of Carrillo's employees. Duffy had received information that Carrillo had received firm orders for 150 of such aircraft, pending trials in the US, from Iraqi president Saddam Hussein. Inquiries to the US State Department have led to a stalemate.

"What is it with police and suicides," Judge muttered under his breath as he pulled the fax from the machine. This was just the encouragement he needed to initiate a "discussion" with Milton Fox.

Judge's continued interest in the whole affair had been to tag a name and a face on Connie Lin's murderer, if not personally wring the bastard's neck. He had little interest in educating the public to a scandalous conspiracy between politicians and nations. The more he discovered, the more it appeared that the latter was the root of this mystery.

Despite his efforts, he had been unable to find Ponce Gutierrez. Short of approaching Carrillo directly about the man, he had found no one else that knew him other than by sight; and Ponce, from all accounts, would have been hard to miss.

Judge had refrained from asking Carrillo about Ponce for fear that the "man from the US" that had often been seen with him might be alerted, therefore making Ponce harder to find. That conclusion was reinforced further after seeing Duffy's body hanging in the wardrobe.

Judge's assumption that a large conspiracy was afoot, and his sudden relationship with Michelle had moved him towards a decision. Questions that had haunted him in the past were now becoming more, it seemed to him, a matter for federal authorities.

To that end, he was overdue a visit to Gibbon's office. A visit he was now prepared to make and to put this whole sordid affair in the hands of the FBI. It would be public knowledge soon anyway, now that the conspiracy was beginning to appear in print.

He could end his participation with ARI with little more than the nagging guilt that he had played an unwilling participant in events leading to the deaths of two good people.

"Don't you want them sent over to Rhoda?" Milt was saying into the telephone as Judge stood in the doorway.

Who the hell is Rhoda? Judge wondered.

Seeing Judge, Milt motioned him to a seat. "All right, all right we'll ship them straight to Mexico City," he continued speaking into the telephone. "No later than next Friday." Another pause, then he said, "You have my word." And he finally hung up.

Judge was ready for a confrontation. "You set me up," he said quietly, his jaw set. Judge handed him the faxed newspaper article. Milt looked at it, assessing his best response to Judge's accusation.

He switched his gaze to the fax, raising his eyebrows when he got to the point about the gunships and Iraq. He looked Judge straight in the eye as he handed the article back. He said, "It looks like someone is trying to cause trouble. Where did you get that?"

"It was faxed to me from one of the men we worked with in England on the Luke project."

"So what do you want me to do?" He shrugged.

"I want you to shut down the program," Judge replied quietly. "My agreement with you, Milt, was that I would have nothing to do with this kind of program."

"Your contract says that you would have nothing to do with a program not sanctioned by either the State Department or the FAA. This one is sanctioned by both."

"It won't be when the FAA reads this," Judge replied.

"Now, Walt," he cautioned, "the FAA has more of a level head than to respond to every crackpot newspaper article that makes an overseas edition."

"It is illegal," Judge stated. "Have you ever heard of the Arms Export Act, or the Kennedy legislation of 1976? There is an arms embargo in place against Chile. We'll be in violation of US import-export laws."

"We are not violating the law," Milt defended. "We are not selling anything except our services, and only Chile gets the helicopters, not gunships. The State Department is with us on this one. Don't you realize that if we shut down this program, we're going to have to lay most of you guys off? There is just not enough business right now to keep this place going. Try explaining that to the rest of your staff."

"I thought we just received a new investor?" Judge said, remembering a recent conversation with an employee.

"That investor will pull out if we shut down the Chilean program," Milt replied.

Judge bristled at the news. He had not realized that there was a connection. How could the State Department be approving the selling of gunships to Iraq?

"Walt, don't do anything rash."

Judge turned and walked out of Milt's office without saying anything. Milt heard the glass doors to the front entrance bang open and watched from his office window as the big man crossed the parking lot and got in his car. He winced as he saw Judge, usually calm and collected, roar from the parking lot.

Staring out of his big office window, Milton Fox sighed heavily. He hated confrontations. If Judge was walking out, he would have to tell Carrillo the bad news. It would slow everything down, and at a crucial point. If deliveries could not be made soon, Milt knew Carrillo's customers might cancel the order altogether, and that would upset Craig Wright.

Wright had told him that without Judge and his specialized skills and knowledge, there would be no project.

He knew Milt could never hire the needed expertise in time. Without this program, Milt knew he could lose his company.

Mounting a gun or a rocket pod on a helicopter was child's play, worth maybe thirty grand profit a copy. Those cheap systems required a gunner and an untrained crew and would last a few minutes in combat.

The weapons systems that ARI sold, however, would be extremely profitable. The single pilot systems that Judge could put together, equipped with secret radar evading technology, would readily sell for three million a copy with a third of that profit.

Getting Judge to cooperate had been a major struggle, forcing Milt to seek an alternate route for reaching his fully integrated goals. The projects in Indonesia and England had allowed him to break the project up, which concealed his ultimate plans. Information was gleaned from Judge one program at a time.

Milt had been nervous about the deal Wright had brokered with Iraq. He knew he could be getting into legal trouble, but the thought of all that profit was just too irresistible.

Twenty-One

Judge had expected to spend a few days brooding over his decision to leave ARI and giving up any whims he had about finding Connie Lin's killer himself. The police, it seemed to him, had made more headway in that regard in the last few days than he had in a year.

He found himself the next morning, however, feeling rather relieved and unburdened. It was time, he thought to himself, to find Gibbons and bring him up to date. He could then move on with his life.

Jenkins was in the office when Judge arrived and put in a call on the radio to Gibbons, who agreed to drive to the station immediately. Jenkins chatted briefly about his kids and family and found, to his mild surprise, a willing listener in Walter Judge. It had not occurred to the sergeant until now what it must have been like for Judge to have lived for so many years with no family or relatives.

Gibbons came through the door and, to Judge's relief, seemed friendlier than he had been during their previous meetings. Gibbons actually greeted him cordially, his former hostility gone.

"Well, Mr. Judge?" Gibbons began, looking in the direction of his captain's office. "Shall we go for a drive?"

"A drive?" Judge asked, perplexed.

"We'll explain in the car."

Gibbons led the trio to his car, and they proceeded north on I-35 towards Fort Worth. Jenkins pulled the unmarked car into the parking lot of a diner that resembled a railroad caboose. "Cup of coffee?" Jenkins asked.

"Fine," Judge agreed as the three men entered and took up a booth. After they had ordered, Judge waited for one of the officers to speak.

Finally, Gibbons looked at Judge. "Our captain has informed us that we are off the case."

Judge stared blankly back at him and then at Jenkins. "I wondered why I hadn't heard from you," he said. "I nearly expected you to be waiting for me at the airport when I returned from Chile."

Jenkins spoke up. "We had tried to look further into Cox and Atterbury's most recent activities when Captain Stillions pulled us into his office and told us to close the case. He got a call from the governor's office to have us reassigned."

Judge, raising an eyebrow, said nothing.

"We explained to him how we think those two may lead us to Connie Lin's killer. He said it was all just a coincidence, that we needed more proof, and that he wouldn't reopen the case on just that," Gibbons added.

"So that's it, case closed?" Judge asked.

"Not exactly," Jenkins added, a weak smile on his face.

"We asked the Captain to explain the death of Pauline Casey and how you and she were supposed to have met that night," Jenkins explained. "When the captain saw that her description matched Michelle Lofton's, he looked into Ms. Casey's death himself with the help of the Norfolk Bureau. There's no question she was murdered. He told us he'd give us a little more time, but not officially. He's under pressure to close the case, but he smells a rat just like we do."

"What else have you found out?" Judge asked.

"We were hoping you might have something to tell us," Gibbons replied. "For instance, how would anyone have known that you were supposed to meet Ms. Casey at that café?"

"ARI has a professional security company that warned all the employees that the phones could be monitored. All the big corporations do that," Judge replied.

"Then it shouldn't be that difficult for us to make a few inquiries with the security company," Jenkins said. "If the phones are monitored by their staff, they'll be obligated to give us the names of those assigned to the task, or hand over any tapes. We'll follow up on that end. It means there must be a connection between someone at ARI and whoever was after Ms. Casey."

"Do you have any idea at all what Ms. Casey wanted to talk to you about?" Gibbons asked.

Judge pulled the fax he had received from London from his pocket. Handing it to Gibbons, he explained about his meeting with Duffy and the journalist's relationship to Pauline.

Jenkins moved close to Gibbons so he could read it too. Whistling under his breath, he said, "Wow, that's pretty heavy stuff. It could certainly explain a lot."

"This should buy us a little more time with the captain," Jenkins said. "It will keep the case on Ms. Lofton open a while longer, but it won't help us with Connie Lin's case. Anything else?"

"Well, you guys were right. Ponce Gutierrez is definitely tied up in this thing. I'm not sure how yet. He seems to show up at Carrillo's facility fairly frequently with some big shot from the US, but he never showed while I was there," Judge replied. "You said he worked for someone in Colombia?"

Jenkins looked at Gibbons and back at Judge. "We didn't exactly say that. Fact is we're not sure. We know he was assigned to the Colombian Embassy, but he might still be somehow associated with the men in the photograph. What are you thinking?"

"Well," Judge was thinking aloud, "Pauline and Duffy probably wanted to prove that the Indonesian and British programs that I worked on were related to the Chilean project. Any way of finding out?"

"We're getting stonewalled by the NSA. But the Captain has some old friends in both the FBI and US Customs, so we'll check with him. Maybe we can find something more," Gibbons replied. "We're going to pull your Milton Fox in for questioning. Unfortunately, we don't have much, and he may refuse to tell us anything. We'll need your help to get us something more solid."

"Hold on, fellas. I left ARI. This is in your hands," Judge told them.

"What? You quit?" Gibbons cried. "You're the inside man. With our hands tied, you're the one that can get the goods on these guys. Don't you want your girlfriend's killer found? We don't even have a motive yet to get her case reopened."

Judge gave Gibbons a surprised look. The lieutenant appeared to have done an about-face towards him. Now he found himself sympathizing with the officers' problem.

"You led me to believe this Gutierrez character was the man we were looking for," Judge said. "I just haven't figured out why he would have gone after Connie. I never met him or anyone he works for that I know of."

When Judge realized that Gibbons and Jenkins were back at square one with their case, he added, "There's a party at Fox's this weekend. It could be an opportunity to patch things up and to learn something more."

The two G-men quietly took Judge back to his car at the station and left him to his thoughts.

Judge thought of going back to ARI right away and digging around, but thoughts of Michelle and his recent discussion with Jenkins about the sergeant's family could not be put out of his mind.

Instead, he called Michelle and talked her into an afternoon away from the hospital. Together they took in the beautiful spring weather at the Dallas Arboretum with Heather.

The Dallas Symphony held their first outdoor concert of the season. Given every year in the open air at the Arboretum, the music drifted with the spring breeze between the long rows of crepe myrtles and azaleas. The three of them drifted with the wonderful classical music of Bach and Beethoven, beneath the afternoon sky, keeping the cool air, blowing in from Lake Ray Hubbard, at bay under a two-person poncho, with Heather tucked between them.

He told Michelle briefly that he had left ARI, and she had accepted it without comment as they huddled together listening to the music. But as they were driving back to Fort Worth, she wanted to know more about his trip to Chile. Secretly she knew that it had been a source of pain that went beyond his loathing for this curious aircraft project.

He related his evenings with L'eon De Padilla and how the man had lived alone in a bungalow Carrillo had once owned.

At one point, Judge did remember asking L'eon what he expected to do when the "crop duster" project was completed and the aircraft were shipped. He had said he would be going to Europe soon to begin another project.

Other than that, Judge was secretive. He evaded most of her questions about Carrillo, and she gave up asking about anything related to the project.

When they arrived at Michelle's home, they were pleasantly surprised to see Helen Lofton in the drive.

"Hi," she greeted, "I just dropped by to see if I could take Heather for the evening. Richard and I want to take her shopping in the morning!"

The child was delighted at the prospect and excitedly helped her mother gather her things for an evening with her grandparents.

"Are you hungry?" Judge asked, longing to keep Michelle out a while longer.

"I am," she replied. "But I'd rather cook up something here than go out, if that's OK with you?"

They stood in the doorway waving as Helen drove off with Heather.

Judge turned to Michelle. Pulling her to him. "You look tired," he said, kissing her softly.

"Not too tired," she said quietly between kisses.

"I'm glad." He smiled.

"C'mon," she said. "You can help me cook." Her eyes shining, she turned and led him into the house.

Her home was warmly decorated in a Mediterranean motif complete with ornate mirror frames, busts of Greek Olympians, and mocarabe-style furniture.

By the time they had sizzled up some spicy shrimp and warmed the lobster bisque, they were both ravenous. The bed of pilaf for the shrimp kept them a bit longer however. To complete the meal, Michelle prepared a Caesar salad while Judge set the table.

Before sitting down, Michelle slipped from the kitchen. Judge listened as Kenny G's soothing music poured from hidden speakers. Michelle returned with a lit candle. Turning the lights off, she gently kissed Judge on the cheek and thanked him for such a wonderful afternoon.

Their hunger satisfied, they settled into the soft pillows by a fire in the den, the sax still softly sounding from the stereo. Judge found her lips in the dancing firelight as she tucked herself against the warmth of his chest. They caressed each other until they had to have one another's lips again and again.

Finally, as if coming up for air, she pulled his head down against her breasts, stroking his hair and softly begging him to stay. Lifting her gently as she wrapped her long graceful legs around his waist, he carried her effortlessly to a room off her back deck. A large spa was partially set into the floor in the center of the room. Michelle began pulling at his shirt, stripping him of his clothing, her lips never leaving his.

Michelle stood and gently pushed him onto a cushioned lounge, controlling him, taking charge if only for the moment. She finished stripping him of his clothing as she led him to the hot tub. He gave no resistance, feeling her soft hair teasing him like a feather.

Michelle slipped in front of him as they lowered themselves slowly into the hot foamy water. Her hands began massaging his stiff neck and shoulders. With the warm jets and Michelle's loving touch, he could feel the energy slip from him as he slid back against the rim. She could sense it too.

Refusing to let all his energy slip away, however, she refused him any peace. She found his lips, her tongue caressing, probing. His ebbing energy transformed at her touch, growing into a lust for her that she craved. She was working him with her tongue, the soothing jets, her stroking hands. Their bodies were incredibly slippery, the sensation exceedingly erotic.

He arose slowly from the water, straining to keep his grip on her with her legs locked around him, her head thrown back. Stepping out of the tub, he lowered her to the cool marble vanity, her back against the mirror.

Each forceful move against her was met with an equally opposing motion. Each of them wanted the upper hand. Slowly, the gradually increasing sensations began wearing her defenses. She could be the aggressor no longer. Clutching tightly, her eyes rolled back, she hung on, accepting the delicious intensity as her cries of ecstasy echoed through the house.

Twenty-Two

The Glass Slipper rocked gently as the wake of a distant sloop finally pushed its way under her bow. Oblivious to the hypnotic sway, dozing on her foredeck, Michelle was lying against the windscreen, which had just the right incline for a nap in the sun. A tennis cap shielded her pale complexion.

A hint of a cool breeze awakened her to catch Judge peering over the side at his own reflection in the mirrorlike water.

The Marina at Eagle Mountain Lake looked like a picture postcard, sitting serenely in the distance above the calm water, filtered pink by the afternoon sun.

Judge stood deep in thought, casting his lure from the aft deck of the "Glass Slipper" while Michelle lay on the foredeck.

Michelle's attention and Heather's bright spirit had engulfed Walter Judge, keeping the recent gloom of reality from enveloping him.

The morning had been sunny and mild with just enough breeze to fill the sail and provide a fun cruise from the marina out past the dam and all the way to the north shore. Judge had prepared lunch, and to the girls' delight everyone had watched a country club sailboat race from the deck of the "Glass Slipper" while they dined.

By early evening, the wind had died and the "Glass Slipper" bobbed lazily in the fading sun on the glass smooth water. Michelle settled on the deck with a book while Judge rigged a pole for Heather.

"I caught one, Heather!" Judge suddenly called to the child in English, trying to get her attention. His only catch of the day was tugging vigorously on the end of his line.

Heather scampered up from the galley and jumped up and down gleefully, clapping her hands. "Fishes, fishes," she said in English.

"One fish," Judge said, smiling at the bouncing child.

"Two fish," she responded.

Judge looked at her curiously. "One fish," he repeated.

"Red fish, blue fish," Heather added, giggling.

Judge burst out laughing. Michelle looked up from her reading. She had not recalled hearing Judge laugh. She looked over at him chatting with her little girl from her prone position on the foredeck. She had felt always that he had a quiet and gentle way with her; yet he also had a powerful presence that instilled respect and even fear from everyone else. From the start, Heather had felt nothing but warmth from the man with the huge hands and dark eyes.

Now, Judge was effortlessly reeling in a two-pound bass. He unhooked it and held it up for Heather to inspect. She grimaced, then got up her courage and touched its slimy scales. Snatching her hand back, she closed her eyes tight, shuddered, and then ran back down into the galley.

Splashing his hands in the water as he released his catch, Judge set his pole down and took up a seat next to Michelle. They looked at each other for a moment. Impulsively, she reached up and pulled the man's head to hers, kissing him warmly.

"You should at least put in an appearance at Milt's party tonight," Michelle said softly, referring to Milt's son's homecoming.

"Not a chance," he said. "I wouldn't leave you for all the tea in Boston."

"Don't be silly. It will take me two hours to get ready on this boat. You make a run for it," she said smiling, "but hurry back."

He was feeling guilty about letting bad business get in the way of socializing with the people he had worked with so closely these past few years. "I don't want to get cornered by David and Milt and spend the whole evening defending my position on the Chile program."

"But you don't want to alienate everyone else," she added.

"OK . . . you're right," he said slowly, remembering what he had promised the two lawmen. He asked, "What time can you and Heather be ready?"

"No, no." She shook her head and held up her hand in resistance. "You go. Mom and Dad are coming to take Heather for tonight and Sunday. Just make an appearance to reassure everyone that your beef is only with Milt. I'll call and make reservations at the 'Carriage House' over on Commerce Street, my treat. I'm taking you for a late dessert if you think that iron man physique of yours can stand the calories. I'll be ready by the time you get back."

Judge agreed and left Michelle to make the reservations. He strode up the floating walkway towards the Marina parking lot. If he hurried, he could be back within an hour or so.

Milt and Emily Fox's estate stood majestically on a knoll, overlooking the Fort Worth Country Club. Their home had become a favorite retreat for many of their dignitary friends during the Byron Nelson Golf Classic, which was held every year during the late spring. With no less than eight bedrooms, they had ample room for many guests.

Now, looking out over the balcony, Milton Fox caught sight of his son's bride-to-be, Maria, clinging to Chad in the garden. She was indeed a beautiful girl. Thinking how much he would have enjoyed having her around while Chad was away, he sadly realized that it might be too difficult for her.

Milt knew that his wife, Emily, had had her heart set on Chad marrying a local girl, perhaps from Highland Park.

She had been stunned and bitter at Chad's announced engagement and had shut herself in the bedroom for hours.

Now, he noticed Judge standing near the bar and wondered where Walt's new girl was. He had recently heard that Judge had a new love. Rumor had it that she was that young doctor who had nearly got him killed. He descended the stairs to mingle with his guests.

Judge had parked along the long drive lined with expensive cars, leading to Milt's estate. He noted a couple of news vans parked among the Volvos and BMWs. With the news media present, even if it were only the social and fashion reporters, he had wondered if Carrillo was there.

He stood quietly by the bar sipping a JD, gleaning what he could from others' conversations. He soon learned that Hector had made a brief appearance and left a short time ago. Carrillo had been in town, having flown to Fort Worth unannounced, in his private jet.

There had been some very heated discussions heard from the front offices at ARI. Carrillo had apparently been furious with Milt about Judge's departure.

Everyone was worried about the project. The prototype was due to be shipped any day from Santiago, and the company had little direction on how to continue.

With Duffy's death still in the back of his mind, Judge felt it best to say nothing of details he could not for sure connect yet.

Milt forced his way through the crowd milling about in the vestibule and walked over to where Judge was standing. Judge had been working his way towards the door when Milt spotted him, but Judge politely smiled and waited for Milt, picking up a glass of chardonnay from a passing tray.

"Walt," Milt called from only a few feet away, raising his voice to be heard above the chatter in the room, "I'm glad you could make it. Come on, I want you to meet Chad."

"Listen, Walt," he began as they excused themselves through the crowd, "I want you to reconsider. We'll double your salary for the duration of the project." Milt wondered if anyone had called to encourage Judge to reconsider. The fact that Judge was here at all made him curious.

"I'll tell you what, Milt," Judge countered, seeing an opportunity. "You tell me the truth, and I'll consider coming back to finish the program."

Milt eyed Judge suspiciously. He knew Judge was no fool. Milt knew if there was anything that could be construed as illegal, Judge wouldn't finish the project no matter what he had said.

"What do you want to know?" Milt asked.

"One, are the weapons systems ARI's selling going to Iraq? And two, who's your liaison with the State Department?"

"The weapons systems that we just sent to Mexico? Iraq? Of course not! You saw the shipping docs, it's approved through the State Department and the Department of Commerce."

"The Mexicans don't have half that many aircraft capable of using that system," Judge insisted.

"You saw the export license. Everything is in order. I don't know, maybe the Mexicans have gotten permission to sell them to someone else." Milt stopped before he said anything else. He could tell Judge did not like his reply.

"You know I can't tell you who the government program director is. Look, he used to work for a Senator on some big committee. He has lots of close ties with groups with deep pockets. He takes direction from a guy he refers only to as 'The director.' They help us set up these little contracts like you work on, and it keeps us going and legal. Come on, Walt, you know the FAA is on board for this one. Isn't that enough?"

"Who's the director?" Judge wanted to know.

"I don't know, honest," Milt lied.

Judge looked carefully at Milt. He could detect the deception in the man's eyes. "I'm sorry, Milt," he said. "You'll have to get somebody else."

"Walt! Please! There just isn't time. The director is already upset. You don't know these people!"

Judge looked keenly at Milt, sensing a potential threat. "The government has lots of resources, Milt. This industry has plenty of experts just as capable as me."

"No, no, you don't understand. I don't have time to find other resources, other experts."

"Then you have a real problem, Milt," Judge said, turning and walking away.

Milt, wringing his hands, chased after Judge, but Emily stepped in front of her husband and grabbed his arm, whispering something in his ear. His expression changed from anxiety to outright fear as his wife pointed to the den.

The evening was mild, and guests had begun spilling out into the back gardens.

After seeing her husband to his unexpected visitor, Emily chased after Judge. Catching up to him, she reached for his hand and gave him a hug. Then, she pulled him aside where she could talk to him privately.

"Please don't leave without meeting Chad," she asked him urgently. "It's so important to Milt and me." She continued quickly, as if afraid of losing his interest. "If you could only speak to him, Walter. We're so worried about his marrying this girl. He can't even speak her language. You're a man of the world, and Chad has heard so much about you. I know he'll listen to you."

Looking down into her concerned face, Judge replied, "Emily, you know that whatever I say will have no effect on your son. He's in love—it's obvious. He needs to make this journey on his own."

Seeing the woman's dejected expression, he added, "Look, he's going overseas before the wedding. That will give him plenty of time away from her. If he gets cold feet, so be it. Meanwhile, why don't you take that time to get to know his fiancée? If your son is in love with her, you know as well as I that there's something within her that you'll love too."

Nodding slowly, Emily took Judge's hand and led him to her son. He was standing proudly in his military dress blues, his hands clasped behind him at parade rest. Maria was smiling at his side, occasionally nodding to questions from people who didn't realize that she had little knowledge of the English language.

As soon as Judge had been introduced to Chad, the younger man began asking him questions. He had always wanted to be a test pilot and planned to apply for flight school as soon as he returned from the Persian Gulf.

Judge tried changing the subject several times, but to no avail. Finally, Chad ran out of questions and paused to gaze at his fiancée. Smiling, he turned to Maria, whose adoring eyes had not left him from the time he; and Judge had begun speaking.

Judge's opportunity finally came to excuse himself from Chad and his bride-to-be. He had learned little to report back to Gibbons and realized now was his chance to leave. He would have been proud to bring Michelle to this gathering, but was glad he hadn't mixed business with pleasure.

Once back at the marina, he parked his car near the edge of the water and saw the faint lights of the "Glass Slipper" in the distance. Eager to return to Michelle, he ran down the floating walkway and through the maze of slips, eager to see her welcoming smile.

The cabin entrance was open below deck. Judge called to her and, receiving no reply, went to the aft stateroom. Her purse lay on the bed with her white silk shawl.

She must have stepped out for a moment, he thought to himself. Perhaps she left to get some ice from the marina restaurant. But something wasn't right.

A feeling of apprehension began to rise within him as he raced up the floating walkway to the cafe.

He passed an elderly man sitting quietly, smoking a pipe on the deck of a nearby boat.

"Say, buddy," Judge called out. "Did you see a pretty blonde lady walk by? She would have come from those slips over there." He pointed towards the "Glass Slipper." The old man looked over at Judge. "Tall, good-looking blonde, wearing a white dress?" he asked, never taking the pipe from between his teeth.

"Yes," Judge said, biting his tongue. *She must be up at the café,* he thought.

"Yep, real classy," he came back. "Passed by about a half hour ago. Headed towards the parking lot."

Judge turned towards the walkway, wondering if she had gone up to feed the ducks with Heather. Maybe they had just missed each other, he thought.

"I'd be careful," the old man called after him, chuckling. "Her boyfriend was pretty big, even bigger'n you."

Judge whirled around, nearly losing his balance. Running back up the ramp to the old man's boat, he demanded, "Say that again."

The old man pulled the pipe from his mouth, surprised at Judge's reaction. "Big guy," he said, "kind of Latin looking. Had his arm around her," he continued. "Kind of strange though," he hesitated, tilting his head and looking off in the distance.

"How's that?" Judge asked grimly. He was beginning to sweat.

"He was smiling, but she didn't look too happy. I notice things like that, you know," the old man said, turning his head back towards Judge. "They got into a big Lincoln."

With a sinking feeling, Judge asked, "Was there a little girl with them, about six years old?"

"Nah, the little tike left earlier with a nice-lookin' older couple—maybe her grandparents."

Judge stood leaning on the side of the old man's boat, reeling at what he had just been told. He closed his eyes, trembling with rage and frustration.

Then, he trudged back to the "Glass Slipper" to call Lieutenant Gibbons.

Sam Jenkins was in the office working late, but when he heard what had happened, he agreed to call his lieutenant at home and to meet Judge at the Fox's estate.

It was time, they both agreed, to put pressure on Fox. It seemed that he was the only tangible suspect they could question concerning the connection between Judge and Pauline Casey, and now Michelle. Judge said he would meet them at Milt's place.

There were a few stragglers wandering out to their cars as Judge pulled up to the Fox's estate. He saw Chad saying goodbye to a small number of guests.

Judge jumped out of the car and walked briskly to the front door. Although he had called his FBI friends, he had no intention of waiting for them before speaking with Fox.

"I need to speak to your father," Judge said abruptly, all politeness a thing of the past. "He's on the telephone, in the den," Chad replied with a concerned look. "Is there something wrong?"

Judge looked into the young man's eyes and remembered the words of one of his special ops instructors. "Your anger will kill you. Never be angry in this business."

With effort, he smiled at Chad. "Sorry if I seemed rude. Just a little misunderstanding I need to clear up with your father."

"I'll show you, just this way," Chad replied.

He led Judge to the rear of the house. The door to the den was closed.

"Dad," Chad said, opening the door. "Mr. Judge wants to talk to you."

Milt was in plain sight, slumped over his desk.

Rushing past Chad, Judge reached Milt first. He checked the older man's pulse at the carotid artery, then stepped back, stunned.

He looked down at Milt, conflicting feelings running through him. The old man had been testy and stubborn, but he had treated him well. They had spent several years together working on projects of mutual interest.

"Christ!" Judge muttered. "What next?" Running a hand through his thick hair, he moved towards the phone to call 911, leaving an ashen-faced Chad to cradle his father's head.

Twenty-Three

The coroner had initially ruled Milton Fox's death a heart attack. However, upon closer examination, the coroner found what appeared to be a small needle mark just below his left ear. An autopsy had been ordered, and the results would be forthcoming in a day or two.

Judge and his FBI friends suspected that Michelle's disappearance and Fox's death were definitely related; however, it appeared for the moment that they could not have both been committed by the same person. Gutierrez was high on their list of suspects for one of them.

It also seemed apparent that those responsible were unaware that the FBI was looking for Gutierrez by name. Judge reminded Gibbons, Jenkins, and their captain of this and noted that this could work to their advantage.

Gibbons agreed, and Captain Stillions had refrained from issuing an APB for Ponce Gutierrez and was not providing either the NSA or the CIA with his name until better cooperation with them could be assured.

Michelle's disappearance did not appear to the local police to be a kidnapping. The few investigators who suspected it, namely, Gibbons and Jenkins, were keeping a tight lid on the investigation for the time being. With no real proof of a connection between Michelle's disappearance and the Chilean program, rumors and public speculation could drive the culprits further underground.

As soon as the kidnappers contacted Judge, and he knew they must, he'd get closer to the answers he so desperately sought—and, he hoped, to Michelle.

The Sunday sun had come and gone by the time Judge had finished formulating his plans. Despite the fact that someone had Michelle, Judge was going to make things more difficult for those he felt were responsible from here on out. The fact that he did not know who they were exactly was only a minor inconvenience. He would find them all.

Except for Gibbons and the Loftons, the phone had not rung. No one had called to give him instructions or to confirm that Michelle was being held until his cooperation had been secured.

To Judge, the connection had been obvious. However, after twenty-four hours, he was beginning to have doubts.

Both he and the local contingent of the FBI felt that Gutierrez might no longer be in the US. Judge had known that Carrillo traveled by private jet and quite probably was traveling with Gutierrez. When he told Jenkins that Carrillo had been at the Fox's estate the night of the party, the sergeant had quickly set out to retrace the Chilean's recent movements.

It hadn't taken the FAA long to trace Carrillo's aircraft entering and leaving US airspace from Texas to Mexico City. No record of a woman matching Michelle's description had been reported at the US Customs.

Meanwhile, Jenkins and Gibbons were trying to make a connection between Carrillo, Fox, and Gutierrez. The CIA was not cooperating, which didn't surprise Judge, but they were getting some help from other police contacts. In fact, they had found the names of the men in their photograph of Gutierrez.

To Judge's surprise, they were members of the board of a relatively new private endowment organization known as the American Democracy Endowment, or ADE. The ADE was a grant institute headed by a US senator and led by a board of directors made up of current and former cabinet members.

The ADE received all of its operating capital and grant funds from the US Department of State. The ADE provided monetary grants to supporters of democratic movements in developing countries. *Like the recent election in Chile*, Judge thought to himself.

The man standing at the podium in the photograph was Senator Stan Roberts of Illinois. Gibbons and his captain were looking further into the relationship between the ADE and Gutierrez. The "director's" name, however, kept eluding everyone.

Judge knew that Michelle's survival depended on two things. The first, he concluded, was his immediate compliance in solving the copter problems, even to the point of integrating the weapons systems. Milt had never approached him about it in his attempts to keep the weapons part of the program secret from Judge. But Judge now realized that his participation in the weapons integration would surface soon. As much resistance as he had exhibited concerning that subject, he wondered if somehow Carrillo had made other plans. The burglary of his safe suddenly began to fit into place.

Judge held the key to the software required for sighting and tracking with ARI's system. This was his first trump card. If they thought they had what they needed from his safe, they were sadly mistaken.

Indeed, they must have felt that now Judge had the ideal incentive to finish the project and to avoid going to the press or the police. With no other witnesses for the police to go to, they would be confident that any ensuing investigation would be useless.

Judge had consulted again with Van Warren without revealing what was precipitating his inquiries. Van Warren had told him that the CIA had been under close scrutiny by Congress since the Iran-Contra scandal. Perhaps, Van speculated, the administration was funding covert activities through State Department grants to endowment groups like the ADE. It was soon after the Iran-Contra scandal that the ADE had come into being.

The ADE had been criticized for loose accounting and little accountability. It was referred to by some members of Congress as a "loose cannon."

Judge was jolted from his reverie by the sound of the mail truck. He dashed out to meet the mailman just as the carrier was putting the mail in the box.

"Thanks, I'll take them," Judge offered, holding out his hand.

As soon as the truck had driven off, Judge eagerly began thumbing through the mail. *Where was it?* he wondered. *Where was the damn letter from those bastards? Would they be foolish enough to put something in writing?*

And then he saw it. Holding the airmail letter he'd been waiting for, he took a deep breath and then ripped it open. Inside the envelope, in his name, was a one-way ticket to Santiago, Chile.

Twenty-Four

Chile to Pay US in Envoy's Slaying—"The new Government of Chile agreed in principle today to pay compensation for the killing of Orlando Letelier, a Chilean exile leader assassinated in Washington 14 years ago."

—New York Times, ***May 13, 1990, p. 1***

Judge had been gritting his teeth for so long his jaw ached by the time he deplaned in South America. He could not remember a time when he felt so determined yet fearful. Fear for the life of a loved one was something new for Judge. It unnerved him, making him question his every move. He knew what he had to do, but he found himself wondering if he had decided upon the right way to go about it.

After the plane ticket had arrived, with all that it implied, he had driven back to ARI to tell David that he was willing to continue working on the project.

"You're too late," David had said.

"What do you mean?"

"Carrillo called and said he wasn't going to ship the prototype."

"Did he say why?"

"No. He just said he had things under control and that they would do the testing down there. I wonder who he found to do it for him."

Judge had held up his plane ticket.

"You?"

"I'm going down there and find out what's going on, and I'll call you when I know something."

Carrillo had a driver waiting for him when he arrived in Santiago—but it wasn't De Padilla, as Judge had expected. The driver, a tall man who introduced himself as Cesar Torres, held himself proudly and seemed the perfect image of a chauffeur.

"So L'eon De Padilla gets the day off?" Judge quipped. In truth, he was hardly disappointed not having to put up with the sullen L'eon.

"L'eon's out of town," Cesar replied amiably.

"Vacation?" Judge inquired, knowing that L'eon would not have gone on vacation. "He deserved it, he was a really hard worker."

"No, he's on a special job for Senor Carrillo."

"Oh, that's right," Judge improvised. "He told me he was going to Europe to work that other end of the helicopter project." Judge eyed Torres for any semblance of a response, but the driver simply nodded his head.

"Yes, Spain I think," Torres offered.

Quickly changing the subject, Judge asked, "Cesar, who's manning this extra checkpoint?"

Although he had been closely inspected at this very location on his last trip, this time he and Cesar were quickly waved through. "These people are part of the CNI. To the rest of the world, they are thought of as the National Information Center. Chileans will always think of them as the National Intelligence Agency. They are a cross between the American CIA and the Soviet KGB."

Cesar's English was impeccable. "You must remember, Mr. Judge, that we are still a dictatorship."

"I thought Aylwin had been elected," Judge pointed out.

He was pleased that Cesar was talking freely, apparently unfazed by Judge's previous questions about L'eon.

"To the rest of the world, we are a democracy. However, it is a controlled democracy, ruled only by a very few men. Pinochet is still a powerful man. He was appointed General of the Army, right after the election."

"You are quite knowledgeable," Judge remarked. "What university did you attend?"

"King's College," Cesar replied with a slight smile.

"Cambridge?" Judge was impressed.

Cesar's smile broadened. He obviously enjoyed surprising people—and Judge immediately felt more at ease.

His family had been members of the Christian Democrats and close friends of one of Allende's cabinet members.

"Do you know who Allende was, senor?"

"Of course," Judge replied. "He was your President until the coup that installed Pinochet into power in the late 1960s."

"My family fled to the US immediately after Allende's assassination by Pinochet's men," Torres continued. "They were living in Washington DC with their friends, the Leteliers, whose father had once been Chile's foreign minister. Pinochet's agents went to Washington DC and murdered the Leteliers. Pinochet suspected that the Leteliers had access to members of the US Congress. From DC, my family fled to England. We lived in England until after I graduated from the College at Cambridge, where I met my wife."

"With your background," Judge wondered aloud, "why are you working as a chauffeur?"

Ignoring the unintended insult, Cesar replied, "It's not easy finding a well-paying job here in Santiago. I couldn't find any work at all until L'eon spoke to Senor Carrillo on my behalf. I would have preferred to work at the University, but I could never afford the lifestyle I want for Ester on a professor's salary." Judge could see that his chauffeur had a deep romantic streak. He was obviously still very much in love with his wife.

They drove to a beautiful hotel on the outskirts of the city, the Hotel Blanca Pinera. They could see it in the distance across the emptiness of the canyon that fell away to their right at the roadside.

The vineyards growing to their left rose from beyond the crest of the hill. Large alders grew at equal distances, every hundred yards or so at the edge of the road, creating a continuing strobe of shadow and light.

Torres pulled under the large verandah adjacent to the hotel lobby. Momentarily enthralled with the beauty of the place, Judge slowly got out, taking in the view. As he stood gazing at the magnificent bougainvilleas, draping over the pillared entrance, Torres said, "I wonder if Senor Carrillo has made an error?"

"What do you mean?" Judge asked sharply. He wasn't ready for another surprise.

"This is the hotel where Mr. Hector houses his political guests, men in high places with dubious intentions. I do not think he intended this place for you."

Judge considered this information, and then asked, "Why does he bring them here?"

"Well, Senor Carrillo owns the Hotel Pinera. He finds it easier to keep an eye on certain guests. It can be also be very convenient if he needs to have a reporter catch a certain politician with a woman who is not his wife, if you know what I mean."

Judge smiled briefly and shook Cesar's hand. "Thanks for the ride and the good conversation." Then, he added, "You know, I think Senor Carrillo had you bring me here quite deliberately."

Torres stared at Judge for a long moment, and Judge wondered if his new friend was regretting some of their conversation.

As he went to the front desk to check in, Torres called after him, "I will pick you up at seven in the morning. Senor Carrillo does not like taxis at the Air Park anymore." Judge chaffed at the news. He had been hoping to have more independence than to be chauffeured about.

The hotel was a two-story structure of classic Spanish architecture with virtually all of the rooms opening onto an interior verandah.

Each room faced a central courtyard that boasted the requisite fountain and lush garden with sitting areas.

He smiled at the receptionist and slipped her a few extra pesos, thus assuring him a first floor corner room. It was ideally situated. The room had windows that opened out onto two sides of the building closest to the main drive, which led down the hill to the village center. Judge would now be able to see anyone watching his room from the outside along adjacent sides of the hotel.

And if the coast was clear, he could step down from either window and disappear into town.

Judge did not have long to wait. As he began to get the lay of his surroundings, he quickly recognized the two Iraqis from his previous visit. Pleased that they had been so predictable, he watched them closely for a while. He was depending on them being there.

They had stationed themselves outside his hotel room. One, the smaller of the two Mukhabarat, positioned himself at a seating area across from the fountain in the courtyard, where he could keep a close eye on anyone that came to or from Judge's hotel room door. The other sat patiently in a dark Mercedes, parked not far from the corner of the hotel, in clear view of both of Judge's exterior windows.

Judge peered through the curtains at the Mercedes, smiling to himself. "Amateurs," he muttered as he unpacked his bags. We'll see how long it takes to shake them.

Twenty-Five

True to his word, Torres appeared at seven o'clock the next morning. The Iraqis, having stood their posts during the night, followed them to the airfield and then abruptly vanished.

Carrillo's secretary ushered Judge into Hector's office. Judge immediately noted the two swarthy men who were sitting in front of Carrillo's desk. Apparently, this was the new crew, having relieved the two men who had kept an eye on Judge the night before.

It made little difference to him—the men were interchangeable and would serve him just fine when the time came.

The two fresh Mukhabarat now stood as he entered.

"Senor Judge," greeted Carrillo warmly, a glint in his eyes, "so nice to have you with us again." His voice dropped in mock sympathy. "Oh, and I was so sorry to hear of Senor Fox."

He did not introduce his two companions, who remained expressionless.

"Please, Senor Judge, have a seat, we have much to discuss."

"Before I do, I'd like you to ask your friends to wait outside," Judge countered. "We need to talk alone."

Smiling, Carrillo replied, "These are my friends, senor. Anything we discuss can be shared with them."

Judge turned and opened the office door. "Either they go, or I do."

Carrillo suddenly frowned. "Senor Judge, these are customers. Please do not be rude."

Judge smiled to himself. It had not taken many words spoken in English to affirm that these two newcomers did not understand English.

"These are not customers, or friends," Judge said, squinting slightly, looking at the Iraqis as he spoke. "They are Mukhabarat! Your customer's apes. If they do not leave now, I will call their colonel and have them shot for interrupting our work!"

Carrillo feigned a smile. "Come, gentlemen," he said to them in a tongue that Judge was unfamiliar with. "Leave us for a moment. This discussion is about business that does not concern you and will bore you."

Judge was not the least bit surprised to see the two men calmly follow Carrillo into the reception area outside his office.

Returning, Carrillo closed the door behind him and said to Judge, "You are lucky, senor, that they do not understand English. You have embarrassed me just the same. What seems to be the problem?"

"Why the Mukhabarat?"

"They are not for you, senor," Carrillo said, raising his eyebrows. "They are here to keep the press away from me."

"There is a pair of them watching my hotel and following me everywhere."

"Then they must be making sure the press does not approach you either. They are very nervous about spies and the press. The Iraqis, they are still worried that the shipments might be interrupted by foreigners."

"So you admit the aircraft is not a crop duster."

Carrillo frowned, hesitating slightly. "Senor Wright said you had had a change of heart, so I thought you knew these things. This surprises me."

Judge suddenly realized that he might have misread Carrillo. How deeply involved Carrillo was in all of this was yet to be determined, but at the very least, he had apparently not been communicating with Milt and Wright on the same level of trust.

"I do . . . that is . . . Milt told me," Judge said, recovering. "It's just that, now that we are in Chile, we don't need to continue the deception about the crop duster angle." He was watching Carrillo's expression closely for any sign of wariness to his sudden behavior.

"Ah, yes." Carrillo threw up his hands with a big smile. "I see that Milt was wrong about you. I told him that even you must have a price despite your reputation."

"You were right," Judge replied. Carrillo seemed to be accepting Judge's "change of heart" at face value.

Carrillo put in, "On the other hand, now Senor Wright, he is angry at you, yes?" He laughed. "It is Wright who must pay you now out of his profits, no? Now I understand why he was so angry when he called me." He was being surprisingly candid and easy to talk with. Just the same, Judge didn't trust him.

If Carrillo was unaware that Judge was cooperating under duress, it would do no good to cause trouble with him. Even so, Judge had to get to Gutierrez and this Wright fellow somehow.

"Who is Senor Wright?" Judge asked.

Carrillo looked at Judge in disbelief. "Wright, he is the big boss, yes?"

"He's not my boss. Who does he work for?"

"Ah, but of course, you have not met him. He makes the arrangements between ARI and my company. Now that your Mr. Fox is dead, surely you will be hearing more of him."

"Your men," Judge continued, getting back to the Iraqis, "their commander, is he a very large man?" he asked, thinking of Gutierrez. He remembered L'eon telling him about Gutierrez, so Judge knew Carrillo must know him as well. Gutierrez, on the other hand, did not know that Judge knew about him yet, and Judge preferred to keep it that way by not mentioning him by name.

"I tell you, senor," Carrillo insisted, "they are not my men. But no, he is not too big. He is, how you say, chubby? It is his relationship to his brother-in-law, Saddam Hussein, that his men fear most. His men are nothing to me, except for when the journalists show up."

Another dead end, Judge thought. He had originally thought that Gutierrez was working for Carrillo. Now he wasn't so sure. Judge had always figured that Gutierrez must be the strong man doing the dirty work, but if not for Carrillo, then whom? Wright perhaps, or the mysterious "director." Maybe Wright was the "director."

"What made you change your mind and decide to move the flight testing down here?" Judge asked. "You know the FAA wanted the testing done in the US. They have not agreed to accept any test data unless they can witness it."

"This was not my idea, Senor Judge. You see, I did not really care if the FAA was involved or not. Senor Fox and Senor Wright said that it would keep you with the project and keep visibility off your US State Department until the problems were worked out and we could fly the aircraft. The FAA services were free, so I went along with it."

"So what happened?" Judge asked earnestly.

"Time, Senor Wright said. My customer is in a hurry. Besides, you could better concentrate on the project here, where outsiders could not influence it."

Outsiders like the police, the public, and the FBI, Judge thought to himself.

"My customer is now willing to accept a demonstration instead of an FAA type certificate," Carrillo continued.

Judge looked sharply at Carrillo. Demonstration? He wondered if the Chilean had realized he may have just handed Judge his biggest trump card.

Twenty-Six

Carrillo's announcement that there would be a demonstration for his Iraqi customers provided Judge with an idea about how to flush Wright into the open.

"Hector," Judge began, "I must tell you. I am here to help you get the aircraft ready, but I will not be doing the flying."

Carrillo frowned suddenly and looked at Judge. "But, senor, didn't you know? You will be the test pilot."

Judge shook his head adamantly. "I'm afraid that will not be possible. Your Mr. Wright has not lived up to his end of the agreement," Judge bluffed.

He knew a stalemate would be short-lived, but he felt certain someone would come out in the open and try to remind him of what would happen if he didn't do their bidding.

"What are you saying?" Carrillo asked. "There was never any mention of using another pilot."

"I understand that you are a pilot."

"Yes, but not a test pilot!" Carrillo suddenly was suspicious. Did he suspect that Judge might sabotage the plane?

Judge watched Hector Carrillo closely. "Is it more money you want?" the Chilean asked. "What agreement has Senor Wright forgotten?"

"He said that he would call me and discuss the arrangements for payment," Judge lied. "He has not called, so I assume the deal is off." Judge shrugged.

"He has not paid you? Not anything?"

"Nothing, ever," Judge maintained firmly.

"This is outrageous!" Carrillo cried. "After all I have invested!"

He paced the floor, waving his hands back and forth agitatedly. Then, he turned to Judge and said, "You told me that even you had your price."

Judge nodded. "Yes, I did. I admitted that everyone, including me, has his price," Judge repeated. "Wright knows my price and agreed to pay it. But he has not. I will not demonstrate the aircraft or test it without payment."

Carrillo was crimson with anger, and Judge quietly placed his hand on the man's shoulder.

"Calm yourself, Hector," Judge said. "I'm sure Wright will come to his senses. Maybe a call from you would remind him. Perhaps it was an oversight."

Slowly, he walked out of Carrillo's office, leaving the Chilean fuming.

Judge smiled to himself as he sauntered to the workbench near the prototype and aimlessly thumbed through the blueprints. *It should not be long now,* he thought.

The big man had been correct. Barely ten minutes had passed before Carrillo's petite secretary came scurrying towards him. "Could you come with me, please, Senor Judge?" she urged, indicating that he was needed urgently in Carrillo's office.

Carrillo was standing at his desk holding the phone in one hand. Wordlessly, he handed it to Judge, then walked quickly from the room, taking his secretary with him. Judge put the receiver to his ear. "Mr. Wright, I presume?" he said calmly.

There was a slight hesitation on the line, an unfamiliar voice came back, seemingly from far away.

"Just what the hell are you trying to pull?" the voice was condescending. "You get that damn thing flying right or your girl is dead."

Judge remained calm. "Nice to meet you too. However, I do nothing until I hear from Michelle," he said firmly. "She calls me today, or I get the next plane back to the States."

There was silence on the other side. Then Judge added the zinger, "She calls me every day or I'll see to it these aircraft never make it to Baghdad."

"You're insane," the voice snarled. "And you're in no position to give orders," Wright growled.

"I just hope you haven't already killed her," Judge continued, "because if you have, I suggest you watch yourself very closely. You know I can be very unfriendly if I have to be."

"I'll have her killed and you with her!" the voice threatened, getting louder.

Judge smiled, knowing he was fully in control. "You know, Mr. Wright, you're so close to all that money that you can smell it. You just can't touch it yet. I believe Michelle is safe with you for the time being. I just want to be reminded that I'm right on a regular basis." With that, Judge hung up the phone.

Outside the office, Judge told Carrillo that he would remain there for the rest of the day. "If Wright lives up to his agreement, we will begin testing tomorrow afternoon. If not, I will be leaving in the morning. Nothing personal, Hector, just business."

"Senor Judge, please. I will pay you. Wright can pay me later. What is it you wish?"

Judge shook his head. "Wright has some property that I want. He took it from me. It is worth more than all you own, at least to me, but it is worthless to him." For a moment, Michelle's face swam before him. He tried to shut it out, unable to even imagine what she was going through. His face red with anger, he turned to Carrillo.

"This is between Wright and me," he told him. "Besides, I don't think he'd want you to cross him by paying me. Not only won't you get your weapons systems—you might get hurt," he cautioned, a note of empathy in his voice.

"It's best that he and I settle this," Judge said. "Don't worry, Hector, Wright will come through. I can sense it." Judge turned and walked out, heading towards the flight ramp.

The flight ramp was a paved area adjacent to the main factory, which must have been a hundred yards square. There were now nearly two dozen used LongRanger helicopters, evenly spaced along both sides of the tarmac. All were waiting their turn at the conversion process. The ramp led out to a short unpaved runway turf that was perpendicular to the tarmac.

Trying to appear nonchalant, Judge took a cursory look at some of the specimens. All appeared flight-worthy. Some still had their batteries intact, and all had fuel on board.

Carrillo had been right to be suspicious about flying the aircraft. Judge was too clever to bring it up to perfection and then walk away. Both he and Wright were wise not to let anyone but Judge demonstrate the aircraft the first time.

Judge was aware that he was on shallow ground. If something were to happen to him after the aircraft was safely airworthy, Carrillo and Wright might think they had no further use of him, or Michelle. They might mistakenly believe that his stolen hard drive contained all they needed to know about setting up the weapons systems and using the countermeasures to conceal the radar signature.

However, such a move would carry risks. The odds were that up to half of the aircraft could be lost to a British embargo. Surely they would keep him around until they were completely confident that the entire system worked perfectly.

This wasn't much of an insurance policy for himself and Michelle. He knew that once the aircraft were flown safely, he and Michelle could be facing a much shorter life span.

Twenty-Seven

Iraq Warns Kuwait and Emirates on Exceeding Quotas Set by OPEC*—New York Times, *Jul. 18, 1990, p. D1

The songs of the chiricocas and turks rang and chirped melodiously in the early morning air. To Michelle, however, the sounds were piercing and nagging, forcing her awake well before she was ready. Holding her head gently, she rose to a sitting position on the soft feather mattress and hoped this new position would settle her stomach.

Her surroundings were mildly familiar. Although she'd awakened before in this place since arriving, this was the first time she could sit and move about without vomiting.

The room seemed small, maybe a dozen feet square. A small window looked out over a long, narrow valley. Below she could see the city lights and wisps of spent fires from ovens and fireplaces curling above the homes.

From an open doorway to the left of the bed came the telltale drip from a faucet.

She remembered heaving over the side of the commode by the sink. Michelle wished for a tub to lie in, which the half bath did not provide. She made her way once again to the basin. This time she did not lean over it. The water was cool and clear as she ran it over her fingers. Bending slightly, lest she lose her balance, she rinsed her face, holding her wet hands against her aching forehead until her palms became warm again.

The chain at her ankle rustled loudly like a stubborn serpent, reminding her of the limits of her freedom. Confused and angry, Michelle carefully lowered herself once again to the bed.

Heather's giggles were still fresh in her mind. The image of Walter Judge dangling his fish in front of Heather brought a smile to her lips, despite her circumstances. She had waited a long time for a man like Walter to come into their lives.

God, she hoped he'd find her. She cringed, remembering the other big man—a monster, who had put his hands around her throat, gagging her into silence, and then sticking a needle into her arm. Soon, she was nearly paralyzed, unable to resist him.

"Burundanga," she moaned to herself. Burundanga, a derivative of scopolamine, was a potent sedative that caused submissive behavior. That was it, she affirmed to herself, shaking her head. The drug had given her mild amnesia and put her into a near hypnotic state during her abduction.

Oddly, she recalled reading a medical paper describing how Central and South American prostitutes often used the drug to enable them to rob or kill their clients.

"Instant morality," she said to herself wryly.

Michelle only vaguely remembered the plane ride, and then another, and another. Or had it been a single trip that she kept dreaming about over and over in her aching head.

Walter had protected her from those men that strange night when the lightning flashed. She had come to feel safe when she was around him. Now she was remembering what Tony had said to her. He had not liked Walter Judge, had not trusted him. Michelle knew he had to be wrong about Walter, if only Tony could see the gentleness in the big man.

But now she wondered about what he had said. There had been a time when Michelle had held Tony in a similar light. She respected him. He was a trained police officer. If he did not trust Judge, then there was something he knew that she didn't.

All this violence that had come to her could, in fact, be related to the reason why Judge was so deeply troubled. Perhaps it was that project in South America or something in his past—like his murdered ex-girlfriend.

Whatever it was had certainly engulfed her too, she thought. Thankfully, it had missed engulfing her daughter by mere minutes. Thank goodness she'd sent Heather off with her parents moments before she had been abducted.

Sitting again, Michelle's gaze followed the chain to the opposite end. In the shadows, she could make out a shackle, held fast to the leg of an old radiator. The chain was heavy, much larger than might normally be used to tether a human. *It could probably hold an elephant secure,* she thought.

The light through the sheer curtains suddenly shone pink. She arose and gingerly made her way towards it, dragging her tether noisily and pulling the drapes aside, letting in the morning sunrise.

How she longed for fresh air!

She pulled the window up. To her delight it opened, albeit barely a few inches, but enough to let in the fresh air of the morning.

She knelt and placed her face against the opening, letting the cool morning air blow across her aching head.

"I must be up north," she reasoned, in Montana or Colorado. Michelle had once visited Leadville, Colorado, high in the Rocky Mountains. The air there had been thin, giving her a headache after a day's hike.

She knew that this time her throbbing headache had been drug induced and that the air here was much easier to breathe than that of Leadville.

Feeling momentarily weak again, Michelle made her way back to the bed. The chain barely could reach the door to the tiny room, and she vaguely remembered trying the door once in the night. It was, of course, locked.

Her thoughts again turned to Walter. Her captors, she felt sure, had some business with him. But if they wanted ransom, wouldn't they have taken Heather too?

Suddenly stricken with fear, she caught her breath. Who was to say they didn't also have Heather? She couldn't bear the thought and pushed it out of her mind. One crisis at a time, she told herself. Whatever the reason, Michelle had a feeling she'd find out more soon. After all, her captors would have to bring her something to eat.

She felt that if she had been taken for some sick reason, like a sex slave, that she would have been molested already, and she was certain that she had not been.

Then, she heard someone else stirring in the house. It sounded like a man's shoes shuffling along the slate floor. A door creaked, and then there was the unmistakable sound of a man urinating. Afterwards she could hear him banging about in the kitchen.

She was unprepared when, a few minutes later, the door to her room rattled as a lock on the other side was removed. Michelle caught her breath. Sitting upright again, she wound her arms around her legs and waited for the door to open. She gasped when she saw who was entering her room.

It was her captor. Michelle had thought she had only dreamed that he was so huge. Now, she trembled as his hard, mean eyes roamed over her.

The man was so big that he had to duck his head and turn each shoulder in order to enter the room. Clearly, he must be a head taller than Judge.

Gutierrez moved past her bed to the radiator and, producing a key, undid the hasp on the shackle at its base. Suddenly, his hand was around her neck, lifting her from the bed. Half throwing her to the door, he said, "You cook now. You run, I break your legs, then you not need chain."

Laughing at her expression, he dropped the loose end of the chain, forcing Michelle to drag it with her.

The kitchen was very small, almost too small for more than one person. A door to one side led to the outside, but she barely gave it notice. She knew she was not up to running. A short drain board was immediately to the right of the door, and the sink was to the right of that. A tiny window above the sink added daylight to the otherwise dimly lit pantry. A gas stove was on the far wall, barely a step from the sink, and a small refrigerator was in the corner. A table, barely two feet square, was against the wall opposite the sink; and with her captor sitting at the table, she was never more than an arm's reach from him.

When she had set out a couple of eggs and cut a slice of ham, he laughed again. "That must be for you. Now you cook me mine. Six eggs, with pepper."

Michelle reddened. If only she had enough strength to shove this paring knife into his fat stomach, she mused. Deciding against it, she didn't think she could even penetrate the brute's skin the way she was shaking. You just wait, she promised him silently. You'll get yours.

The smell of the eggs and meat on a greasy skittle was almost more than Michelle could tolerate. Her stomach was upset, and she was tense and fearful.

When Gutierrez had finally begun shoving down his breakfast, she gained enough courage to speak.

"What do you want with me?" she asked as steadily as she could under the circumstances.

Gutierrez looked up from his plate. His direct glare frightened her again. "First I gets my money," he said. "Then I find out how good a woman you are. Then I makes you scream."

He laughed, in the process spitting out some of his half-chewed food.

She looked away, her stomach beginning to heave.

Michelle picked up the chain, as much as she could carry, and stumbled back into her room. As she slammed the door behind her, she could still here him laughing at her.

At least her head was beginning to clear, she noticed as she sat on the bed. She had managed to keep down a glass of apple juice and a slice of toast and jam. Still holding a length of the chain in her lap as she leaned on the edge of the bed, she eyed the open window and wondered if she could free herself and make it down the mountain to the distant town.

As if in response to her thoughts, the door burst open, and Gutierrez wedged himself through the door. He yanked the chain away from her and secured it to the radiator once again.

Grabbing her around the neck, he pulled her to him, burying his stubbled face in her breasts.

She realized that it was futile to struggle against him. It was like battling a force of nature. Resigned to enduring whatever he meant to do, she lay passively when he pushed her onto the bed and began yanking at the front of her dress. It had just begun to tear when the ringing of a telephone made him hesitate. Cursing, he released her. With a last burning look at her, he left the room, locking the door behind him.

She moved to the locked door and listened intently, her heart still pounding. But the one-sided telephone conversation was in Spanish, a language she had never learned. How she wished she had!

Looking again at the hasp on her shackle, she remembered the old key that the big ape had kept in his pocket. It was an old-fashioned key like the one her grandmother had used for an old hope chest that sat at the foot of her bed. Michelle, always a curious child, remembered being able to open it once using a piece of bent coat hanger.

Now, she was again searching for something to use on the lock, but there was nothing in sight.

A shelf projected from the wall to the left of the locked door. Below it was fastened an empty clothing rack. There was nothing under the bed, and the bureau by the window held half a dozen empty drawers. Searching them, Michelle found several pairs of men's socks, too small to belong to the man that held her captive.

She also found a pair of sweatpants and an old sweatshirt. The sweats were extremely baggy, even for a man. At first she passed them over, thinking there was no way she could put them on with a chain on her leg.

Then, she reconsidered, and went back to the sweats, holding a pant leg against her waist.

Michelle quickly pulled her dress off over her head and stretched one of the baggy cuffs until it tore at the seam. She stuffed her head through it. It was a tight fit; however, she got one arm and shoulder through it as the seam opened a little more. She managed to get the pant leg on over her midsection. Nearly falling over, she stood for a second with both legs and her tiny butt crammed into one pant leg.

Finally, she pushed the sweats down to her ankles and stepped one foot out and pulled them up normally. Encouraged by her own cleverness, she continued searching the room.

It was a relief to be out of her dress and into something warm and clean. Michelle hoped the excessively baggy sweats would also make her less appealing to her captor. She put on a fresh T-shirt and the socks.

The man to whom they belonged had been neat and tidy. Everything was nicely folded and clean, albeit several sizes too large for Michelle. But it was certainly better than her party dress.

Dismayed at not finding anything to open the lock with, she flopped back onto the bed. She would have to look for some cutlery to confiscate from the kitchen during her next cooking shift, she thought sourly. At least the long bulky sleeves of the sweatshirt would make it easier to conceal a fork.

Michelle turned her head suddenly and looked at the headboard. It was a bookcase style with two small sliding doors at each end. She slid the door on the left to the side and removed a couple of books. A quick glance proved them to be written in Spanish. Sliding the door open on the right, Michelle found a man's unused handkerchief with something wrapped inside it. It had been hidden behind a couple of paperbacks. Trembling, she unwrapped it to find a man's large stainless steel watch. Her captors must not have seen it. Turning it over, she gasped in shock when she read the inscription on the back: To My Walter, Our love is for all time! Connie Lin.

Twenty-Eight

Deep in thought, Walter Judge struggled with the task of reducing the risk to Michelle if she could be found.

Judge wondered how the FBI agents from Texas were doing. He knew it was time to call them and update them on his progress. Had they connected Wright to the senator on the ADE board? Who was the director? Who had killed Milt?

As for the Iraqis, their role in the sordid affair seemed simpler. They were in Chile to protect the project and keep journalists and spies away. Judge doubted there was any significant exchange of funds between Carrillo and the Mukhabarat.

If anything, the Iraqis were an annoyance. Saddam Hussein must desperately want the gunships, even to the point of risking the presence of the Mukhabarat to quash any premature press releases. Judge wondered who had eliminated Pauline and Duffy because they had gotten too close to the truth.

Judge worked late into the evening, expecting to be called into Carrillo's office at any moment. When it didn't happen, he wondered if he would have to resort to his alternate plan. Escaping with his life would be the easy part, but he wouldn't stop until all responsible had suffered the ultimate punishment.

Judge visited the flight ramp often, usually with a soda and a bag of chips. The lazy big American was taking another break.

The gate guards had become used to his visits, and he began to chat with them, trying out his pitiful Spanish to build rapport with them. At least one of the Iraqis was always in sight.

On the opposite side of the building, he noticed several loading ramps. Although he had not paid much attention to them previously, he now noticed many large crates. Judge strolled over to have a look and noticed that a couple of workers were lifting a disassembled tail boom into one of the wooden boxes.

Must be where the aircraft are packaged for shipment, he thought. Since the only area of the aircraft being modified was the flight control system, it would seem that much of the aircraft could be packaged and shipped soon after being disassembled. Then it could be reassembled on the receiving end. In fact, the weapons system could be installed while the final flight controls configuration was being completed and shipped.

Reading the shipping labels on crates that he knew held the tail booms, he tried to memorize the Spanish wording.

He repeated the address in his mind. The words Rota, Spain, were clearly marked. Another mystery solved.

At eight thirty, he slipped back to the guard gate, having asked Torres to pick him up at that time. The Iraqis should be following him and Torres to the hotel within a few minutes.

Torres was just stepping out of the limo as Judge passed through the gate.

"Good evening, Senor Judge." He smiled. "You are working very late this evening."

"Indeed." Judge sighed heavily, getting into the car. He asked Torres to take him to the Carrera Hotel and not the Pinera Blanca. Torres was curious about the request, but said nothing.

As he and Torres drove, Judge reflected on his conversation with Blake, after receiving his fax from London concerning Duffy's death. Judge had called him before he left Texas. Blake had explained, much to Judge's surprise, that British Intelligence had become involved in the case.

Duffy, it turned out, had been working with MI5 and had been providing information to them about suspected arms deals. They were especially interested in the gunship deal with Iraq. Now, finding Duffy's killer was also a priority, considering his father's standing in British society.

Judge had decided that they could help each other and asked if MI5 had a man operating in Chile. Blake had responded that there was, but that the operative had not been able to come across any new information. Judge managed for the three of them to meet in Santiago after his arrival.

Torres had promised Judge that all his driving needs would be met. Renting a car would be considered an insult after such a fine gesture. At any rate, Judge concluded, he could get much more information through casual conversation with Torres than he could by himself in a rental. When it came time for alternative transportation, he would find it.

Contrary to the custom, Judge preferred to ride up front with Torres, who seemed to accept western casualness. Now, he smiled and said that he would be glad to take Judge wherever he wished to go.

Judge noted with some interest that the Iraqis were nowhere in sight. It could be, he thought, that while he was in Torres's car, they could follow at a more leisurely distance.

When they arrived, Judge strolled into the Carrera Hotel's cantina, glad that he had picked an early hour, before other guests were due to begin filling the place. It was nearly nine, the time between dinner and when the late-night entertainment began. It was perfect timing.

"Walt!" a voice called out, as Judge stepped over to the bar.

"It's good to see you, Blake," Judge replied. "I'm glad you could make it."

"Your call was a welcome surprise," Blake continued. "When I sent you that fax, I wasn't sure you could be of assistance."

"Blake," Judge interrupted, holding up a huge hand, "we haven't much time. I'm being followed everywhere by the Mukhabarat. They'll be walking in any minute."

Blake Johnson quickly turned and motioned to another man sitting in a booth by the window. The man quickly approached.

"Walt, this is Reynolds. He's MI5, British Intelligence, as I mentioned on the telly."

"Pleasure," Reynolds said formally. "I've heard a lot about you. We were beginning to worry that you might not show."

"What's this about the Mukhabarat?" Blake asked.

"There are four of them, working in shifts. Those two pulling up in that Mercedes," Judge began, motioning out the window, "are the 'day shift.' Doesn't appear that they speak much English, and they're never in uniform. The night shift ones look like Abbott and Costello. I recognized them from the last time I was here. I am certain that the Mukhabarat killed Duffy. Apparently, their job is to keep the press away from the project. I still don't know who their commander is, but here's what I've got for you so far." Judge handed Reynolds a folded paper. He also gave him the shipping address for the helicopters and his address at the Pinera.

"Call us at this number if you get a chance," Reynolds said, handing him a card with some letters and symbols on it.

"It's coded, but just reverse the alphabet and use a corresponding number starting with eight. Every three letters, add an additional seven, you know the sequence. There'll be a bird on the line who will fetch us or take your message. If she doesn't answer with the name 'Isabelle,' hang up. Cheerio then."

Both men turned and disappeared out the far entrance to the cantina. A moment later, the Mukhabarat entered.

Judge was intimately familiar with the odd British intelligence system for coding short messages. It wouldn't take him long to unscramble the code.

He accepted two hot cups of coffee from the barkeep. Turning towards the two Iraqis entering the lounge, Judge feigned a smile of recognition and offered each of them a coffee.

Taken off guard, they both reached for a cup. Faster than an eye could focus, Judge dropped the containers, simultaneously grabbing each man's outstretched hand. He flipped the man on his left completely onto his back. Barely had the surprised Mukhabarat hit the tile when his companion crashed on top of him.

Holding both men down, one atop the other with an enormous knuckle in the middle of the upper man's chest, Judge raised his left hand high as if ready to karate chop the man's throat.

Judge leaned over and snarled loudly so that the barkeep could later translate for the two. "I do not like being followed." Then he stood erect and sauntered out of the cantina.

The two stunned Iraqis shakily got to their feet, confused and angry at having been taken by surprise. Too embarrassed to ask the young man behind the bar for a translation, they ran outside after Judge.

As they spotted Judge and Torres speeding off in the limo, they broke into a run for their Mercedes. Had anyone been nearby, they would have heard a vehement burst of Arabic expletives when the pair arrived at the car, only to find that their steering wheel had been torn from the column.

Torres looked at Judge, shaking his head solemnly he said, "You should not antagonize those men. They are dangerous."

"Not to me," Judge replied, still gripping the Mercedes steering wheel in his hands. "I wanted them to know I am not afraid of them. Carrillo will not deny me a little fun." He motioned at a corner filling station. "Pull over for a moment. I need to call the factory."

Torres stopped at the nearest pump and took the opportunity to clean the windshield and top off with petrol. Judge went inside to use the phone. He had no intention of calling the factory, but the less he revealed to Torres, the better he felt. He exchanged a few bills for a handful of pesos and dialed for an operator to get him through to the FBI.

"We have some bad news," Jenkins told him immediately. "The NSA and the CIA have moved into ARI. They're taking all the computers and blueprints."

"When did this happen?" Judge asked, surprised.

"Just this afternoon. We were questioning ARI's security agency about their phone monitoring when the G-men walked in."

"Did you find out anything?"

"Just that the agency did remember your call from Ms. Casey. We were talking to the man that monitored the call when it came in. They don't monitor all of the calls, but they do record them all. They were under orders from Fox to turn over all overseas incoming and outgoing calls to him."

"I suppose the NSA and the CIA still aren't talking," Judge said, dismayed.

Jenkins added, "Actually, that's part of the bad news. They're not only talking to us, they're blabbing to the press. It will be all over the papers by morning. They're trying to cover their tracks. It doesn't look good for you here. The only good news is that they don't know yet that you have been working with us."

Judge closed his eyes. The public furor would force the government to tighten the embargo against Chile and unite the European community against them as well. Carrillo would never get his aircraft out of the country, and Michelle would receive a death sentence.

"Damn it!" Judge cursed. "How did that happen?"

"Some newspaper in England broke the story to the reporters at the *Fort Worth Star-Telegram*. When the press publishes Carrillo's history as the third world's largest arms merchant, it will make our job even more difficult than it's been," lamented Jenkins.

"Do they know about Gutierrez and Wright? It seems obvious that they are operating independently of the US government."

"They don't seem to be letting on about Wright or Gutierrez. As far as we can tell, they believe that ARI was operating independently and that you and Fox had a beef and that you left the country after his death. No one can vouch for your whereabouts at the time of his death. The police want to talk to you. Oh," he hesitated, "we believe Wright is currently not in the States."

Judge gave no sign that Jenkins's revelations bothered him. He would have reached the same conclusion had he been the police. He would clear all that up in time. Right now he had his hands full.

Judge filled in the sergeant about his contact with Wright and that he had insisted Michelle be able to call him. If Wright knew about the story that was about to break, he would be unlikely to follow through. Judge's heart sank. It had been nearly eight hours since his call from Wright.

"Neither Wright nor Gutierrez are here in the US," Jenkins repeated. "We've been able to get some information from Customs as to when they left," Jenkins added after listening to Judge's account.

"We traced Wright to the Colombian Embassy. He used to work for the CIA and has been working with the consulate there. He was at Fox's party the night he was killed and is our chief suspect so far. Fox's wife said a man with his description asked to speak with him at the party. Let us know as soon as you think it safe, and we'll have a chat with the police about him."

"Suspect? So Fox was murdered? For sure?"

"The autopsy report came in yesterday afternoon. There's no doubt."

"What about Wright's ties to the Colombian Embassy? Doesn't that connect him to Gutierrez?" Judge asked.

"We believe it does, as well as the two spooks you dispatched the night Michelle was first attacked."

"Has Gutierrez shown up there in Chile?" Jenkins asked.

"No," Judge replied. "What about the men in the photograph? Have you been able to identify any of them?"

"Yes, the man at the podium was a Senator Roberts from Illinois. Most of the rest were CIA. It seems that his endowment group, the ADE, sometimes uses the CIA to transfer funds to some of their recipients when other means are not appropriate."

Judge suddenly felt he had misjudged the entire conspiracy. Dismayed, he hung up.

For every new revelation, there was a corresponding setback, he thought bitterly, as Torres drove him back to the Pinera.

The hotel room phone was ringing when Judge burst through the door. Lifting the receiver, he answered, "Walter Judge."

Dead silence. It seemed to last for minutes as Judge waited.

"Walter!" Michelle's voice was forceful if strained. And then, "Let go!" she demanded of someone.

Judge heard a scuffle, a loud thump, and then more silence. Gripping the phone, he forced himself to hold on, praying she'd return.

Michelle had shoved Gutierrez away, revolted by his stinking breath as he pushed his face in front of her, reaching for the telephone.

"Walter," Michelle said again, speaking deliberately now. "Walter, our love is for all time . . ." Then, there was more scuffling, and silence returned. His palms were too large to fit between the ear and mouthpiece, or they would have snapped under his grip.

"So," said a deep voice with a Latin accent. "You see she lives. Maybe she call you tomorrow and maybe no." The line went dead.

Twenty-Nine

How could that be possible? Michelle had found his watch. He had read that inscription nearly every day for over a year. There was no mistaking it. She must be at L'eon's bungalow.

Oddly, Judge realized he felt calm. Sitting on the edge of the bed, he mulled over her message. He had convinced himself that Michelle was being held in the US. Obviously, Wright had wanted to keep the project out of the US. In order to be in total control, Wright must have wanted Michelle out as well. As relieved as he was at knowing Michelle's whereabouts, he knew that no one in the US could help him now.

Whether Wright was acting for someone higher up or not was immaterial now. It was obvious by Michelle's call that Judge's services were still needed. Otherwise, why keep her alive?

Judge pulled the hotel room curtain aside to see if the Iraqis had made it back to the hotel yet, but there was no sign of them.

Spreading a sectional aviation map on the bed, he made a quick survey, jotting notes on a pad. He then left the hotel, racing down the drive to a café he had seen earlier with a pay telephone. He didn't want to risk using a phone in the hotel that Carrillo owned.

"Isabelle" answered promptly and put him through to Blake.

Judge, unwilling to risk being overheard on either end of the line, avoided mentioning Michelle. He alone would handle that problem. Now, he needed help in other matters. Tersely, he told Blake and Reynolds exactly what he wanted.

They assured him they wanted to help, but would have to clear it from above. "'Isabelle' will have an answer for you by noon tomorrow," Reynolds promised. It was the best he could hope for, and Judge hung up, exhausted.

It was after midnight when he returned to the Pinera. The Iraqis were still not in sight, and he quickly completed his preparations for what he hoped would be his last night in Santiago.

Having lived through highly dangerous experiences with little sleep, Judge had conditioned himself to go to sleep when it was most needed. Just as he could separate his consciousness from pain, so could he separate stress from his autonomic nervous systems. He knew that, without sleep, both he and Michelle would be dead within a day.

Even so, he awoke early and met Torres before sunup for a prearranged pickup to the hangar.

The aircraft was ready when Judge arrived, and he quickly gave the orders to move it onto the flight ramp. While it was being fueled, Carrillo called Judge into his office for a flight briefing. The Chilean pulled out a map and spread it onto his desk.

Carrillo elected to fly chase, a term used in the business for a chase aircraft to follow each risky test in case a precautionary landing had to be made. Unfortunately, it would also limit any exploration of the surrounding areas that Judge hoped to carry out.

Before Judge climbed into the cockpit, he had Roberto open the panel leading into the lower flight controls area. Judge then had Roberto help him remove one of the newly designed bell cranks. Reversing it, they reinstalled it in the opposite position.

"But, senor, I can assure you it is exactly as you had us draw it on the blueprints."

"I know it is, Roberto. I was reviewing the design myself last night, and I realized that I had made a mistake. Trust me. We have it correct now." It had been Judge's way to guarantee the aircraft would not fly correctly if ill fortune had befallen him. Had they not changed it, the aircraft would have crashed. A ruse he apparently had not needed.

It was the perfect opportunity for some advance planning, as well. Without any helicopter mechanics around, Judge took advantage of the situation to secure some advanced supplies.

He pointed to the fuel gauge, which was working perfectly, and told Roberto that the fuel pumps were malfunctioning and would need to be replaced soon.

"Roberto, we're going to need a couple of boost pumps. See if you can get a couple of new ones out of stock and leave them by the work station inside."

Roberto, unaware of the deception, ran off to do as he had been told. Judge would need those extra pumps once he put his plan in motion.

Rolling the throttle to 100% rpm, Judge then checked the beep range of his linear actuator. Satisfied for the moment that the engine could be controlled at flat pitch, he began making note of a few other necessities. The torque gauge reading, oil pressure and temperature gauges, and the operation of the radios all seemed acceptable.

Rotor track and balance of both the main and tail rotors seemed acceptable, probably because they had not been removed or their configurations changed during the rebuild process.

Just as he had done in the hangar, Judge now slowly cycled the stick forward and aft, only this time the blades were turning. The rotor seemed perfectly in phase with a forward motion tilting the rotor down and vice versa. Lateral cyclic motion resulted in the appropriate response as well.

Finally, he slowly brought the aircraft to a hover. The aircraft appeared to hover with the same flight characteristics as its former LongRanger self. Both longitudinal and lateral step inputs in a hover also elicited the correct response. This proved his changes to the flight controls had not adversely affected the rotor phasing.

Judge hover-taxied to the unpaved strip to conduct some controllability exercises. He felt it important to verify his control margins and stick position gradients during cross-control exercises in left and right sideward flight.

To satisfy himself that he was ready, Judge conducted several hovering throttle chops. He did so at increasing skid heights, until he was finally at about eight feet, using full up collective before the skids touched the ground. *Good enough*, he thought.

With everything in order, Judge announced to Carrillo that he was ready to take the aircraft "over the fence."

Judge evaluated the stability for both climb and descent, adding collective until he was using full takeoff power for climb for that altitude, and full autorotative descent.

He purposely flew to the extreme corners of the test area that Carrillo had outlined for him. Carrillo had kept silent throughout the test, only radioing to Judge when he was getting too close to the Santiago Terminal Control Area or when acknowledging Judge's announcements to a change in direction.

Visibility was good despite some smog from the city. Judge could make out the pacific shoreline on the far western horizon from his altitude and made a mental note of the magnetic direction of what appeared to be a corridor on the ground, which was rather sparsely populated. He had not recalled anything of note on the map for that area, which led all the way to the sea. Arial navigation maps did not show much detail about what was not aviation related.

Finally, he decided to turn and head back, with Carrillo in trail. He did not want Carrillo to get suspicious.

They landed to the cheers of several dozen of the workers, who had labored long hours to see this happen.

Carrillo bounded out of the LongRanger even before the rotor stopped turning, beaming with delight. He motioned Judge to hurry and shut down, and before Judge could exit the copter, he had reached in to shake Judge's hand excitedly.

After a short debriefing, Judge quickly made for the factory exit. Torres stood by the passenger door as Judge approached, grinning. "Mr. Hector insists that you join him for lunch," he announced.

Thirty

Michelle, although still feisty, was now watching her captor with some caution. He was a violent man, and his unpredictable outbursts made her suppress some of her rebellion.

To her dismay, he had cleared the kitchen of any cutting tools save for the butter knives. Even the forks were missing. He insisted she cook for them, but when she had served him his last meal, he had produced a fork for himself, but insisted she eat with a spoon.

Afterward, he had slapped her with a whopping backhand when she resisted being shackled to the radiator again. She was saved from more violence when the phone rang again. "I'll be back to finish this." Grumbling, Gutierrez left to answer the phone. He had not returned until it had rung again. This time, he had fetched her fighting like a bobcat until she realized she was to speak into the receiver.

The call had taken her by surprise. Had she not been holding Judge's watch and been reading the inscription for the tenth time, she would have been too flustered to remember exactly what was imprinted upon it.

Even so, she had had to blurt it out quickly. She hoped Judge had heard all the words.

When she had first found his watch, Michelle had bristled with anger. The thought that Judge had been in this very room had given her the idea that he was responsible in some sick way for her being there.

After the call, however, the attacks seemed to stop abruptly. Gutierrez began muttering angrily in Spanish but refrained from hitting her or trying to fondle her. Perhaps one of his incessant phone calls had been a warning to leave her alone. She wondered if it had been from Judge.

As the evening advanced and the dark shadows of the room foretold yet another night to be spent in this awful place, Michelle heard the sound of an approaching vehicle. It was dark enough that she could see the shadows caused from the headlights as it turned into the short carport on the opposite side of the bungalow from her room.

A single car door slammed, and footsteps came up the gravel driveway. Michelle moved from her position by the window to the door. She listened as the door was opened without a knock. She knew Gutierrez was still in the open room by the fireplace, sitting in an overstuffed chair. The overpowering smell from his cheap cigar filtered in under her door.

Gutierrez did not get up when the man entered. The stranger burst into a tirade as soon as he came through the door. "Damn it all, Ponce, how the hell am I supposed to get to sleep with you smoking those damn rags all night?"

"I only have one at nite. Wot, you theenk me reech?" His accent was so thick Michelle could barely understand him, but at least they were speaking English. "Why you not stay in hotel? Maybe keep an eye on Judge?"

"Screw him! Carrillo's got the Iraqis watchin' him like a hawk."

"How'd he do that?"

"He convinced them that Judge was a spy and wasn't to be let out of their sight if they wanted the aircraft delivered. They know we got something on Judge to keep him working for us and that he can't be trusted. They're stuck on him like stink. He must be scared shitless with the Iraqi Mukhabarat on his ass. I'm sure Judge thinks they kill every reporter that gets near Carrillo."

"Yeah? You not so smart if you theenk heem scare easy. I work with Cox and Atterbury a long time. Good agents, tough like me. Judge broke their bones with his bare hands. He'll squash you like a bug when he catches you."

Michelle caught her breath at the sound of all the familiar names.

She heard Gutierrez blow another long puff of smoke. "You here early. Why you not stay in the US for a while? You give me more money, and I'll stay there a long time."

"Not if you know what's good for you. The director told me the story's already out in the UK. Said he couldn't protect me much longer. Told me to tie up the loose ends and go back to Colombia for a while."

"How come the director of the CIA can't protect you? He can do anything."

"Not against another scandal like this will turn out to be if Iraq attacks Kuwait."

"What loose ends you need to tie up? I thought you got Judge's reporter girlfriend a long time ago?"

"Yeah, the one your stupid 'tough' buddies mistook that doctor broad for. What a bunch of morons. No, you idiot, Fox. He was getting ready to spill his guts to Judge. Fox couldn't control the guy or keep his big mouth shut. I made it look like a heart attack. Damn it, can't you put that thing out? At least open a window. Never mind, I'll do it," he said, opening a window.

Michelle bristled with hurt and anger. Judge had not told her that she had been mistaken by Cox and Atterbury for one of his old girlfriends. Surely Judge must have known. Why did he not tell her? She gritted her teeth. Her anger fueled her determination to keep listening, despite the smell from the cigar.

No sooner had he opened the window than Michelle's room began filling with the foul odor as the cigar stench seeped faster under her door. She had to cover her nose to keep from gagging.

"So why do you have to stay here? Why can't you stay in hotel?" Ponce persisted. Clearly, he had a certain disdain for the American stranger.

"Staying here is safer. I spotted a guy I used to run into at the Agency that works for British Intell. He finds out I'm in town I won't get a moment's peace," the new man said. "Besides, I only came to see Hector and persuade him to get me more money. So I get here and guess what? Says he won't give me another cent until Judge demonstrates the aircraft."

"When?"

"Carrillo says maybe tomorrow."

"How much you gonna get?" Ponce asked.

"Another hundred thousand," the stranger said disgustedly. "He owes me more than that. He said he'd give me an advance for getting Fox to ship the weapons kits early. It will get me by until Hussein pays him when the deliveries start, if Judge will quit dragging his feet. If we don't deliver before the last week of July, we won't get a nickel."

Ponce was not listening. He was slouched in his chair with his head tilted back, blowing smoke rings, to the consternation of his guest. "What're you going to pay me with if you can't deliver on time?" His eyebrows were raised, and he was staring directly at the small man.

"Oh, knock it off," the stranger replied nervously.

"No," Ponce interrupted loudly, sitting up and pointing a finger at Wright. His abrupt change in octave startled Michelle. "You knock it off, Wright! You haven't paid me in a long time. *I* will go and collect your money for you. That is how it's gonna be. You unnerstan? You're going to stay here with the girl till we get the rest of our money. Then I get to go play in Bogota!"

"OK, OK," the stranger said nervously, afraid to disagree with Gutierrez. "We'll make it. Just relax." Then, getting up, he said, "Just keep the girl alive until Judge gets done. We may need her to keep him moving when he learns what he has to do for us in the Mediterranean."

Thirty-One

Iraq Deploys Troops Near Kuwait Border Amid Dispute on Oil*—New York Times, *Jul. 24, 1990, p. A9

Judge met Carrillo at the Hereford Grill, not far from Providencia. Carrillo was already seated and apparently alone. He stood politely as the host escorted Judge to his table.

Raising his glass, Carrillo toasted, "To our success! And many more!"

Judge sat down and raised his glass, going through the motions.

"So, Senor Judge, you think you have solved the problems with our helicopter?"

"I have fixed at least one problem. I'm not saying there couldn't be others."

"Others?" Carrillo asked, lowering his glass. "Let us hope not."

"Hector, Fox once told me that you went to Hurst Helicopters for help before you went to ARI," Judge asked, conveniently changing the subject.

"Sure, Hurst did the original design study for me. Cost me a quarter million dollars. But when it came to working on my aircraft, well, you know, with the embargo, they were too afraid to be involved."

He continued pouring himself another glass of wine. "So I asked one of your congressman if he could lend some assistance."

"Congressman?"

Carrillo continued, pouring himself another glass of wine. "I asked an old friend, one of your senators, if he could lend some, how you say? Assistance? An old classmate from the University of Utah, where I went to college."

"Who?" Judge asked again.

"A very helpful man named Roberts. He is now a US Senator. Do you know him?"

"I've heard of him," Judge replied. His interest was piqued, recalling the name from his last conversation with Gibbons and Jenkins.

"He has been helpful in the past, but . . . how shall I say it . . . expensive, if you know what I mean?" Carrillo said, rolling his eyes.

"No, I do not know what you mean."

"You are indeed a bit naïve, my friend. His helpfulness always has a price, as so many of these political matters do."

"I thought Roberts was getting money for you. Are you telling me that you have to pay him?"

"Getting money for me? Oh, you mean the ADE contributions. Yes, well, it works both ways. You see, his group gets me grants to support Aylwin, but in return, I must help them get helicopters to Iraq, at my expense."

Judge was dumbfounded. "Roberts is having private endowment funds diverted to you so you can develop inexpensive gunships for Iraq?"

Carrillo began to look uncomfortable. "Senor Roberts communicates everything to me through Senor Wright. Wright brought me the initial funds. He is, how you say, liaison? You make it sound like I am doing something bad, senor. I am doing exactly as your government has asked me to do. I support Patricio Aylwin and sell aircraft to Iraq."

"It sounds like you are doing the US government a favor," Judge interjected. "But I think Wright is trying to trick you somehow." Judge had no idea if this were true. It was a thinly disguised ruse to keep Carrillo talking.

"What do you mean?" Carrillo demanded.

Judge poured the man another glass of wine. "It appears to everyone else that you are in business with Wright and not the US Government. I think Wright is not giving you all the money given to him by the ADE." Judge cocked an eyebrow at Carrillo, hoping to drive a wedge between the two.

To his surprise, the man smiled wryly. "You are very wise, senor. Yes, you are probably correct. But you know, I have no choice. You see, senor, there is no aircraft manufacturing in my country. I needed assistance and expertise. Senor Wright is told by your government to assist me in getting the aircraft built. He makes a deal with ARI to provide assistance, but I have to pay for it."

"Hold on a second." Judge frowned. "I thought you just said that Wright brought you the money. You're telling me that you have to give him a kickback?"

Carrillo shrugged. "I know he is a cheat. I tried going around him to Senator Roberts to get the ADE to pay for ARI's work directly. Senor Roberts, my friend, had to protect himself and said I had to deal only with Wright. So I give Wright money, Fox money, and I use what is left to build the aircraft. Once I deliver, we all make the big money. President Hussein pays cash!"

As Judge digested all this, Carrillo continued, his tongue loosened by the drink. "I even paid that other helicopter outfit in Hurst a quarter of a million dollars for the preliminary design, but they wouldn't go in with me to develop it into a prototype. Finally, I went back to Wright to set up a deal, and he brought in ARI and Senor Fox."

"Don't tell me," Judge offered, "Fox agreed to build the weapons kits for just the materials and labor in exchange for a percentage of each sale." It had always been Fox's way of getting a percentage of the profit from all future aircraft sales, even though ARI wasn't building the aircraft.

"Yes, you are correct again, senor. When my customers begin paying for each aircraft, ARI and my company will split the profits."

"What about Wright?"

"He works for your government. The money he has cheated from the ADE funds is all he will get." Then Carrillo lowered his voice to a whisper, "But he doesn't know it yet. He thinks he will get more with each job you do for me." He chuckled.

"What happens if the aircraft don't get delivered?" Judge asked.

"Naturally, I have the most to lose. Of course, no matter what happens, I must pay Mr. Wright as part of our deal for your flight today. In fact, I will make my last payment to him tonight."

Judge stopped chewing. It was an involuntarily lapse, but one that Carrillo noticed. The Chilean smiled. He had caught Judge. "So, senor. Your questions are more than idle curiosity, yes? It is as I suspected. There is still a problem between you and Senor Wright. I was wise not to trust him."

Carrillo was not smiling any longer. "You think I am telling you so much because I cannot hold my wine, senor? You are foolish if you think that."

Judge squinted at Carrillo, realizing that he had played into the Chilean's hands. It had been fortunate for Judge that Carrillo's agenda nearly paralleled his own.

"I think I know what you want. You're telling me all of this so I'll turn Wright in to the American authorities and get him out of your hair. That way you won't have to pay him."

"You are very perceptive." Carrillo was smiling again.

"He was holding me over your head, wasn't he?" Judge said, thinking aloud to Carrillo. "He needed some assurance that you would pay him. If you didn't pay him, then he would force me to stop working for you."

"Indeed, senor. You are most clever! But as you have guessed, now that the aircraft is flying well, I do not need either of you anymore. You are free to deal with him as you like."

"What about the weapons system integration?"

"I have made other arrangements. I have found another way to get the aircraft systems completed at a better price than Wright will charge me."

Judge was suddenly worried. If Wright was cut out of the deal, Michelle was as good as dead.

"Have you told Wright yet?" Judge interrupted anxiously.

"No. I must speak with my new partner first so I do not upset him."

"Who, Wright? You're going to upset him plenty when you tell him your cutting him out of a chunk of the money."

"No, no, not Wright." Carrillo laughed. "There is a great huge man. Much larger than you, that works for Wright. Wright owes him a lot of money, so I will pay him instead, and he will work for me. He will not hesitate to leave Wright for more money."

Judge had seen the name coming as soon as Carrillo had begun to describe Gutierrez.

"Ponce Gutierrez!" Judge said, trying not to grit his teeth. "So he does work for Wright!"

"It is a strained working relationship at best, Senor. Wright met him through his work in the CIA. He hired Ponce for himself after Ponce got fired from his security job in the US. Ponce is very rough with women, senor."

"Where is he now?"

"He is staying at L'eon's bungalow, up in the mountains. I used to own it, but gave it to L'eon as a gift. Ponce is using it while L'eon is in Spain."

"And how exactly is he going to help you get the weapons systems and countermeasures integrated?" Judge inquired.

"I understand he holds the plans and codes for completing the work. He will get the extra help he needs to do the job. He can be very intimidating, senor. I will not need Hussein's men to keep the press out of my business anymore. Ponce also speaks Arabic, he will have many uses."

"Why not have Gutierrez get rid of Wright?"

"You do not understand politics very well, senor. Mr. Wright has very close connections with the CIA, and the CIA and Chile have a long and painful history together. Patricio Aylwin does not wish to have problems with the CIA and his new government. They will not have Wright arrested even though we know he has done things the CIA will not protect him for. No, senor, I know you. I can tell you wish to deal with Wright yourself. Better you than anyone in Chile."

Carrillo dabbed his mouth with his napkin and motioned for the waiter to bring the check.

"Senor Judge, I may come across to you as a ruthless businessman. I prefer to use the word, how you say it, shrewd? However, I am not a murderer."

"What about kidnapping?"

Carrillo suddenly looked at Judge, indignant. "What do mean, kidnapping?"

"Where did you go after you left Fox's party?" Judge asked.

"I went on to Miami," Carrillo said testily. "I own a property investment company there, SwissInc if you must know. In fact, it's the same one that purchased much of ARI's private stock. So you see, Senor Judge, in a way, I own you."

Judge said nothing, and Carrillo asked, "Why do you ask?"

"You left in your private jet?" Judge asked, ignoring Carrillo's question.

"No, I went with Senor Wright on a commercial flight. He put Ponce on my plane and set him back here to Chile."

Judge had no doubt that Carrillo was telling the truth. It appeared evident that the Chilean had no knowledge of Michelle's disappearance. Carrillo was simply an innocent businessman who was stuck doing business with the likes of Wright. Shrewd, but innocent; Judge decided to use Carrillo's innocence to gain advantage.

His mind racing, Judge said, "OK, Hector, I'll get Wright out of your hair, on one condition—that I can borrow one of those old LongRangers you have awaiting conversion. Just for a few hours, I would like to do some aerial sightseeing while I am still in Santiago." Judge held his breath. It would be easier than having to steal one from the airfield.

His answer came without hesitation. "But of course," he said, waving his glass. "After what you have accomplished today, it is the least I can do. I will have an aircraft for you within the hour. You can fly it anytime you like."

"Thanks, Hector," Judge said, relief flooding through him. Casually, he clinked Carrillo's glass in a toast, and the two men downed the contents of their glasses.

Thirty-Two

As Carrillo left the restaurant, Judge turned to his chauffeur and asked, "Torres, where is Mr. Carrillo going? Maybe it's none of my business, but I forgot to ask him something."

"Of course, senor," replied Torres. "He must attend a business meeting at the Café de Brasil."

Judge nodded grimly to himself. Carrillo was going to meet with Wright. He had run out of time.

Torres continued, "I must pick Senor Wright up from the cafe in an hour and take him to the airport. If you need to speak again with Senor Carrillo, I will bring you to the café and then take you to your hotel."

As much as he wanted to meet up with Wright, it was not his highest priority right now.

"So you wish to come, Mr. Walt?" Torres inquired, interrupting his train of thought.

"No, it can wait . . ." Judge replied. "Thanks anyway."

Torres headed the big car towards the Hotel Pinera. Neither man spoke. Judge was focused only on what he had to do next.

It was after eight and quite dark. The way the bungalow was situated, anyone driving towards it during daylight would be spotted, and Judge needed the element of surprise.

Tonight Judge knew that the sky would be pitch-black, with the moon obscured by some high clouds. He had checked the forecast earlier with Carrillo under the guise of a legitimate test flight preparation.

When Torres dropped him off at the hotel, Judge waited until the limo was out of sight then raced to his room and called Blake. Blake picked up on the first ring.

"How did you do on the other information we talked about?" Judge asked.

"It's all set up," Blake began and proceeded to rattle off a bunch of numbers, which Judge carefully wrote down.

"Good luck, buddy. And be careful!"

Judge looked through the curtains as he hung up. There they were. His Mukhabarat tail was back on duty. This time, a lone driver was sitting in a rental car under his window.

Swiftly, Judge opened the window and climbed out. He trotted over to the driver's window. Then, tapping on the window, he smiled at the surprised Iraqi driver and motioned to him to roll it down.

Recovering from his surprise, the driver, not trusting the unpredictable Judge, pulled a silenced .38 from his belt and began rolling the window down. Before the window was halfway, Judge's huge fist slammed into the side of the man's temple, knocking him unconscious. "Amateurs," Judge muttered under his breath as he shoved the man aside and took the driver's seat, tucking the .38 in his own belt.

Judge roared out of the hotel parking lot and made straight for De Padilla's bungalow in the foothills north of Renca. He had thought of securing the helicopter for the task at hand, but anyone at De Padilla's place would have heard it coming.

A quarter mile from De Padilla's tiny abode, he hesitated. De Padilla's place was isolated along this stretch of countryside. He had noticed the absence of other houses on his previous trip. The bungalow sat alone only a few yards from the road, a flickering light coming from the window. "Good, they have a fire lit," Judge said to himself.

He pulled the unconscious Iraqi from the front seat, removed a couple of long plastic tie wraps that he had taken from the flight line, and bound the man's hands and feet together behind him.

He then opened the back passenger door and tore out the rear seat cushion. Ripping a sizable chunk of foam from the seat, he made his way towards the bungalow.

The place was so dark that Judge could not see the ground in front of him. He crept slowly towards the flickering light and looked into the den window. A figure sat by the fire in L'eon's overstuffed chair, nodding lazily in and out of sleep.

"This man is too slight of build to be Gutierrez," Judge said to himself. He could see past the figure and down the short hallway to the kitchen, which was dark. The door to L'eon's bedroom was open, but it too was dark.

Suddenly, Judge caught sight of the hasp securing the door to the bedroom where he had once slept. His pulse quickened. Ghostlike, he slipped past the window and around to the far side of the bungalow.

To his dismay, the window was open about six inches. Surely if the window were not secured, Michelle would have escaped. He began to worry that she was not there. *But if she was not inside, why would there be a locked hasp on the outside of the door*, he wondered.

Confused, he applied upward pressure on the window. It moved. Soundlessly he inched it up, a fraction of an inch at a time. Finally, after what seemed like hours, he silently entered the room.

Pulling his penlight from his pocket, he flicked it on, cautious as a cat in a junkyard.

A bed, the very one he had slept in, loomed in front of him across the room. A figure was lying motionless under a thin sheet. Dousing the light quickly, he moved slowly towards the bed, fiercely aware of the time.

"Walter!" whispered Michelle's voice. "My god, you're here!" Instantly she was in his arms. Tears welled up in her eyes as he held her tight, then lifted her effortlessly from the bed. But her chain cut short their attempt to flee.

"Bastards!" he muttered. "Are you hurt?"

"I'm fine," Michelle replied. "It's tied to the radiator," she whispered, now trembling with excitement. "Just get me out of here. Please."

Setting her down, he covered her mouth with his hand and whispered softly, "How many are in the house?"

"Just one man, but there's another one due back any minute. He's gigantic, Walter, we have to get out of here. They're going to kill us!"

"You wait here," Judge whispered. "I'll be back in a minute."

Michelle nearly screamed at him for making such a stupid remark, but she bit her tongue.

Judge slipped out the window as soundlessly as he had entered. Picking up the piece of foam that he had left outside the window, he moved towards the other side of the house.

Despite his size, he easily climbed to the top of the stone chimney. Once there, he stuffed the foam into the flu. Then, he crawled onto the roof and moved silently to the back of the house.

Wright responded as Judge had expected. Too smart to use the front door, he pulled up the window leading to the back of the house and crawled out. He looked in every direction for the man who had smoked him out—except up.

Ponce Gutierrez had been accurate when he told Wright that Judge would squash him like a bug if he caught him.

The only sound was the sudden cracking of his spine as Judge's 240 pounds came crashing down on him. Wright crumpled to the ground writhing in agony.

Judge relieved him of his pistol and grabbed him around the neck, lifting him to his feet. Wright, whose legs were numb, was unable to kick but tried pounding Judge feebly with the only arm that seemed to work.

Judge loosened his grip around the man's throat. His thumb and forefinger were nearly touching. "Bastard!" Wright hissed hoarsely. "You broke my back!"

"Mr. Wright, I presume." Judge said, "We finally meet."

Wright tried to curse but only managed to spit all over himself.

"Now tell me, who is the 'director'?" Judge asked.

"Go to hell!" Wright croaked.

Judge caught the man's flailing hand and snapped Wright's arm at the elbow. Tears rolled down Wright's cheeks as he screamed in agony.

"Do you remember what happened to your buddies, Cox and Atterbury?" Judge asked. "If you want to live, you'll tell me who the director is."

"They weren't my buddies! And you won't kill me, Judge! You're too moralistic!"

Judge took Wright's pistol with his free hand and put the slide in his mouth. He pulled the grip with the slide in his teeth, cocking the .40. Sticking the silencer into

Wright's crotch, he said, "You're right. I won't, at least not yet. But I won't hesitate to blow your balls clean off."

Wright's eyes grew even wider. "OK," he screamed. "It's Williams, Casey Williams."

"Casey Williams, the CIA director?" Judge repeated incredulously.

"He'll have you killed for this, Judge!"

"For what? Saving him the trouble of getting rid of you? I doubt it."

"Oh, by the way, Wright," Judge continued, "hasn't Carrillo told you? He fired us today. He has found another way to finish your precious helicopters."

"You're lying!" Wright croaked hoarsely.

"He hired Ponce to work for him. Seems nobody needs you anymore, Wright. You know what I think? I think Ponce went to get that money Carrillo owed you. Carrillo's going to hire him and pay him in advance. What do you think Ponce will do to you when he comes back with all that money and finds you lying here without your gun?"

Wright thrashed on the end of Judge's arm. Disgusted, Judge threw him on the ground, as if tossing out the garbage.

"Judge, you can't leave me here, Judge!" Wright screamed.

Ignoring his plea, Judge rushed back to Michelle's window and somersaulted through it.

"Hurry, Walter, I have a bad feeling that the other man will be back any second!" Michelle cried excitedly.

In two strides, he crossed the room and kicked down the locked door. Smoke poured into the room from the plugged fireplace.

Judge reached around the door casing and lifted the keys off the nail. He quickly unfastened Michelle's bindings.

Judge knew if Carrillo said much to Gutierrez about their luncheon conversation that Gutierrez could put two and two together and figure out Judge's next move. He could be rushing back to De Padilla's bungalow. Judge also knew Ponce would not come barging into the bungalow like a bull. Instead he would do as Judge had done: approach with stealth, and with a bigger weapon than the one Judge had.

"Where are we going?" she asked. She couldn't imagine crawling out a window instead of rushing out the front door.

"We have to be careful about everything we do now," Judge said quietly. "The big man that you are afraid of may already be back and is not about to rush in here if he thinks I might be armed. If he's out there, he'll be out front waiting to gun us down the second we run out that door."

"Wait," she said suddenly. Michelle turned and reached behind the headboard and removed Judge's watch. When he reached for it, she turned her back to him. "Nothing doing. Finders keepers. Besides, I earned it. You have to earn it back."

Silently, they left through the bedroom window. Judge caught a glimpse of a wire going up the side of the house. Thinking it might be a new telephone line, he grabbed it and tore it free. It was indeed a telephone line. He reached as high as he could and cut it with a penknife. Then, he ripped the lower end from the side of the house.

Far down the road, as the winding road made its way along the valley wall, he could see a set of headlights moving at abnormal speed making its way up the mountain.

Breaking into a run, Judge grasped Michelle's arm and quickly led her into the darkness in the direction of his acquired automobile.

Thirty-Three

Michelle sat with her eyes closed, shaking her head slowly as they drove. "Can't we go to the American Embassy? Surely they would help us."

"I am not sure we would be safe there either. The US Embassies are an extension of the US State Department. US Embassies are basically safe houses for CIA operatives. I just can't take that chance."

"CIA?" Michelle cried. Judge realized he had a lot of explaining to do. He began telling her as much as he could on the way into the city. Michelle added pieces of the mystery by relating the conversation she overheard between Gutierrez and Wright. She was especially agitated at Judge for not telling her about her being mistaken for one of his old girlfriends.

It took longer to get to the highway leading to the turnoff to the airpark than he had hoped. He was worried that Ponce might have had time to get there first, ahead of them.

"Michelle, do you think you can drive?" Judge looked at her.

"Yes, of course," she said, rubbing her ankle. "What do you want me to do?"

"Are you ready for a little adventure?"

She looked at him, frowning. "Well, let me see. Since I've met you, I've been attacked by killers, struck by a car and hospitalized, kidnapped and flown nearly 5000 miles to a foreign country, and chased by ex-members of the CIA. Just what sort of adventure did you have in mind?"

"Do you see that big building over there?" he asked, ignoring her sarcasm and pointing to the Museum of Natural History. They were in Quinta Normal, heading northbound. The airpark was only a couple of miles up the road just past Renca.

"Yes," she replied, nodding.

"OK, we're going to go past it up this road to the turnoff to Carrillo's factory. After you let me out, I want you to drive straight back down this road to that museum. Drive around to the parking lot in the back. The lot is not lighted. Park out of sight off the street, to the north of the lot. You'll see a couple of limos parked there. I think the museum uses them for escorting special visitors. Park next to them. Stay down out of sight," he ordered.

"I am going to land there in one of Carrillo's helicopters in about forty-five minutes. When you hear the helicopter, turn your headlights on. If I don't show up by ten, then drive back up this road to the first hotel you find. There will be one on your right up about a mile." He handed her

Blake's number. "Call this number and ask for Blake and tell him where you are. He'll come and get you and try to get you out of the country. It will take him some time, however, and he'll have to hide you for what could be days or weeks." Judge pulled a map from his satchel pocket. He showed her where they were and the short route to downtown and the hotel.

"Why can't he just take me in at the British Embassy?"

"Too risky. You're not a British citizen. I'm sure they would be forced to hand you over to the US Embassy, and then we'd be right back where we started. The CIA could find just as much value in keeping you cooped up as Wright did."

She was angry with him, relieved that she was free but angry with her rescuer just the same.

That had been his backup plan. However, if he could get her out of the country without having her imprisoned by anyone, he was going to do it.

The two of them switched seats, and he had her drive the rest of the way to the airpark to make sure she could manage it. She seemed much improved, if a little shaky. Judge reached overhead and removed the bulb from the dome light.

When he opened the door at the guard gate to get out, the inside of the rental remained dark. The guard could not see inside, but when he recognized Judge, he motioned them to go ahead and enter. Judge shook his head. "Ningun, ello es nomás. Él es ir hogar," he said in poor Spanish.

The guard simply shrugged and opened the gate for him. Michelle turned the car and roared away, back down the road.

Making his way to the far end of the facility, he was relieved to see a crew busily washing one of the LongRangers on the flight ramp. Carrillo had been true to his word.

The crew was surprised to see him. The lead crewmember, one of the few who could speak a little English, approached Judge, smiling. "Senor Judge, we were not expecting you tonight."

"Well, when Mr. Carrillo offered me the use of a LongRanger, I couldn't wait to fly it at night over Santiago and see the city lights," he lied.

The young man stopped smiling. Noticing Judge's torn and soiled clothing, he said, "But, senor, you are hurt?"

"No, no," Judge stammered, trying to smile. "I was helping Torres change a flat tire, and the spare rolled down the hill in the dark." He feigned a sheepish expression. "I tripped when I ran after it."

The young man looked at Judge with a blank expression, as if trying to figure out what he had just said. Suddenly, he began laughing. He turned to the two kids helping clean the aircraft and babbled the story to them in Spanish. They joined in the laughter.

"Ah, but, senor, there is no fuel until morning. The fuel depot, she is locked. Only Mr. Hector and the day foreman have the key."

"How much fuel is in the aircraft?" Judge asked, trying not to panic.

The lineman shrugged.

Judge pushed by him and reached into the cockpit to the overhead panel. Turning on the battery, he tapped the fuel gauge. To his relief, it read almost half a tank. "It has enough." He smiled. "I will only take a short ride." Judge borrowed the man's flashlight and double-checked the fuel state by peering into the tank with the filler cap removed. The tank appeared to be about half full.

The young man shrugged again. "It is up to you, senor."

The cowling was off, which made it easier to get a closer look at the machine. The transmission oil was clear, if only slightly yellow in the sight glass, as was the 90 box. More of a sign of age than wear. Older used aircraft usually had a dark, even purple stained sight glass, so this was a good sign.

The cockpit held no surprises either. It had the usual horizon gyro, but it also had a Directional gyro and Turn coordinator with eyebrow lighting. This would be essential for flight over the water at night. To his surprise, it had an emergency locator transmitter; a transmitter that activated a homing signal in the event of a crash. Judge wondered how he might use it to his advantage.

He excused himself and announced that he would draw up a flight briefing. He slipped into the shop, where work was continuing on the production line. Gathering up some nylon tubing, the boost pumps and radio, he threw them into his small satchel with a few small tools.

There was a vending machine in the break area; and he filled the bag with pastries, chocolate bars, and sodas.

Returning to the flight ramp, the crew looked questioningly at the satchel. Judge pulled out a Coke, and they smiled.

The LongRanger started smoothly. He had no trouble keeping the TOT gauge in the yellow during the start, and that gave him a little bit of a warm feeling that maybe the engine was healthy. At least the battery was healthy if nothing else.

Judge wasted no time in lifting off and turning south towards the museum. Keeping dangerously low to keep from getting into the Los Carrillos Airport radar, he used the city lights to help him.

Were it not for the museum's size and lighted domed roof, he would have never found it. Being unfamiliar with the city, he had a struggle finding his way. It is always easier when the map and the terrain match, but at night one cannot see the terrain.

The area north of the museum was pitch-black. He knew the parking lot to be there, but he could not see it. Suddenly, a pair of headlights illuminated.

Making a hasty approach, Judge set the aircraft down only yards from where Michelle had parked, turning the landing light on only as he sank below the top of the museum.

Judge did not want the Los Carrillos tower to see the landing light. If he had been able to avoid their radar, he wanted to keep out of sight.

The radio was tuned in to the Los Carrillos Control Tower frequency, and Judge had heard nothing from them concerning an unidentified aircraft. Unfortunately, he only had the one radio, and a warning could have been given to other aircraft on departure control or the approach control frequencies.

Michelle stepped out of the limo and rushed towards the helicopter. Judge helped her strap in, and he lifted off as soon as he knew the cabin door was latched.

They headed north again, keeping so low that it frightened Michelle.

He waited until he was over the airpark before he turned to the west. If Ponce was to set up a chase, Judge wanted him following out to the sea.

After tightening the collective friction, Judge reached for the satchel and pulled out the portable Trimble GPS that he had gotten from Blake. GPS was new this year, and Trimble had the best to offer. He put the saucer-sized antenna as far forward on the glare shield as he could. The huge windshields of the LongRanger would allow for enough signal until he could land outside the city and tape it outside in a better location on the cowling.

Flying dangerously low was one thing; blasting through Chilean restricted airspace was another. He headed northwest to intersect the road leading to Casablanca, and then to the coast. It led through less populated terrain, but also led through two restricted areas that he had to be sure to avoid.

The SCR31 restricted area due west of Santiago and south of El Noviciado only was active to 3500 feet above the ground, but he had to stay at treetop level in order to keep from being noticed by Santiago radar. Judge was able to avoid the area by just skirting the road to the south.

With the exception of the occasional streetlamp, the terrain was pitch-black. He had to follow the road using the landing light. Fortunately, the road completely avoided the SCR68 restricted area around El Bosque, but it led right into the one surrounding Casablanca and encompassed all the terrain from there north to Valparaiso and west to the sea.

Just past the village of Curacavi were two roads leading north from the main road to Casablanca. The roads straddled a stream, which ran along the valley floor between several small mountains. The mountains only rose some two thousand feet above the road, but it was enough to shield them from the Santiago radar and still give him some breathing room.

They could also keep enough altitude to spot a vehicle's headlights for several miles north along the road. The road led to the tiny village of Lopa. A single light, coming from a bungalow, marked the spot with the help of the GPS.

Blake's buddy was supposed to have the fuel drums set up just north of the road as it made a sharp turn heading west, just north of Lopa. The stream continued north for several hundred yards, and the streambed widened until it was nothing but a sandbar.

Judge slowed to about twenty knots and strained his eyes to see up the valley. He swung the helicopter around to see if he could see headlights coming up the road behind him. All was dark.

Suddenly, Michelle grabbed his arm and pointed. Judge turned his gaze and instantly spotted what had caught her attention. Several fifty-gallon drums sat upright along an outcropping of rocks. Perfectly hidden from the road, they would have been easy to spot from the air or by any passing hiker. Fortunately, any hiker would have had little use for them.

Judge settled the aircraft just north of the outcropping so that they too would be mostly out of sight from the road, at night anyway. Much of the aircraft would be in plain view during the day, but the headlight beams would all pass short of the spot at night. Judge cut the engine and let the rotor come to a stop. All was quiet.

Thirty-Four

They climbed out of the helicopter and inspected the drums, four in all, nearly full.

"My god, they must weigh five hundred pounds apiece!" Michelle exclaimed. "How are we going to get them in the helicopter?"

Fortunately, Reynolds also left a couple of wooden two by six planks. "We'll use these," Judge said, picking up a board.

At nearly four hundred pounds apiece, they would have been tough for him to load into the helicopter without the planks.

He opened the big side doors on the left of the aircraft and rolled the drums up the planks. Once inside, he had to tip them right side up. Four drums of fuel were a tight fit. In fact, they did not all exactly fit on the floor. Judge had to set two of them on the forward facing backseat panels.

"Can it lift all that weight?" Michelle asked, staring at the squatting LongRanger.

"If we can get it off the ground, we'll make it. We're going to burn a lot of fuel pretty fast at this weight, so we won't be too heavy for long."

There was no interior in the back of the LongRanger, which made the job easier. Using a couple of hold-down straps attached to the seat belt anchors, Judge secured the aft drums to the aft bulkhead, which was also the aft fuel cell's forward bulkhead.

He then removed the aft fuel-indicating probe and stuffed the neoprene hose into the cell. The other end was connected to the boost pump that he had stuffed in his satchel. A crude four-into-one fitting, which he had fashioned from some AN fittings, was screwed into the pump inlet; and each leg of the fitting had a hose, which he pushed into the small opening at the top of the drums.

Unscrewing those top plugs would have proved a real problem if Reynolds had not also left the tool for that purpose. Judge wondered how many other things he would discover that he had forgotten to bring.

Two wires to the battery buss and a handheld switch made the system operational. It took only a couple of minutes and two more wires to install the fuel flow meter in the fuel flow line at the back of the engine combustor.

Michelle stood by, nervously watching the road for any approaching headlights. She shivered.

"Michelle, hold this gauge and this switch. I'm going to need you to help me with the fuel transfer once we get going." If they could stand the smell of fuel from the open fuel cell and the open drums, they would have enough fuel for at least five hours of flight, or about six hundred nautical miles.

Judge directed Michelle to turn on the pump as he held a penlight in the aft tank opening. When the tank was nearly full, he motioned her to turn it off. It took ten minutes to fill the aft tank. He would have to use the fuel flow meter and his watch to estimate the tank state. He didn't want to overfill the aft tank and have fuel pouring into the cabin, but he didn't want to be running the tank dry either.

In all, it had taken less than half an hour to get the aircraft ready. Despite the night air, Judge was drenched in sweat. Michelle was shivering.

After searching the night sky and the road for signs of traffic, Judge started the turbine. So far, if anyone was looking for them, they had not been spotted.

"OK, here we go," he said, lifting off again. Despite the cool air, the turbine didn't put out enough power at 100% torque to get them off the ground. They bobbled briefly as the rotor strained against the weight. Judge gritted his teeth as he overtorqued the transmission, and the aircraft lifted a foot into the air. Gingerly he nosed the aircraft over the embankment to gain the advantage of translational lift. Finally gaining it, he eased back on the torque as the aircraft began to climb.

They headed west. The sea was an empty blackness as they approached the shore. Judge descended as low as he dared, turning on the landing light momentarily, just long enough to reset the altimeter to zero. Then, rising eighty feet, they headed northwest out to sea.

His fear and apprehension were extreme. He was flying out over the open ocean, in a single engine helicopter, with open fuel drums, at night, low level, at over a hundred knots. Judge knew he had broken every rule in the book, along with more laws than he cared to count.

Trying to scale the Andes would have been tougher, both for the helicopter, and for them, particularly at night. The Chilean Army had several high altitude helicopter outposts scattered along the border with Argentina. There was no way to tell exactly where they were located, but most likely would have been near any mountain pass that they would have chosen to sneak through. The weight of the aircraft with enough fuel for the journey could never have climbed high enough.

Blake had said that they could not depend on his help if he went into Argentina. Judge tried to rationalize that flight into Argentina would have been riskier than flying out into the Pacific. The reasons for his decisions were not reassuring.

His bitterness was intense, but Judge did not know to whom he should be directing it towards, other than himself, for having gotten into such a mess in the first place.

He spoke to Michelle over the intercom to help her find the spare GPS battery packs. She was still shivering, perhaps from fear. She had placed all of her trust in him.

"Is this it?" she asked, holding up a tiny box.

"That's it," he said, "put it in your pocket, we're going to want to change it quickly if the ones in the GPS go dead."

He unbuckled the ELT from its mount. Turning it on, he listened for the beat of the ELT on VHF 121.5. The tone was loud and clear. Sliding back the side window, he tossed the beacon out. It continued to transmit after it hit the water. By the time they had traveled another twenty miles, however, they could no longer pick it up on the radio.

When they were a hundred miles out, he turned on the landing light. Judge was startled to see the water so close. The wind had picked up, and the swells had become white capped and choppy. Judge knew they would run right into the water if he let it hypnotize him, so he turned on the taxi light. Each light made its own spot on the surface of the water. By keeping the two spots the same distance apart, he could keep a relative reference above the surface.

The horizon and the altimeter were a better help. He soon found he could just reset the altimeter using the lights-on-the-water method from time to time, and then turn the lights out.

At two hours out, Michelle changed the GPS batteries. Judge felt a brief stroke of panic when the GPS did not come back online right away. After a few moments, however, it realigned.

He was getting sloppy with his altitude and felt it safe to climb another hundred feet. When he was sure that they were over international waters, he climbed another hundred feet.

Judge tuned in 121.5 again—the international VHF emergency frequency—and keyed the mike.

"Tango Hotel, this is Whiskey Java, do you read, over." There was no response. They were still fifteen nautical miles from the rendezvous point, so he did not anticipate an answer just yet due to his low altitude.

Judge wanted the assurance of someone else close by. Feeling the need for a little more altitude, he climbed another hundred feet. Turning on the landing light again to get a brief check of the water, he was stunned to see only the reflection of the light coming back at them. They were in the clouds at three hundred feet!

He quickly descended until he could see the light on the water. The sea had really become rough. The waves were over ten feet.

"Tango Hotel, this is Whiskey Java, do you read, over." There was still no response. Judge found himself shivering. He could see Michelle's wide-eyed expression in the reflection of the instrument lights.

She tapped the flowmeter with her finger and looked questioningly at him. Judge nodded as she turned the boost pump on again. Before the ten minutes were up, however, the usual hum that the pump usually made changed tone and became more erratic.

He glanced over his shoulder and could see the pump shaking in an erratic fashion on top of one of the drums. It was cavitating. He shook his head. "Michelle, the drums are empty. You do not need to worry about that switch anymore."

"How much fuel is left?" she asked, trying to remain calm. *Judge did not seem worried*, she thought. *To him, this seems like all in a day's work.* "Will we get there in time?"

"Of course. The mains are nearly full. We have plenty." He knew, however, that even if they found the ship that he didn't think he would have enough fuel to make it back to shore. "Put on the vest," he said. "Just in case, and remember, do not pull the lanyard unless you are outside the helicopter. That little cigarette-pack sized thing in the satchel, . . . yeah that one, that's the strobe. If we get in the water, push that little rubber nipple to turn it on."

As she slid the water vest over her head, Judge held the cyclic with his knees and did the same, trying not to think about the rising sea state.

"Tango Hotel, this is Whiskey Java, do you read, over." Again, there was no response. They were less than ten miles from their coordinates. At low altitude, he figured the VHF should at least be good for ten miles. He began transmitting every two minutes.

At five miles, according to the GPS, he still could not raise anyone on the radio.

They were over the spot now, and Michelle must have noticed the tension in his voice as he made another call. "Tango Hotel, this is Whiskey Java, do you read, over."

"Whiskey Java, this is Tango Hotel, we read you two by." The signal was very weak. Michelle grabbed his arm in excitement.

"Tango Hotel, I read you two by . . ."

"Loud and clear now, Whiskey Java. Head to coordinates South 28 degrees 10.33 minutes by West 79 degrees 8.74 minutes, over."

Rain and mist began hitting the windscreen as Judge fumbled with the GPS and the cyclic. When they were finally turned to the correct heading, he could see from the GPS that they had another five miles to go to the new coordinates. He turned on the tail strobe.

With their hearts pounding, they finally saw the ship looming ahead. It was a big cargo container ship. Judge could see an area amidships that appeared to be the ship's helipad. *At least*, he thought, *it could be used as one*.

"Tango Hotel, can you turn the ship directly into the wind? I think I can approach from the stern."

"Roger, Whiskey Java, we already are. That lighted area is not a helipad," Tango Hotel replied, as if reading his mind, "it's one of the cargo hold doors. It won't hold the weight of the aircraft. You will have to ditch. We have a crew standing by with a lifeboat."

Judge's heart sank. Michelle was not strong enough to swim in these waters, even with a vest. "Negative, the girl is too weak. I'm going to try and hover over the cargo door, and you guys come and help her out." Judge was shouting into the mike.

He could not tell if the boat slowed or not, but he knew that he and Michelle were running out of time. Pulling the helicopter into a hover over the middle of the pitching ship, he could not keep a constant distance above the hold.

Once, the skids touched the lid, and then they were ten feet in the air again. Michelle gritted her teeth. She was no quitter. When she could see a half-dozen men struggling on the deck below her, she pushed open the door and climbed onto the skid.

With the door banging her on the butt as she faced Judge, she began bending her knees with the rhythm of the rise and fall of the ship.

"You have to come too, Walter. Please!" she yelled at him above the din of the engine. Her headset had been unplugged for her exit, and the intercom system no longer allowed normal conversation.

"If I don't go back now, it will just happen all over again. You'll never be safe with me! You give that little girl a big hug for me!"

Then she was gone.

Judge swung the helicopter over the side of the ship and disappeared into the storm.

Thirty-Five

Hurrying along the Avenida Balmaceda on the way to De Padilla's place, Ponce Gutierrez pressed harder on the accelerator. He should have known that Carrillo no longer needed Judge when Wright had told him that Judge would soon be flying the prototype. After hearing about Carrillo's offer to loan the American a helicopter, Gutierrez had jumped up and rushed out of the room, nearly forgetting to collect what he had come for.

A hundred thousand American dollars was more money than he had ever seen at one time. Gutierrez smiled to himself. He had secured his new position with Carrillo weeks before, unbeknownst to Wright. He imagined the look on Wright's face when he learned the news and hoped he could get to him before Judge did.

Things had certainly changed between him and Wright since their first meeting during the early Pinochet years in the '70s. Wright had been working for the CIA in South America and had heard about the big Chilean. Finding Gutierrez out of work, Wright had decided to hire him.

He had employed Gutierrez through a CIA front organization for a while, a security company in Illinois. It was a great assignment for Gutierrez, learning to get around in the US and being around American girls. When he got into trouble with female staff members, however, he had been fired from the CIA.

Wright, knowing Gutierrez's usefulness, was able to hire him personally and bring him into the Colombian Embassy as a private operative. Wright paid Gutierrez out of a fund that he always seemed to struggle to keep liquid, a problem that often seemed to have the big Chilean working for free.

Wright assigned Gutierrez to Cox and Atterbury, two other ex-CIA private operatives that Wright employed, as an agent in training.

Now, Gutierrez turned off the headlights as he rounded the last bend in the road before reaching De Padilla's place. He didn't want to be seen or heard if Judge was already there. Stopping the car a quarter mile from the bungalow, he got out, opened the trunk, and pulled out a .308 rifle.

Suddenly, he heard a movement in the tall grass. Crouching low and swinging the rifle around, he used his off-center vision to spot the source of the sound. He dimly made out a lone figure struggling in the weeds.

Approaching cautiously, he discovered the Iraqi, bound and gagged. Gutierrez quickly cut the man's bindings.

"What happened to you?" the big Chilean asked in Arabic.

"Judge tricked me," came the obvious reply. "I fought him, but he is too big," the man lied.

Gutierrez knew it was useless to question him further and handed the Arab a pistol from his belt. The two crept towards the distant house.

The place was dark as they approached. It seemed that Judge might have departed with the girl, with Wright in pursuit.

Gutierrez explored the smoke-filled house, then opened the windows to air the place out. The fire was still smoldering, and he doused it with a pan of water.

Hearing a cry from the Iraqi, who had been scouting the surrounding area, Gutierrez moved again out into the fresh air. His Middle Eastern partner was kneeling by a figure on the back lawn.

Wright was wincing in pain and shivering from lying on the cold ground. "Gutierrez! Thank god, you're back. That bastard Judge broke my back and left me here."

Gutierrez reached up and exchanged his rifle for the pistol from the Iraqi. Then he waved for the Iraqi to move out and keep surveying the area.

"I told you he'd squash you like bug," he said to Wright.

"Did you get my money?"

"No," Gutierrez said, cocking his pistol. "But I got my money."

"What are you doing?" yelled Wright as Gutierrez pointed the pistol at his head.

"Carrillo fired you. You're not needed. Judge neither."

"What, are you crazy?" Wright cried. "We can't integrate the weapons systems without him. I can get him back. He'll never stop working for us. I'll show you how."

"Sooner or later, Judge keel you, maybe me too. I don't need to work for you anymore."

"We need him, don't you understand!" Wright said urgently. "He's the key to putting everything we've been working for together. Don't you see? For every aircraft we deliver, we get fifty grand. There's a hundred aircraft, Gutierrez? That's five million big ones! I'll split it with you!"

"I forget to tell you. When you were knocking off that reporter in Virginia that night, I was getting Judge's notes and stuff outta his safe. Fox told Carrillo that Judge keeps all his secret stuff at his house. How you say it? Piece of cake. Carrillo's men decode it. Found all Judge's weapons computer stuff. We don't need Judge anymore."

"The girl, the girl can finger you to the cops!" Wright cried desperately. "I can help you get her. She'll never testify."

"Cops, what cops? I don't worry about US cops. I don't need the US, just their money!" He laughed, holding up the satchel of bills that Carrillo had given him. "I don't need the girl, and I don't need you for nothing!"

Except for Gutierrez and the lone Iraqi exploring the grounds around De Padilla's remote villa, no one heard the single report of the silenced .38 doing its job against the crippled Mr. Wright.

Thirty-Six

Judge had barely made it back to the shores of Valparaiso the night he had flown Michelle out to the ship. Thanks to the approaching storm from the north, he had been aided by a brisk tailwind.

He spent most of the night getting enough fuel to return to Santiago. He had finally returned the helicopter to Carrillo's flight line just as Hector had shown up for work. The Chilean had been in a jovial mood and, much to Judge's relief, appeared not to be aware of any additional need for Judge. Carrillo and Gutierrez were not yet aware of the weapons systems integration problems that they would soon be facing.

Judge had learned from Carrillo that Ponce would soon be on his way to Spain following a quick stop in Bogota. There was no mention of Wright. It appeared to Judge that his predictions concerning what would become of Wright must have come to pass, so he quickly boarded a flight for Colombia.

By the time Judge arrived at the Eldorado International Airport outside Bogota, he was exhausted and irritable. Although the trip seemed to take too long, the flight had actually arrived in Bogota nearly an hour earlier than scheduled.

Deplaning through the customs area proved easier than he had thought; the customs officers looked at each other, sized up the big American, and shrugged. After checking his luggage for weapons, they motioned him to move on.

Colombia is different than most Central and South American countries. Customs does not look for illicit drugs coming into the country. They're only watching for those that leave.

Guns, however, are a different matter. A ten-year prison term is not unusual punishment for being caught with a gun in Colombia. Ironically, the number of murders in Colombia easily exceeds virtually every other nation.

Daylight had slipped away just as Judge had hoped. He shivered once in the cool twilight. Exhausted, he grimly resigned himself to surviving what he knew could be a long, painful night.

Judge hailed for a cab to take him to the Tequendama Hotel, located about five minutes by taxi northeast from the Centro International, the central business district.

The driver, who called himself Pedro, handed Judge a card. "Please, senor, call me whenever you need a taxi."

"Sure thing," Judge replied, grateful that Pedro could speak English.

He settled back in the seat, readjusting to the locale of Bogota. He would need to remember as much as possible if he wanted to survive the next twenty-four hours here. Skyscrapers loomed in the distance as the taxi drove south. More immediately to their left and right, Judge could see beautiful colonial style mansions majestically standing in the twilight. They must be passing the rich La Candelaria district, Judge calculated.

They drove past what seemed like hundreds of glass greenhouses. Judge remembered how famous Colombia is for its orchid trade. Most Americans knew only of the drug traffic, and of course, Colombian coffee.

Bogota was teeming with life, even though the time was into the eight o'clock hour. Most shops, which had closed for three hours during the afternoon, were still open; and many shoppers were about once again.

The evening chill might keep some folks inside, but Judge doubted they'd stay there long. The temperature was a cool fifty-five degrees. Although it was only eight hundred miles from the equator, Bogota, at 8600 feet above sea level, did not suffer the heat of cities close to the coast.

It did, however, like Denver, Mexico City, and other high-altitude metropolises, suffer from acrid air pollution.

"On the left—over there," Pedro announced as they left La Candelaria, "is the Bullring. The Plaza de Toros Santa Maria," he announced. "The main season is over now, but the local *toreros* have small bullfights there in the mornings. You can see them sometime, if you wish."

"That's OK," Judge commented. "If all goes as I expect it to, I'll be on my way out of here tomorrow."

They were entering what must be the downtown area, with tall modern-looking buildings that reminded him of a recent taxi ride through New York City.

"The tourists call this section, 'Little Manhattan,'" Pedro added as if reading Judge's mind. "This is the Centro Internacional. Your hotel is just up ahead."

The cab rolled up to the Tequendama Hotel. As the driver lifted his bag from the trunk, Judge could not help but notice the hotel's elegant appearance. The entryway was laid with red marble from floor to ceiling. The steps, the huge pillars reaching skyward, even the reservations desk appeared to be made of marble. He could hear running water from a nearby fountain as he entered.

"What do I owe you, my friend?" Judge asked Pedro.

"Three thousand pesos, senor, and please, senor, Colombian taxi drivers—we do not accept tips," he said almost apologetically.

To his embarrassment, Judge suddenly remembered that he had no Colombian currency. After all, he had not intended on staying in Colombia for long. He handed the driver four one-dollar American bills, which Pedro nodded was close enough and said goodbye.

"Hold on," Judge said, handing the driver a few extra bills. "I'd like to hire you as my driver for tonight."

"Si, senor. I will wait for you over there with the other cabs." He pointed to a cab stand, and Judge admitted.

Judge checked in and was directed to the elevator. He pushed "7" and rose to the seventh floor. To his satisfaction, the room was large and quite luxurious. Mahogany lined the walls leading to the window, which took up the entire west wall of the room. The curtains were drawn, and the lights of the city kept the room from darkness, with no added illumination.

Judge removed his toiletry bag from his luggage and took out a tiny brown bottle labeled "rubbing alcohol." In truth, it was chloroform. Slipping it into his pocket, he knelt down to zip up his bag on the floor. Leaving the light on, Judge shut and locked the door and headed out to meet Pedro.

Getting into the cab, he asked Pedro to drive him to the La Zona Rosa, the red light district of Bogota.

"senor, are you sure? It is not a safe place at night. If it is women you wish for, I can arrange for a girl to come to your—"

Judge interrupted Pedro with his hand. "Thanks just the same, but I'm going to meet someone. Just see if you can find La Zona Rosa for me, OK?"

"Ah, yes, senor. I know it well, it is famous. I will not have to look for it."

As Pedro drove by a bed-and-breakfast inn after entering the Northern Zone, Judge reached forward from his seat in the back and touched Pedro on the shoulder.

"Stop here at La Casona, Pedro. You wait for me here. I could be a short while or a very long while." He handed the driver a hundred-dollar bill. "If you wait for me, I'll double this when I return."

Pedro's eyes grew wide at the sight of the currency. "How long is a 'very long while,' senor?"

"If I'm not back here by daylight, I'll be dead. Can you wait 'til morning?"

Interpreting Judge's comment as a joke, the driver laughed. "For two hundred dollars, senor, I will wait for two mornings."

Judge jumped out of the cab and hurried down the street. Three blocks further north on Viva Calle, he turned right, heading north out of La Zona Rosa. Finally, he arrived at Calle 85, the corner where the action from the Copacabana nightclub was spilling out into the street.

To Judge's surprise, Ponce was better known in the streets and barrios of Bogota than he had dared to hope.

Ponce, Judge knew, had an addiction to cheap whores and an even greater passion for beating them up. It didn't take Judge long to find a disgruntled victim who was more than willing to sell Ponce out for some American dollars.

Apparently, Ponce spoke freely when he had too much to drink.

The bouncer at the Copacabana made no attempt to intimidate Judge, as he would have any other gringo of smaller stature. Judge gave him a tight smile, then ignored him and walked in like a regular. He picked out a table for himself along the wall across from the bar. Two pretty young girls already occupied the table.

They looked suspiciously at Judge as he sat down. They were dressed in extremely short skirts and low-cut bright red and orange rayon tops. Their nipples pushed through the shiny material, and Judge knew that one of them—the one with the dyed red hair—was probably ready to offer her company for the night to the tune of fifty thousand pesos.

The other girl, however, looked frightened. A natural beauty, she had her hair tied back in a long dark ponytail that curved over her shoulder, covering one breast.

"This table is taken," she said in excellent English.

"I know," Judge said. He had noticed three drinks on the table. Obviously, the owner of the third beverage must be in the john. "I'm not here to cause any trouble," Judge began. "In fact, I have an offer for you. I'll give each of you fifty thousand pesos if you'll help me find someone."

"We already have a boyfriend," the redhead replied.

"He has both of you, then? Lucky man!" Judge grinned. Then, turning serious, he said, "No, you don't have to leave with me. I'll pay you here."

"We don't know anybody," the brunette insisted. She looked as if she wanted to leave, but her friend put a restraining hand on her arm.

Judge watched them struggle with their decision, and he decided it was time to remove a hundred-dollar bill from his pocket and place it on the table. The girls regarded the currency with interest, but neither made a move. Then, the redhead asked, "Who are you looking for?"

Before they could answer, a well-dressed tall Latin man appeared. Sizing up the situation, he whirled upon the girls and began speaking angrily in Spanish.

Judge stood, towering over the man, and held up his hand smiling. He told the girl who spoke English to tell him that Judge was an old friend who stopped by to pay an outstanding debt. He'd be leaving in just a moment.

That seemed to calm down their pimp, who accepted Judge's handshake. He sat down at another table and watched Judge and the girls from a short distance, never taking his eyes from them.

"OK, who are you looking for?" asked the redhead, urging Judge along. The presence of her pimp made her nervous.

Judge described Ponce Gutierrez above the din of the bar music.

"We do not know him," the girl said nervously. Judge could tell she was lying. Removing another hundred from his pocket, he placed it in front of her.

"I can promise you, you will never see him again," he said convincingly.

The girl looked at the determination in the big man's eyes. "You need to speak with a girl named Marianna," she finally said. "She hangs out at the Casanova. Word is all over the barrio that Gutierrez knocked one of her teeth out last night."

"What does she look like?"

"I have never seen her. When her boyfriend beats a girl, word gets around quickly. Usually a father or brother or another boyfriend would go after him, but no one goes after the Big One, that Ponce."

Judge left the girls and his hundreds at the table and walked out of the bar in search of the Casanova. He found it near the Carulla supermarket near Calle 85. It took him longer to find the girl named Marianna than the nightclub.

Finally, a bouncer pointed to a young girl with a grotesquely swollen cheek and lip. Despite her appearance, she was still trying to pick up a boyfriend for the night. Judge found her nearly begging an Italian tourist to take her for thirty thousand, a mere pittance to what she would normally require.

Her back was to him as he approached from the bar of the Casanova after the bouncer had pointed her out to him. A large wide-brimmed *toquilla* hat hid much of her profile. Her long silky jet-black hair flowed from underneath it. The blousing of her bright yellow halter top accentuated her ample breasts and tiny waist. She wore form-fitting blue jeans that hugged her flesh all the way to just shy of her delicate ankles. A pair of black patent leather heels peeked from the shadow under the table and matched her wide belt. Leaning forward on her elbows, she slowly drew on a cigarette, removing any hint of innocence from an otherwise stunning picture.

She neither looked up, nor motioned him to sit, as he slid into the iron chair across from her. Now in front of her, he could see her face, save for her eyes, which were somewhat hidden by a pair of tinted designer glasses. Another attempt, Judge soon realized, to hide a wicked shiner. He too was momentarily shocked at seeing her disfigured face.

Judge felt immediately sorry for her.

She spoke something to him in Spanish, and Judge suddenly realized he might not be able to learn a thing from her.

"I'm sorry," he said. "I don't speak Spanish."

"I said," she repeated in English, much to Judge's relief. "Please do not run away like the others."

"Don't worry," Judge replied, relieved. "I can tell," he continued, "that you are extremely beautiful, even after what that Ponce did to you."

"You know heem? You are his friend?"

"I am not his friend. But I have some business with him. I need to find him, and I hope you can help me."

She looked at him in disbelief. "You must be a crazy gringo," she said. "Nobody looks for Ponce. I was stupid. He offered me good money, but now I cannot work for weeks," she said disgustedly. "You keel him for me, I pay you, I promise. I can pay you little each week." Judge reached out and handed her a couple of crisp hundred dollar bills.

"Just help me find this guy who hit you."

"Find heem?" She nearly yelled it, pocketing the money. "I no have to find heem! He stay at Santa Fe Hotel!"

Thirty-Seven

Arms to Iraq: The Chilean Connection

—The Washington Post, ***Aug. 5, 1990, p. D7***

The seemingly endless open Texas landscape northwest of Fort Worth is interrupted by two enormous structures trying to compete for title of biggest aerial landmark. The first can literally be seen for tens of miles from the ground and is testament to the size of Texas itself. Rising to meet the wide-open sky is one of the largest grain elevators in the entire southwest.

It is the second largest landmark, however, that has become the target of interest for a growing line of traffic on this unseasonably sultry early summer morning. The Aircraft Certification Office of the Federal Aviation Administration nearly requires the entire converted World War II dirigible facility that houses it just to hang its sign.

Michelle Lofton stood in one of its conference rooms with her parents. Huddled close around her were Sergeant Jenkins, Lieutenant Gibbons, and several other officers. Many others soon joined them.

"Are you sure you want to go through with this?" Michelle's mother asked, looking at her daughter.

"Things could get pretty ugly from here on out," Gibbons pointed out.

"Ugly for whom?" Michelle blurted out angrily. "For me? Just how much uglier can things get?" Her anger was directed at the lieutenant. His constant presence the past few days had worn on her. He had even sent her flowers, a deed for which he was severely admonished for by his captain as well as Michelle's father.

"All I'm saying," Gibbons responded defensively, "is that maybe you shouldn't put too much stock in anything he told you. After all, it was he who has caused you all this grief in the first place."

"That man never lied to any of us," returned Michelle testily. "All he ever did was what he thought was right. Every one of us was deceived. He has protected me from the day I met him." Michelle's lips trembled, and she turned her back to them, struggling to regain her composure.

She had a lot to say in that conference room that morning, but she would have to be less emotional. Michelle's mother placed an arm around her in silent support.

Tony Gibbons began to say something to her, but Michelle's father held up a hand and shook his head. "You need to give her a little more space, son," he said quietly, leading the lieutenant a few feet away from the women.

Captain Stillions joined them. “Senator Phillips will be here any minute. I wanted to ask you before he arrives, have any of you heard from Judge?”

“Not since before Michelle called from Panama,” Jenkins replied. “Not a word.”

“He’s going to have a lot of questions to answer if he ever turns up alive,” the captain said.

“When Michelle gets through this morning, we’ll all have a lot of questions to answer,” Jenkins added.

“I wish she would let us get further into this investigation before she brings the press into it,” the captain continued.

“When my daughter shows you what she has in that satchel,” the senior Lofton remarked, “I believe you will have all the proof you need to get the cooperation that you’ve been denied. I have to agree with Michelle. Showing you guys, the FBI, the press, and the Senator this evidence all at the same time will keep it from getting quashed by the very people that are trying to stifle your investigation.”

Michelle, having regained her composure, rejoined the small group. She remained silent however, distant with her own conflicting thoughts of what she was about to say before all these people.

Walter had told her that once the floodgates of information were opened, she and Heather would cease to be a target. No one so far had been killed out of revenge. All of the murders to date had been to keep secrets.

But she now worried that Judge would be in greater danger, if he were still alive, from a still yet undiscovered conspirator high up on the political ladder. She shuddered. Evidence linking CIA Director Williams was thin, and there were no facts yet in evidence at all beyond him or Senator Roberts.

In the end, she had to agree with Judge that regardless of how high up the conspiracy was rooted, they would all be much safer with the facts out in the open. The remaining culprits would be too busy scrambling to cover their own tracks to worry about the Loftons.

Judge had explained in painful detail everything that he wanted her to know that could be backed up with either hard evidence or evidence that could be quickly uncovered by the press, the FBI, and the police once the pressure from certain politicians was lifted.

She regretted now how much she had fretted to Judge during the entire flight across the water that night. Michelle had let him know how naïve he had been to be involved for so long. "How could a man so worldly be so innocent?" she had said to him. The shadow of danger that had followed him had enveloped everyone he had come in contact with. She wished now that she had never said anything to him about it.

Michelle had had a rough voyage from the southeastern Pacific to the Isthmus of Panama. Unaccustomed to rough seas, she had been seasick much of the way. The British crew had treated her well, and she in turn had tried to assist the ship's steward with other crewmembers who had suffered the same fate.

Her father had been waiting for her in Panama with her passport, accompanied by a senior agent from the Dallas office of the FBI, an old friend of Captain Stillions.

Tony Gibbons was with them as well. His captain had recommended him when the lieutenant insisted that two elderly gentlemen were not security enough for Michelle in light of the mounting number of deaths in their case. With the blessing of the senior Lofton, he had come along as a friend of the family. Together they had escorted her home through Mexico City and finally DFW.

Judge had surprised her by heading back out into the storm after dropping her onto the boat. She was suddenly no longer angry with him, but frightened for him. She wondered what he was about to do.

She knew that, in a world that had gone seemingly mad around her, he was her pillar of strength and comfort. She longed to be held in his big arms again.

When her nightmares frightened her in the late evening hours, it was Judge who she wished to be beside her. She knew that if he were within her reach that nothing would ever happen to her or her child.

Heather had been delighted to see her mother when she had finally arrived home. Having no idea of her mother's ordeal, she had skipped and clapped and chattered gaily.

Her constant hugging and kissing had brought Michelle out of a worrisome mood.

The child's only forlorn moment had been when she was told that Mr. Judge was gone. She continually begged to go to his house to see him.

Michelle had finally given in and taken her daughter to play Walter's piano. Judge had given her a key and the alarm code the day before their weekend on the lake.

"Michelle," Helen Lofton interrupted her daughter's thoughts, "Captain Stillions just announced that the Senator is outside. He should be here any second."

"I don't know how anyone finds his way around this place. The layout is so confusing," Michelle said.

To accommodate any confused visitor, as well as facilitate a somewhat austere civil service budget, signs pointed the direction of meeting rooms. Special escorts for VIPs were not uncommon; and on this day the ACO manager, Eric Jameson, found himself the unlikely escort for one Senator Grant Phillips.

Neither man was smiling, however, as they hurried along the yellowed corridors of the aging brick structure. They came to a set of double doors at the end of the hallway. The doors were closed, and a pair of uniformed policemen each opened a door for the senator. Stationed beside them were several additional uniformed officers.

A hush came over the occupants of the surprisingly cramped meeting room when the senator entered with

Jameson. It seemed apparent, at least to the senator, that the meeting had indeed been quickly planned. With its old navy gray tables joined end-to-end down the middle of the room, it was not at all what he was accustomed to.

The Fort Worth chief of police reached across the table and shook hands with the senator and introduced him to Captain Stillions of the FBI. Eric Jameson followed suit by introducing the senator to the Tarrant County sheriff and senior agents of the FBI, US Customs, and the US Commerce Department. None were smiling.

Senator Phillips looked to the head of the table where a pretty blonde was seated. She was dressed in a navy blue Seville and looked every part the chair of the meeting. Despite her obvious good looks, evidence of recent stress had taken a toll, and her eyes betrayed her with apprehension.

Lt. Tony Gibbons and Sam Jenkins flanked Michelle. Behind them sat a rather distinguished-looking couple, Michelle's parents—Dr. Richard Lofton and his wife, Helen. At the far end of the table sat counselor Van Warren, who motioned a familiar nod in the direction of the somewhat bewildered senator.

Behind those seated at the table, lining the walls of the small conference room, were representatives of the press including the *Fort Worth Star-Telegram* and the *Dallas Morning News*.

"Senator Phillips," Michelle began. She hesitated just long enough to stand. She wanted everyone in the room to understand that she would begin the meeting and that none of the esteemed attendees were to interrupt before she was finished.

"Thank you for coming, and thank you, Van, for asking your friend and colleague, Senator Phillips, to come on such short notice and under false pretenses."

"False pretenses?" Phillips asked, surprised.

"Each of you has been sought out by name and association. Each of you has, in some way, contributed to an investigation that few of you know the depth of. You were each carefully sought out because of your individual integrity and your long-standing devotion to the law."

Michelle had prepared and given many lectures during her tenure as a physician. None, however, had been as thoroughly rehearsed as the one she gave to the contingent in that meeting hall.

She began, much to the bewilderment of her audience, by telling of the US State Department's directives, namely, the continued alignment of Reagan's South American policy and illicit support of Iraq. She quickly detailed the support structure that the ADE represented and how the CIA was using the private endowment with knowledge of representatives of the federal government.

Before anyone could utter an objection to what had begun to appear to some as an antigovernment diatribe,

Michelle described the murder of Pauline Casey. Detailing the information that Ms. Casey had discovered, she explained how Wright had intercepted the young woman after ordering his two goons, Cox and Atterbury, to follow Walter Judge and kill her before she could pass on any information to him.

Michelle explained how her own earlier attack had been a case of mistaken identity when Wright had been unable to contact Cox and Atterbury and inform them that he had already caught up to the young reporter in Virginia.

Stunned expressions were met with affirmative nods from various law enforcement members who had participated in pieces of the investigation.

Michelle continued to describe ARI's programs in Indonesia, the United Kingdom, and Chile, producing the photographs of weapons systems and gunships, test plans, maps, and copies of shipping documents, some of which had State Department and Department of Commerce license stamps.

A copy of the *London Times*' article brought gasps from some as she continued with the story of Duffy's murder by the Iraqi Mukhabarat. She then moved onto the murder of Milton Fox by the accused Mr. Wright and her own kidnapping at the hands of Ponce Gutierrez.

When she began trembling, Tony Gibbons stood up and moved beside her. He produced the photos of Gutierrez.

Tony persuaded Michelle to sit. Michelle did so, but she continued talking, quieter now, about overhearing conversations between Wright and Gutierrez and between Wright and Judge. She finished with the details of her rescue and how Wright and his organization had been able to take advantage of the capable, albeit naïve, Mr. Walter Judge.

There was silence as everyone gave Michelle a moment of reprise. Then Senator Phillips raised his hand, not in a request to speak, but as a motion to prevent the press from jumping up.

“Ms. Lofton, please forgive me, I am in no position to dispute anything you have presented here. It does appear that there is indeed the makings here of a tremendous scandal to which, I will be the first to admit, I have known absolutely nothing about.”

“You have presented here, with the assistance of our law enforcement, a seemingly bunch of evidence,” he continued. “But—and please don’t misunderstand the intent of the question—but we must be very careful here. Do you have any evidence that could possibly connect this mysterious Mr. Wright to the director of the CIA? Wright seems like a phantom in the midst of all this other evidence!”

Michelle picked up the satchel in which she had produced most of Judge’s evidence. She tipped it over and dumped out three plastic bags. She slid them towards the surprised senator.

One bag contained Wright's ID and passport, which Judge had lifted from him. The other contained Wright's silenced .40 semiautomatic, which Judge had been careful not to blemish. The third contained several mini cassettes on which Judge had quietly recorded his conversations with Fox, Wright, Duffy, British Intelligence, and Carrillo.

"Senator Phillips," Michelle said vehemently, "perhaps you can direct our uncooperative CIA and your colleague, Senator Roberts, to explain these."

Thirty-Eight

Sirens wailed from all directions, waking all inhabitants of Bogota's La Zona Rosa district who were not inebriated or otherwise drugged. Despite the early morning hour, a large crowd had gathered in Calle 85 con 30. Most were curious onlookers, but the number of policia was growing by the minute and began pushing the onlookers away.

Some, however, could not be deterred. They pushed against the uniformed officers in an attempt to get a look at the stranger lying in the street in front of the Santa Fe Hotel. He lay facedown in a pool of his own blood. Shot dead by the local police.

Not an hour before, the streets had been relatively quiet. The bars of Bogota are required to close every morning at one. That was the signal for the remaining hookers who could not secure a boyfriend for the night to lower their fares in a final attempt at having a roof over their heads for the night.

It had been the time that Judge had been waiting for. Having learned that Gutierrez had often been unsuccessful at getting a girl for the night, he knew that the giant Chilean would be scouring the early morning streets. He would be looking for a desperate little whore willing to take on the risk of being with one of Colombia's most dangerous johns.

Judge had found the desk clerk quietly dozing at his post at the Santa Fe and had used the chloroform to ensure a continued slumber. He had quickly looked up Gutierrez's room number, which turned out to be the same as Marianna had indicated. It never hurt to double-check to ensure that the man had not changed rooms.

Judge then had borrowed the clerk's master key to unlock Gutierrez's room. After blocking the bolt to the door and returning the key, he had ventured into Gutierrez's room and given it a thorough search. There were no weapons in the room, which worried Judge. He had hoped Gutierrez would have left his gun in the room before venturing out to drink and chase whores in Bogota. *A man that size really had no need of a gun*, Judge had thought.

When he heard the unmistakable sounds of the big man coming up the stairs, he unlocked the balcony door and slipped out onto the tiny platform, quietly sliding the door closed. He had stood in the shadows and waited.

The walls of the Santa Fe Hotel seemed to shake as Gutierrez trudge up the steps to his third-floor room. His heavy steps reflected his mood, as he had been unsuccessful in getting one of Bogota's Zona Rosa whores. His reputation for slapping them around had preceded him.

One by one they had turned him down. An offer for five hundred dollars had nearly won him a naïve young newcomer, but a quick whisper in her ear from a seasoned veteran of the streets had sent her backing away in fear.

Five hundred American dollars was a lot to spend on a hooker for one night, compared to the seventy-five they customarily received. However, five hundred for a night followed by a month with no business was tough to justify. Patrons in the Zona Rosa were not attracted to girls with smashed faces and broken noses.

The drinks he had imbibed had not helped. He was an angry drunk, and it had often gotten him into trouble with the police. His diplomatic immunity had worked in the past to his advantage however, particularly since he was often caught armed, and he realized then, only too late, that with Wright dead he would soon lose that benefit.

Gutierrez was not altogether without senses. He realized he could not afford to get arrested this night, for he was to be on his way to Spain the next afternoon. The girls of Rota did not know him, and he had high hopes of being more successful in Spain.

Gutierrez turned the key in the door to his hotel room. The light was on, as he always had left it. Out of habit, he leaned to one side of the entryway and pushed open the door. He peered in and, finding it as he had left it, he entered, locking the door behind him.

His jacket slid off his enormous shoulders, and he let it drop to the floor, making no attempt to hang it up. He pulled off the Desert Eagle .50 magnum shoulder holster and tossed it on the bed. The Israeli Arms pistol was by far the largest framed automatic in the world, if not the most powerful. Few men existed that could carry it concealed without making an obvious huge bulge in one's outer garment. Gutierrez could wear it with no one noticing.

He leaned on the wall above the commode as he relieved himself, flushing even before he had finished. The faucet in the bathroom squeaked when he turned on the cold water. He let the basin nearly fill before dunking his head. Finally, he took a stale towel and briskly rubbed his face and hair dry.

Gutierrez reentered the bedroom and suddenly jerked upright, shocked. Calmly standing in the far corner of the room was Walter Judge, holding the Israeli Arms Desert Eagle. The curtain in front of the balcony fluttered in the breeze.

Judge had known how big Gutierrez was from everything he had heard. Standing before the man now, however, he couldn't help but be a little taken aback. He was not used to being in front of a man bigger than he was, and it was disconcerting to say the least.

"You no want to keel me that way," Gutierrez began. He was not thinking particularly fast after all he had imbibed, but he was not altogether stupid either. "I know you. You not shoot a man with no gun."

Judge remained expressionless. He had never killed an unarmed man who wasn't in the act of killing or running someone down. Despite his complete and visceral loathing for the man in front of him, he didn't want to kill one now. "Suppose you tell me why you killed Connie Lin," he finally said.

"Ah, yes, you want to know. Put down the gun, and I tell you."

"You tried to kidnap her like you kidnapped Michelle Lofton," Judge accused, ignoring Gutierrez's words. "Only the tiny woman was too much for the big Ponce Gutierrez."

"My name is Gutierrez!" Ponce said proudly, rolling his R's. "She not tiny, she fat like pig with big belly!" He laughed. "She not do what I tell her. She not let me stick her with needle. All she want to do is fight!" He laughed again.

He could see Judge's veins stand out on his temples and his face turning red. The American's eyes were squinted in anger. "Be careful, Mr. Judge, your anger wheel keel you." He laughed again, mocking the training that he knew Judge had endured. "Yes, your little beetch left you because she was starting to like you. You are such a stupid man. You think girl like her really like mutt like you? She worked for us. I not try an kidnap her as you say. She talk you into going back to work for Fox like we tell her to. She become your girlfren' in Korea 'cause we pay her. Then she get confused and start to like you. Stupid beetch! So she get guilty feelings and leave you." Gutierrez roared with vicious laughter. "When I tell her she not done with you, she say she tell you everything." Gutierrez shrugged. "So I kill her." He shrugged like it was nothing.

Gutierrez could not finish his goading of Judge as the American had launched himself across the room. Holding the ten-inch barrel of the Desert Eagle in his fist and wielding it like a club.

The fight was on. It took only seconds to destroy everything in the room with their thrashing, kicking, and thrusting. Judge was crimson with rage and penned up grief. Gutierrez was taken aback by the American's speed and took several glancing blows from the butte of the pistol before he was able to knock it loose. It flew straight through the window and changed the focus of their attention considerably.

Both men appeared well advanced in their martial arts skills. Despite the wreckage of all the furniture, they were wreaking little injury so far to each other. Judge was much faster than Gutierrez but was at a distinct disadvantage on several accounts. He was some sixty pounds lighter than Gutierrez, who was not by any means an out-of-shape hulk. Judge's rage was working against him, using up his adrenaline, dulling his usually keen offense.

Judge was not as familiar with his surroundings as Gutierrez, whose only disadvantage so far was his lack of speed and his mildly inebriated state. It seemed to Judge, who was not thinking very clearly himself, that the drink had actually served his opponent by dulling the painful onslaught that he was getting.

Gutierrez suddenly had Judge around the waist, lifting him off the floor and slamming him against the wall. Before Judge could brace himself, Gutierrez had charged him again, trying to crush the American with his weight. The wall had given in to over six hundred pounds of flesh, sending the two huge men busting through the wall and into the hallway.

The banister to the stairwell fared no better, and both men crashed down the landing into the lobby, pounding and tearing at each other like two lions of the Serengeti.

Grabbing Judge by the throat and the groin, Gutierrez heaved him into the air and lunged full force at the double entrance doors to the hotel. They exploded through the splintering hardwood out into the street. Slow-moving drunken patrons, street people, and prostitutes instantly scattered in all directions.

Weakening fast, Gutierrez spotted the gun lying in the street. He grabbed it in his oversize fist. Judge was upon him in a second, trying to wrestle the gun from him with both hands. They rolled over and over in the street. Judge's fist was nearly the size of his opponent's however, providing him with but a moment's reprise.

Suddenly, Judge felt the bottle of chloroform tumble from his torn pocket. He jerked his hand violently, causing the gun to fly to the ground a few feet away. Gutierrez leapt from him and onto the pistol as Judge reached for the bottle.

Before Gutierrez could finger the gun and turn, Judge was on Gutierrez's back, smashing the bottle on the ugly man's head. The drug spilled down his forehead into his eyes and across his face. Judge locked his legs around Gutierrez from behind and put both of his enormous palms over the man's face, forcing the chloroform into his nose and mouth. Judge held on to Gutierrez piggyback style, too weak to do much else.

Both men were breathing hard, and the drug quickly went to work on Gutierrez. He finally got a solid grip on the gun and tried to point it behind his head at the American behind him. Judge loosened the grip of one hand from Gutierrez's face long enough to hold off the gun. Judge's left palm was more than large enough, however, to keep a smothering hold on the Chilean's mouth and nose.

Gutierrez began to panic as he realized the chloroform was taking effect. The ringing in his ears had become a loud roar, and he felt the earth beginning to spin. Loud sirens were earsplitting in their approach as the policia began to arrive. His knees buckled, and he went down on one knee. His head began to clear but not his vision.

Unable to hold on any longer with one hand, Judge lost his grip on Gutierrez. He fell to the ground and began to roll as quickly as he could manage, fearing it was not near fast enough; as the blinded and staggering Chilean began getting to his feet, he fired the big Israeli Arms Desert Eagle.

Anyone that had never heard the sound of a Desert Eagle .50 caliber automatic would have thought the military had opened fire with a howitzer. When one of the heavy rounds pulverized the windshield of the nearest vehicle of the policia with the officers inside, every armed man in sight opened fire.

Windows shattered as guns roared and cracked while gunpowder blazed like fireworks until nothing could be made out through the smoke. Then as quickly as it began, all was silent. No one moved. The smoke hung heavy and pungent all about, refusing to dissipate. No one noticed the big silent figure staggering through the smoke and into the darkened shadows.

Thirty-Nine

Iraqi Force Invades Kuwait; Tanks, Troops Storm Capital

—The Washington Post,
Washington DC, Aug. 2, 1990, p. A1

Glancing skyward, Chad Fox continued rushing west to Al Jahra. He could see the smoke darkening the horizon as he raced towards it.

Against orders, he had left his post at his temporary barracks in Kuwait City. He had been assigned there to assist in the evacuation of the US Embassy. The consulate personnel were in a panic, but Chad had hurried out without hesitation. He had not been able to think clearly since his dad had been murdered.

Maria had moved back to her job in Panama, refusing to live with Chad's resentful mother after the death of his father. Chad had been upset when he had found out, but knew that it would be best for her. It had been difficult for Maria to stay on due to the language barrier. Having to put up with Chad's mother had been more than she could bear.

Their wedding plans had been put on hold, much to his mother's delight. It seemed to be the only thing to cheer her up in the days following her husband's death.

No sooner had his father been laid to rest than Chad had received orders to go to Kuwait. He had known that his assignment was to be in the Middle East. However, he had been given thirty days' leave. His leave had been cut short due to the urgent developments between Iraq and Kuwait.

Chad's preoccupation with his personal life had dulled his ability to make decisions. He found himself responding from emotion, not necessarily sound military judgment.

Chad even allowed a buddy to chase after a girl he had met in Kuwait City. Remembering his courtship to Maria, Chad could hardly have refused. The girl was taking her new boyfriend to Al Abraq to meet her girlfriends when the Iraqi Army began advancing across the border.

Now the young American and the girl were fleeing back to Al Jahra, along with most of the Kuwaiti civilians. Chad had to find his friends and find them quickly. The floodgates of hell and horror had opened. Iraq, with an overwhelming force, had overrun the line of defense that the Kuwaiti Army had hastily assembled.

War had not been anticipated by most of the west. In fact, the west had been selling arms at an alarming rate to Iraq, Iran, Kuwait, Egypt, Jordan, and Israel on some ludicrous fancy that it would stabilize the Middle East.

The buildup of Hussein's troops along the border had been known for weeks; however, an actual invasion had surprised most everyone, including the United States.

Now Chad was in a race to get his friend back to the embassy in time for the evacuation. He had taken his commander's jeep and knew that he would suffer the consequences upon his return. In the confusion of the evacuation, he hoped the missing jeep would be overlooked.

The road from Al Jahra was filling with cars and trucks fleeing for Kuwait City. Hoards of people, thousands, carrying whatever they could grab at the last minute, were crowding both sides of the street.

As Chad approached the city, they began swarming onto the highway towards him, making travel in the direction of Al Jahra difficult.

Chad could hear the gunfire now, interrupted by artillery fire. Suddenly, the streets were deserted, and Chad was alone. Most of the people were fleeing in the opposite direction and were now behind him.

He turned north towards the agricultural center, where he was to meet his friends.

A helicopter passed overhead. Glancing up, he thought it looked like an AH-1 Cobra. He waved, but then realized the aircraft was not a Cobra—like nothing he'd ever seen.

As if in response, the helicopter made a sweeping turn, descending to the street a half mile in front of him. It would be the Kuwaiti Army, Chad thought, trying to warn him not to proceed any further; he would have to ignore them. He only had another mile to go. He thought that he would be able to get by with his American jeep and his uniform.

A blast of smoke appeared from the helicopter as it hovered over the road ahead of him. Chad had but a second to realize it had fired on him, but it was already too late. The TOW missile roared over Chad's head so close that he felt the shock wave from it as it passed.

Before he could stop the jeep, another screamed by, missing him by several yards. Realizing that he was the intended target, he slammed on the brakes.

The aircraft lifted to a hover, tilting forward, its tail high in the air like a striking scorpion as it accelerated. Chad spun into a U-turn and fled up the highway, the Carrillo gunship in hot pursuit.

It took only moments for it to be upon him. The pilot, abandoning the errant missiles, began opening up with a continuous burp of gunfire from the turret, spraying 7.62 bullets in all directions.

With the aircraft a few scant yards behind him, Chad was trapped. There was time only to see his short life flash before his eyes, and he had no time to say goodbye to Maria and his grieving mother.

Final

Was Death in Chile Linked to Iraq Deal?

—The Washington Post, ***Aug. 6, 1990, p. D12***

The colorfully dressed South American visitors and US citizens arriving from their southern jaunts welcomed the warm, dry air of the Central Texas summer. The Airbus had been completely full and had become stuffy after the engines were shut down. To add to their discomfort, the plane was taking longer than usual to unload.

One man, standing above the rest, appeared oblivious to the din. If the stale air bothered him, he did not show it. He remained expressionless as a growing number of those about him began grumbling about the slow progress.

Finally, after making their way through US Customs, the tension eased; and the smiling faces returned as long-separated friends and families joined each other in the main terminal arrival area.

Walter Judge soberly observed as a mother and child rushed into the waiting arms of their long-awaited daddy. Exhausted and heavy-hearted, Judge remained in the waiting area of the gate, observing until the last couple had embraced amidst tears and laughter. Finally, he ebbed into the tide of travelers moving towards exits.

Having but a single bag, Judge wandered out to the ground transportation curb and boarded a waiting Super Shuttle. He moved to the back and slid his big frame against the window as the van continued to load.

Judge was not sure if he was glad to be home or just glad to finally be north of the border. Had he been in Asia following an experience like he had recently endured, he would not have felt so alone.

The Asians had often come to him with offers to join a family dinner, smoke a pipe, or play a friendly game of checkers and tell stories over tea and rice rolls. He barely remembered a single night alone unless he was on a mission or otherwise indisposed.

This was not Asia, however, and no one was waiting for him or noticed his bedraggled appearance. He was just a lonely figure amongst a mass of Americans, too involved in their lives to pay much attention to what was happening to the rest of the world.

Looking up, the familiar sights of Texas brought closer his last memories of the Loftons. Dr. Lofton's disappointed expression and Helen's disenchanted look were still fresh in his mind. He longed to call and see how they were doing, but he felt by now they could care less that he had finally made it back to Texas.

Walter Judge placed his head in the big palms of his hands with his elbows on his knees deep in thought. Michelle had been so disgusted with him because he had put them all in danger. It was all his fault. He should have pushed her away like all the others.

What was to become of him now, he wondered. Maybe it was time he left Texas. His life would be empty again like it had been for so many years. But he had been hard and callous then and reveled in his solace. It made him harder, more controlled. But Michelle had got to him. She had brought back all the memories of love and friendship that he had long since buried. The thought of going back to an empty life frightened him now. She had uncovered his emptiness and filled it with love and family again. Oh, how he wished he'd never left the strawberry patch so many years ago. He placed his head in his big hands and wept.

He had called Lieutenant Gibbons to fill him in on everything that had happened. Gibbons had been short with him, and Judge could have sworn that the lieutenant was disappointed he had made it back.

Gibbons had told him that he had brought Michelle back from Panama—words that stunned him. He would have thought that her father would have broken all records to get to her first. Tony said he had asked how Judge had found her and gotten her out of Chile, but she had told him that she didn't want to talk about Walter Judge.

The papers were full of stories of ARI's involvement with Carrillo and Saddam Hussein. The sinister connection of the conspiracy to the young doctor's disappearance was the story that was selling the papers. Of less interest seemed to be the murders of Milton Fox, Duffy, and Ms. Casey.

There had been no direct mention of Judge by name, or for that matter, of Wright or Gutierrez. The CIA connection to the ADE was referred to as being "under investigation."

All of this news, however, was being overshadowed by the latest events in Iraq, which seemed to have hit the American public by surprise. No one appeared overly inquisitive about the US role in the Iraqi arms race. Everyone was tired of political scandals.

Judge's spirits were heavy as the Super Shuttle left Highway 360 and merged onto I-20 en route to the South Arlington string of exits. They passed by the community hospital where he knew Michelle might still be working late. Without him to occupy her time, she could get back to her patients without worrying that she might be neglecting them.

As they approached the exit to Green Oaks Boulevard, Judge suddenly felt claustrophobic. When the van had made the exit, he called for the driver to pull over. He had had enough of sitting in a seat for one day. Grabbing his bag, he stepped out into the fresh air and began strolling towards home.

Despite his gloomy mood, he felt a great burden had finally been lifted from his shoulders. For the first time in months, he could look forward to a night's sleep without the dread of what lies ahead.

Yes, there would be questions from the police, maybe even some from reporters. And then, there were those nagging questions he had about Senator Roberts and Director Williams. He knew he was going to have to watch his back for a long time to come. When he felt better, he would pursue the answers, he said to himself. He would pursue them both. Pauline's death would not go unanswered for. Judge would see to that.

Suddenly, he stopped at the corner of his street. Waiting for a car to pass, he cocked his head, as if listening for something beyond the song of the jays and rustling of the live oaks towering above the street in the summer breeze.

Judge took a few more steps, listening intently. He was sure of it now, as he broke into a run, a bright glow on his dark eyes. There was no mistaking the carefree, happy dance of ragtime piano tunes, filling the air from the open windows of his home.

CPSIA information can be obtained at www.ICGtesting.com
Printed in the USA
BVOW070641180313

315671BV00003B/4/P

9 781479 799053